FINALLY

F-BOMB: SEALS LOVE CURVES, BOOK 9

MARY E THOMPSON

BluEyed Press

F-BOMB: SEALS LOVE CURVES

Welcome to the world of F-BOMB where a group of former SEALs have come together to protect the curvy women they love and the country they call home from the dangers of the world. They have the training and the knowledge, and they have the ability to kick some ass when needed. And it'll be needed.

F-BOMB: SEALs LOVE CURVES

Freedom (free everywhere)
Fiancée (subscriber exclusive)
Forgotten
First
Failure
Friends
Family
Forbidden
Future
Finally

SUBSCRIBE NOW AT MARYETHOMPSON.COM

To you...for sticking with me through this series. I love these men and women, and bringing them to life has been a true joy. Thank you for sharing this journey with me.

1

Welcome to Vermont. Those three simple words shouldn't have been enough to make every cell in Liam Johnson's body tense up, but they were. His fingers tightened on the steering wheel, and everything in him screamed to turn around. But that wasn't an option. Not when a woman's life was on the line.

His childhood wasn't horrible, but he promised himself years ago that he'd never return to the minuscule town he called home for eighteen years. A town that was rundown and worn out long before he was born and had no chance of being more than a passthrough on the way to Canada.

But that was exactly where Liam was headed. Back to East Charlottesville. Back to his past. Back to all the memories of why he wanted to get out of there in the first place.

Liam, English to his friends and teammates, took the next turn into the parking lot of the makeshift welcome center. It was almost three o'clock, and even though he wasn't far from his destination, he needed to stretch his legs.

He parked far from the entrance to the old home that was used as a welcome center and walked out onto the grass. He looked back at the cars drifting by on the small road that wound through Lake Champlain between New York and Vermont. The lake was always a fantasy vacation spot. The kind of place his handful of classmates with money would go. English had never been there, and driving through on his way into Vermont was not as appealing as he'd hoped it would be. Nothing about being back in Vermont was appealing.

English kept walking until he could almost pretend the occasional traffic was the soothing hum of a computer instead of the irritating buzz of vehicles. He closed his eyes and drew in a deep breath. He held it, then let it out slowly, willing the tension to leave his body. Each breath soothed the rattled parts inside him. Until his phone buzzed.

"Yeah."

"Are you almost there?" Dex. English's roommate. Soon to be former roommate once he officially moved in with his girlfriend. And English's friend.

"About an hour to go. Maybe a little less."

"You doing okay?"

English nodded to himself, hoping the action helped his words to be more believable. "I'm good."

"I should have gone with you."

"I'm a big boy," English said. He was the baby of the group, the one the rest of them treated like a kid brother half the time. He was smart and capable, but he was also young and they acted like he couldn't be on his own.

"That's not why and you know it."

The sympathy in Dex's voice said it all. He knew English didn't want to go home. Each of the men on their team had their demons, and because of that, they all understood each other's.

"I'll be fine."

"And you'll call if you're not." It wasn't a question.

"Yeah."

"You don't owe anyone anything," Dex said, his voice softer, like he was speaking to a child instead of a grown ass thirty-three year old man.

"It's a job. That's all. I'll be there for a few days and head home. They can't get into my head in a week."

"You and I both know that isn't true."

English sighed. It wasn't, but he wanted to believe it. His parents were good people, not monsters, but they never supported his choices and weren't shy about letting him know that. His dad wanted him to go to work at the factory in town when he finished high school. Hell, he wanted him to work there before he finished high school. That was the way of life in East Charlottesville. Finish high school, get a job at the factory, marry a local, have kids, rinse and repeat.

English never wanted that life. He knew it for as long as he could remember. But he also knew he couldn't tell his parents until he had another plan in place. Not that it mattered. They were still angry.

"Have you learned anything new about this woman?" English asked. He needed a subject change. And to get his game face on.

"Nothing. We've gone through the basics you found, but there hasn't been much of anything on her. She worked at a church, but I think you know that. She was also a waitress. Lived alone, no family. The friend who reported her missing said it's not like her to go so long without contact. Her bosses said they've had others do this and they usually send in an address to mail their last check. Local PD doesn't seem concerned. No forced entry at her place, nothing out of place. Her car is gone, so the assumption is she left town and didn't want to tell anyone."

"Anything on the friend?"

"Nah. She looks clean. No flags."

"Is she a local?"

"Yeah, her name is—"

English waited. His team just got a new case that was taking all of them. He should be there to help, but instead, he was looking into the missing person case. "Dex?"

"Sorry, man. Meeting. We'll talk later."

"Yeah." English stared at his phone as it went dark. He was alone. His team was swamped, and English was on his own to find Jeanine Waterford. And face his past.

It wouldn't have made sense to bring anyone else. Going in alone under the cover of his parents' party was easy. He knew the town, and he knew anyone else would draw attention. If he was going to get any answers, he needed to draw as little attention to himself as possible.

It was a good thing English was a pro at being invisible.

THE CLOSER ENGLISH got to his hometown, the more he wanted to turn the SUV around and go home. He pulled over to the side of the road a few times just so he could close his eyes and breathe, but he kept going. There was a missing woman, and English didn't turn his back on people in need.

He finally reached the edge of town. The stop sign in the middle of nowhere was out of place, but so was everything else there. Going straight would send him into the heart of East Charlottesville. A right would take him to his parents' house. A left would send him past the high school and the old factory. None of them were appealing.

If he was only there for the job, English knew the left would make the most sense. Get a feel for the area and see the entire town. He flipped his blinker and made the turn. He wasn't the same kid he was when he left more than fifteen years ago. He was successful and strong. It was likely he wouldn't be recognized by anyone because he'd changed so much. And—

"Fuck me," English mumbled.

The old factory sat to his left, a gleaming beacon on the hill. The sign at the road proclaimed it was now West Textiles. The colorful metal and stone declaration said the new owners took tremendous pride in the factory, and the shiny exterior said that extended to the facility itself.

English took a left, curiosity getting the better of him. He had a vague recollection of his parents mentioning the factory was bought years ago, but he put it out of his head, assuming it didn't mean much. The look of the place said that assumption was wrong.

English drove down the long driveway to the parking lot, passing signs celebrating ten years in business. At four-thirty on a Friday, there were a lot of people leaving. All of them smiling.

He got a few curious looks, and some narrowed gazes, as he drove through the lot, pretending to be looking for a spot. His brand new Lincoln SUV stood out against the trucks and cars and SUVs that, in many cases, were older than him.

English swung back out of the lot and onto the main road. The factory was the biggest employer in town, but it had never been well maintained. The pay was not great, and the working conditions weren't any better. But the new look of the place made English wonder if the rest of the town had gotten the same facelift. If the owners had enough money to clean, paint, and spit-shine the factory, it meant more money would be going into the town to do the same to the old buildings there.

Before the thought could fully form, English came up on the high school. The old brick building had green stains from years of skipped pressure washings. The parking lot boasted potholes and cracks that could swallow a small child. Lines were nonexistent on both the parking lot and the athletic fields just past the small school. Kids ran around on the football field and jogged the worn path that served as a track. Just like he remembered.

The factory and the school sitting so close together and looking so different was jarring. Nothing in East Charlottesville was ever fancy like the factory. Nothing. But that wealth clearly didn't translate to the rest of the town.

English kept driving, down the center of town on C Drive. The old movie theater still stood, with a marquee sign telling him the movie playing was six months old. The diner on the corner hadn't changed. The small shops were open, but the faded and cracked paint on the storefront picture windows told English nothing had been taken care of in East Charlottesville.

He reached the end of C Drive and made his left to head toward his parents' house. He was almost there when he thought about Jeanine Waterford. She worked at the diner, but she also worked at the church. English took a quick left and headed toward the border where the church sat.

Holy Trinity Christian Church was one of the oldest churches in the country. It sat on the border of Vermont and Quebec and offered access to both the US and Canada without documentation. A line down the center told visitors where the border was, letting people wander in and out of each country at will. It was only when someone left that they had to show the ticket they received on entry to make sure they went back to the country they entered from.

English parked in the lot and went into the church. A

small chapel was holding an afternoon service, but the gift shop and museum were open. Jeanine Waterford worked in the gift shop.

Trinkets sat on shelves next to religious souvenirs. The place was a popular tourist attraction, as much as anything in East Charlottesville could be. The bored-looking woman behind the register chewed gum and watched her phone while English wandered aimlessly. He picked up a postcard with the church on it and a visor clip for his SUV and carried them to the register.

"Did you find everything you needed?" the cashier asked, barely looking away from her phone as she reached for his items.

"I did. I was wondering if Jeanine is working today?"

The woman shook her head, still ignoring him. "Nope. Hasn't been here in a week or so. She quit."

"Really? She told you that?"

"No, but that's what happens. People work here for a few years, sometimes less, then realize this job sucks, this town sucks, and life sucks, so they get out before they lose their minds." The woman looked up at him, vehemence in her eyes. "That or they go crazy."

"Crazy?" English asked. He didn't know what this woman meant. She was younger than him, mid-twenties at the oldest. He didn't know many women that age, but her clear hatred for her job surprised him.

She shrugged. "There was one woman who worked here like, forever ago. She was crazy. Kept saying she saw people who weren't there. Or things that weren't there."

"Like what?"

She shrugged again, her voice fading back to boredom. "I don't know. I never met her. All I know is I'm not sticking around here long enough to lose my mind. I'm going to New York City to be a star."

English resisted the urge to roll his eyes. "Congratulations."

She flashed him her first genuine smile and bagged his items. He handed her cash and stuffed his change in the bag with his purchase. On his way out, he took note of all the places someone could hide, or could hide something, before he left.

He got in his SUV and sent Dex a text to look into the church and former employees, especially one who went crazy. Dex texted back that he'd report when he had something.

English put his phone back in his pocket and accepted that he couldn't stall any longer. His parents' party was at seven, and it was getting close to five after his detour through town. If he knew his parents, they were going to want to be at the party by six, which meant he needed to clean up fast.

He parked in front of the house he grew up in and turned off the SUV. The yard was trimmed neatly, but the beds around the house were overgrown. The paint on the siding was chipped and peeling. The roof was missing a few shingles. Gauzy white curtains fluttered in the windows, showcasing the lack of air conditioning no matter how warm it was outside for early September.

English grabbed his duffle from the front seat and stepped out. He closed the door and locked the vehicle out of habit. He was halfway to the front door when it opened to his mom drying her hands on a dishtowel.

"Oh, my God, Liam? Is that you?"

"Hi, Mom."

"William! Liam is here!"

"Liam?"

His mom waved English closer, holding the door open while he closed the distance between them. She was in a blue dress he had seen her in before with a white apron around her waist. Her hair was up in her signature bun at the base of her neck with gray streaks throughout. English made it to her and leaned down to hug his mother, inhaling her pencil shavings and freshly baked bread scent.

"Hi, Mom."

"Oh, Liam, I'm so happy you're here. Why didn't you tell us you were coming?"

English chuckled. "Then it wouldn't be a surprise visit."

"This is the best surprise ever."

"I was hoping. It's been a long time since I've been home."

"Too long," his dad said from behind them. "Your mother's been upset."

"Sorry. I should have visited. You guys can come to Niagara Falls sometime. I think you'd like it."

"You know we aren't city people," his mom said quickly.

"Yeah, but it's beautiful there."

"Can't beat here," his dad said roughly. It was the same old argument. Everything a person ever needed was right there in East Charlottesville. Why would anyone ever want to leave?

English simply nodded, not engaging with his dad. He knew it wouldn't end well since neither of them would change their minds. It wasn't worth the fight.

"Good to see you, Dad."

"You're gaining weight. Sitting in front of that computer all the time isn't good for you. Don't you know sitting is the new smoking?"

English almost laughed at his father's words. Sure,

English knew it, but he was surprised his father knew the latest medical advice doctors were sharing. English agreed with it, but that was why he made sure to get in a run every day, lifted weights, and used the punching bag in the office. He was not hurting for exercise. And he hadn't gained weight since he left the military.

"I'll be careful," English told his dad, knowing it wouldn't silence him but was the best he could do.

"If you'd have come to work at the factory, you'd be using your hands and would be on your feet all day. You wouldn't have a chance to get fat."

English resisted the urge to show his father the six-pack under his shirt and simply nodded. "Is it okay if I stay here while I'm in town?"

His father grunted, but his mother was quick to pull him inside and agree. "We wouldn't have it any other way. Would we, William?"

His dad grunted again and stepped back to let English pass. "We're leaving in twenty minutes."

"I'll be ready. I'm going to take a quick shower and get changed." English didn't wait for a reply before he headed down the short hallway toward the bedrooms. His parents' room was at the end of the hall with a private bathroom. His room was to the left with a full bathroom on the opposite side.

English put his stuff in his room and groaned internally at how little had changed. His science awards and movie posters still decorated his room. The space themed bedding he picked out when he was nine covered the bed. The same thin curtains that were in the front of the house covered the closed windows in his stuffy bedroom. He was already suffocating. But he had a job to do.

English grabbed the clothes he packed for the party and

went across the hall. He showered quickly, getting out in less than five minutes. He dressed in the clean clothes and grabbed his dirty ones. He put his phone, keys, and wallet into his pockets, then went back across the hall to drop off his clothes and grab his boots.

It couldn't have been more than ten minutes since he walked into the house, but his parents were at the front door waiting for him anyway. His dad made a point of looking at his watch when English walked out. "Glad you could join us."

"Sorry I kept you waiting," English replied, his tone just as frustrated as his dad's.

"That giant vehicle you parked in the driveway is blocking me in."

"I thought the truck was yours."

"It is, but since there are three of us now, we need to take your mother's car."

"Why don't I drive?"

"That big, fancy thing?" The disdain was more than clear in his tone. He wasn't getting in English's brand new Lincoln if his life depended on it.

"I'll park it on the street."

His dad shook his head and mumbled something about being late to their own party when English walked by. He backed his SUV out and parked in front of the house. His dad backed out right behind him and barely stopped long enough for English to fold himself into the backseat.

"Everyone is going to be so happy to see you, Liam. They've all missed you."

"It'll be good to see everyone," English lied. "Hey, speaking of missing, I read about a woman who went missing last week. Jeanine Waterford. Did you know her?"

His mother shook her head. "Jeanine was a little bit of a

wild one. She probably took off with someone driving through town."

"Without telling anyone?"

"She wasn't really a part of this town. She didn't work at the school or the factory," his mom said. For a town of less than a thousand people, it amazed English that there were still classes. If you worked at the school or the factory, you were part of the in-crowd. If you didn't, you might as well not exist.

"I heard she worked at the church. I stopped by there on my way into—"

"That woman skipping town is nothing you need to concern yourself with, Liam. She was nobody, and there ain't nobody looking for her. The town's better off without a woman like her trying to get half the married men into trouble."

Well, that was something he hadn't read about the woman online. And it just gave him a pool of subjects. All the married people in town.

2

CAITLYN POWERS GLARED AT OFFICER PATTINSON AND TRIED not to let out her claws. The man was as useless as tits on a bull, as her mother used to say. Not that Caitlyn ever wanted to be compared to the heartless bitch her mother was.

"So, you're not doing anything to find Jeanine? At all?" Caitlyn asked, proud of herself for how calm her voice sounded.

The cop shrugged. "There's nothing for us to do. It looks like she left town."

"But forgot to take all her stuff?" Sarcasm dripped from Caitlyn's words and poured all over the desk.

The cop leaned back and leveled her with a glare of his own. "Ms. Waterford's apartment is a crime scene. No one is supposed to enter. Are you admitting to breaking and entering, Ms. Powers?"

"If it's a crime scene, then why aren't you looking for her? It's either a crime scene or she left. It can't be both!"

"There is no sign Ms. Waterford did not leave. But, like I told you three days ago, we turned the case over to the FBI. They're the ones in charge of missing persons cases."

"You also said they would be keeping you updated on their progress. Is there any progress?"

"No. Because she's not missing."

"Then where the fuck is she?"

The cop rose at her screeched words. He leaned over the desk so quickly, Caitlyn had to back up or let him head-butt her. "You will not speak to me that way, Ms. Powers. If you don't leave, I'll have you arrested. And then where will your little investigation go?"

Caitlyn drew in a shaky breath and tried to calm herself down. She'd never been very good at holding back her anger. It got her into trouble more than once when she was a kid, but as an adult, it just landed her on the unemployment list. Getting arrested would give her a permanent spot there, and she couldn't risk that.

Her hands shook with the need to punch the smug son-of-a-bitch, but Caitlyn did exactly what he wanted her to do and left the station without another word.

The bright sunshine forced her sunglasses over her eyes before the first tear fell. It wasn't the first time she'd been on the wrong side of a plea from the police department. But when the cops were spineless assholes she went to high school with, guys who were too scared to talk to her when she was on top of the world and relished in the fact that her current place was squarely on the bottom, she knew she'd get no help at all.

"Did you hear Liam Johnson is back in town?" a woman walking by asked her friend.

"Oh, Patty'll be so happy about that. Is he coming to the party tonight?"

"I would assume that's why he's here. Bob saw him..."

Their voices trailed off as they continued down the sidewalk past the police station and Caitlyn's attempt to eavesdrop.

Liam Johnson.

Caitlyn remembered Liam. He graduated with her, too, but he was smart and kind and too good for her. She also heard he joined the military and was a part of some elite team that helped find people. Not many people made it out of their small town, and the ones who did were talked about in adoring whispers. Like Liam.

For the first time in more than a week, Caitlyn had hope that her friend might be found. Jeanine would come home, and Caitlyn would help her move on from whatever hell she'd been through. Maybe they could finally leave the shit town they lived in and start a new life. Somewhere far away from East Charlottesville.

And the memories the town held.

THE LAST PLACE English expected his dad to go for the anniversary party was to West Textiles. He expected dinner at a restaurant, maybe even somewhere outside of town, but not a catered event at his dad's place of employment.

"Mr. West offered," English's mom said. "He's so kind. He treats his employees like family. He says since he doesn't have one of his own, he wants all the people who work at West Textiles to know he's there for them if they need anything."

"That's...nice of him," English said as they got out of the car. He was more than a little curious about the place, and this way, he didn't have to break in.

The party was set up in a large, open room that looked like a banquet hall. Definitely strange for a factory. But clearly not underutilized judging by the seamless way things ran. The catering company and bar staff had everything set up and ready to go before the first guests arrived.

Everyone sang the praises of their host for throwing the party. English even heard some of them talking about Mr. West footing the bill for most of it, although English wasn't sure his father's pride would have allowed that.

English worked his way through the crowd, thankful he'd changed enough that few people recognized him. He could be invisible and try to pick up any information out there about Jeanine Waterford. Not that there was much.

He leaned against the bar and watched the guests. The bartender slid his beer across the temporary structure and nodded to English like he was anyone else.

Invisible was his forte.

If anyone knew anything about the missing woman, English would bet on it being the staff. He'd learned long ago that if you wanted to find out something, you always blended into the background because people would say things around you if they didn't realize you were listening. Servers were always invisible, and always knowledgeable. He just needed to find one who might be willing to share something with him.

Bingo.

A pretty, young server on the edge of the room was watching him. She was not even close to his type, but that wasn't the point of the mission. The point was to find out whatever he could about Jeanine Waterford.

English made his way toward her, glancing her direction enough to let her know she was the reason he was walking over there. She smiled and ducked her head, like she was embarrassed by the attention. A ploy. She was young and cute with strawberry blonde hair pulled up in an intentionally messy bun. Her eyes were wide and bright, giving her a cartoon look that was definitely perfected with makeup. Her lips were a glossy pink, tempting if he liked that kind of thing. But he didn't.

English preferred a woman who wasn't trying so hard. One who had curves and a biting wit. One who would roll her eyes at the man stalking her from across the room.

He reached the woman's side and took his time looking her up and down before he simply said, "Hi."

She giggled and batted her eyelashes at him, playing up the sweet and innocent thing so well he wondered how old she really was. "Hey."

"You come here often?" The pick up line was cheesy and bad enough that English wanted to roll his eyes at it, but it was effective.

The server giggled again and shook her head. She bit her lower lip, and English let his gaze drift there. He had to play the game with her.

"I'm new. I've only been working for Mr. West for a few weeks. I'm Cami."

"Hi, Cami. It's nice to meet you."

"You, too."

"Do you live in town?"

She nodded. "Yeah. I grew up here. My daddy works here. My mama's gone, though."

A local. Definitely someone who would have information. "Sorry about that. What is there to do around here? Aside from this party?"

She laughed. "Not much, really. Most of my friends go out to the river and drink. There's one bar, but that's mostly old people."

"Wouldn't want that."

She giggled again. "No. My boyfriend and me prefer the river. It's more...private out there."

Boyfriend. Dammit. She was a flirt, but she was making it clear she wasn't available. So much for that lead. "Makes sense. Maybe I'll see you out there later."

"Sounds good. I should get back to work." She bounced away like she hadn't just blown his chances at finding out something useful. Of course, she didn't know that was the only reason he was talking to her.

English stayed where he was against the wall. He watched the rest of the party until he spotted his cousin approaching. English couldn't stop the smile on his face.

"Well, shit, look what the cat dragged in," Adam said in greeting. He clapped English's hand and pulled him in for a hug. They were close to the same height and had both put on a few dozen pounds of muscle since high school. Adam and English were close growing up, best friends and cousins, but it had been years since they'd seen each other.

"I didn't know you were coming to this thing."

Adam snorted. "Couldn't miss it if I wanted to. Mom and Dad insisted I make an appearance."

"Lucky you."

"I didn't know you would be here. How are you? How's life?"

English shrugged. Adam was the only other family member who had an interest in getting out of their hometown. He was a year younger than English, so when Adam left, it wasn't as hard. English broke the mold. Or at least cracked it.

"Life's good. Our team is doing well. I enjoy the work."

"And are you here for work or just a visit?" Adam asked carefully.

English sipped his beer and looked at his cousin from

the corner of his eye. He hadn't kept in touch with Adam and had no idea what he did for a living. He was taller by an inch or two and wider by the same. His matching blond hair was cut short, and his blue-green eyes said he saw things no one else did. If English had to guess, Adam was not a civilian.

"What makes you ask?"

Adam turned with his back to the rest of the crowd. The move was casual enough that anyone who saw him would think he was facing English to say something private. Instead, he flashed a badge. An FBI badge.

"What the hell?" English blurted, the words spewing out before he could stop them.

"It's not my case, but I saw it come through the system. I also saw it was shared with a private contractor organization."

"As far as anyone else knows, I'm here to surprise my parents."

"You can't stand being here."

English shook his head and took another sip. He limited himself to only one drink for the night, but he wanted it to last the whole night. "I'm willing to bet you aren't much happier about this than I am."

Adam shook his head. "Nah, but it's par for the course for me. I go where I'm needed."

"But this is pleasure."

Adam shrugged. "As much as it can be. I'm assuming you have all the files, but if you need anything, let me know."

"Do you know her?"

Adam shook his head. "Never heard of her. Mom and Dad are pretty tight-lipped about her. Tommy and Rick said they heard she skipped town."

"It sounds to me like there's more to all of this. Dad told me she was messing up marriages."

Adam's brows shot up with the new information. "Think they knew her?"

"I hope not. Aren't we here for their anniversary?"

Adam chuckled. "How long are you in town?"

"A week. Maybe more, maybe less, depending on what I find."

"We're attracting attention, but we need to talk. Breakfast tomorrow?"

"I'll be there. Seven?"

"Let's make it eight. There's a cute little server who's been eyeing me all night."

English snorted as his cousin pushed off the wall and stalked through the crowd. He walked right up to Cami and said something to her before she blushed and nodded eagerly.

Guess that boyfriend wasn't so real after all.

Damn. English really needed to learn how to read women.

CAITLYN LOOKED out at the crowd and grimaced. She hated working odd jobs like she was, but that was what happened when all the money she earned modeling as a kid went into a trust that her mother controlled and ran off with.

Not that Caitlyn was still bitter or anything.

Jeanine told Caitlyn over and over again that she needed to get a lawyer and find her mother, but Caitlyn had zero skills. And zero money. Which brought her right back to the event she was working. Because her goals had shifted.

Caitlyn grabbed a tray and made her way around the

room. She stayed to the outside so her wide hips didn't knock over a table, or a client. Her boss had threatened not to let her work again after the last time that happened, but she talked him into letting her work when she found out they needed extra people. And now that she might be able to get some help finding Jeanine, she was even happier she did.

Liam Johnson. She remembered the nerdy guy who sat near the window in her math class. Freshman year, at least. Then he passed her and moved up and up until he was taking college courses before they graduated high school. He was easily the salutatorian of their class, probably should have been valedictorian, but he was the kind of guy who never made anyone else feel stupid in his shadow.

And the kind of guy Caitlyn found herself in need of help from.

She recognized his parents, but being the guests of honor, they were simple to spot. Caitlyn circled the room and couldn't find Liam.

Small town rumors weren't always right, but Caitlyn prayed this one was. He was the prodigal son. Returning home from the war, coming back to celebrate with his parents.

She spotted a man near the bar earlier that vaguely reminded her of Liam, but he was too tall and too built to be the nerdy guy from high school. Caitlyn kept looking, wondering if her quest was a waste of time, when the screech of the microphone drew her attention to the stage.

"Good evening, everyone," Mr. Johnson's voice boomed through the speakers. "Ooh, sorry about that. Patty and I just wanted to thank everyone for being here tonight. This is a special night for us, and we are so grateful you're all here to celebrate. We also wanted to say thank you to our son, who made the trip home. Liam, wave."

Caitlyn followed Mr. Johnson's gaze to where Liam was standing against the wall. He pushed away and lifted his glass toward the crowd.

"Damn," Caitlyn breathed. The man from the bar was Liam Johnson. The military did wonders for him. He was always adorable, but those muscles and the roughness around the edges made him every woman's fantasy.

"You're right, honey," an older lady nearby said. "If I were thirty years younger, I'd be fighting you for him." She winked and kept walking.

Caitlyn smiled back and let the woman believe what she wanted to believe. Caitlyn definitely appreciated the sexy version of Liam, but she wasn't interested in him for his brawn. She needed his brain.

His father said a few more words, profusely thanking Daniel West for hosting them, and announced dinner would be out soon. That was Caitlyn's cue to get back to the kitchen. She was on the far side of the dining hall, which meant she was going to be one of the last ones to get there. And would miss her chance to serve Liam and ask him for help.

Servers were already walking out of the kitchen when she got there. She spotted one of the new ones, a young one who still had the youthful glow Caitlyn watched fade from her mirror a long time ago.

"Hey, are you going to the head table?" she asked.

"Yeah, why?"

"I wanted to let you know this guy on the far side of the dining room asked me about you. He wanted to know if he could have your number." The lie was easy enough to tell.

She blushed and grinned, then looked at her tray.

"Oh, I can take that one, and you can go get another one. He's in that back corner. You won't be able to miss him."

"Thanks, Caitlyn," she said, handing over the tray and bouncing back into the kitchen for another one.

Caitlyn made a beeline for the head table. She wasn't going to risk anyone else getting there first. She was almost there when another server stopped next to the table. Caitlyn was supposed to start at a new table with each tray, but she didn't care. She could lose the job that night and it wouldn't matter.

As long as she talked to Liam.

"Liam," she breathed when she reached his chair. She ignored the glare from the other server and set up a stand so she could put her tray down. "It's been forever. How are you?"

He looked up at her with a smile that didn't reach his eyes. "I'm good. Thanks. How are you?"

"You don't remember me, do you? I know I look a lot different than I did in school. I'm—"

The other server cleared her throat loudly. She was out of time.

He nodded slowly, his gaze searching her. "You look..."

Caitlyn tugged her button-down shirt down and smoothed a hand over her round, not pregnant, belly. Caitlyn's cheeks burned under his gaze. She was a size four when she graduated high school. As a size twenty-four, she was happier, but staring at Liam made her more than a little self-conscious.

"Um, anyway, so I was wondering if you wanted to meet up after this. We could grab a drink and catch up. Here's my number. I look forward to hearing from you."

Caitlyn hurried away from his table without looking

back. She knew she was going to be in trouble, but she had to try to talk to him.

No one else in town believed Caitlyn. They all thought she was crazy. But she knew something happened to Jeanine. She knew her friend wouldn't disappear without telling her where she was. She knew she was in trouble. Or worse.

And Caitlyn knew the only person who could find her friend, dead or alive, was Liam Johnson.

She just hoped he called.

3

———————

English watched the server hurry away. He couldn't shake that she looked familiar, but as he watched her disappear into the crowd, he still couldn't place her.

He stared at the number and memorized it, then pocketed the slip of paper. He struck out with the young server, but he still needed information. If the curvy, sexy one was offering up herself, he wasn't opposed to mixing a little business with pleasure.

Just because English didn't remember her didn't mean he couldn't get to know her after the party. He just hoped she didn't live with her parents or have space sheets on her twin bed like he did.

"Liam Johnson," Daniel West said, taking a seat next to English. His parents introduced them on the way in, but Daniel was talking to the caterers and couldn't say more than hello.

"Mr. West."

Daniel laughed. "Oh, please, call me Daniel. Everyone does. I don't like formalities."

English nodded at the man. He was another one who

looked vaguely familiar, but the three years difference between them almost guaranteed the familiarity was from growing up in the same town. English remembered when Daniel's parents died in a house fire. English was a senior in high school, and Daniel was away at college.

"It's wonderful you could be here for your parents. Your dad speaks so highly of you."

English pasted on a grateful smile. Outside the house, his father was the doting father and man he should be. Inside was where the truth came out. But English wasn't about to share that with his father's employer.

"Thank you. I see you've done some amazing things here. The factory looks great."

"Oh, thank you. After my parents died, I floundered for a while. I wasn't really sure what I wanted to do with my life. I invested the insurance money and worked for a few years, but wherever I went, it wasn't home. When this place was listed for sale, I knew this was where I was meant to be."

"The town is grateful to you for it. My parents sure are. They've done nothing but sing your praises to me since I got here."

Daniel tipped his head back and laughed, exposing his neck. A small patch of dark stubble drew English's gaze and made him like Daniel even more. He put on the act of being personable and real, but he didn't look like a man who could be approached in his navy suit and red pocket square. His fancy shoes and shiny cufflinks added to the too perfect look. But that patch of his beard he missed shaving made English believe the man had flaws just like everyone else.

"Your father has been very kind to me over the years. Losing my parents when I did was tough, but everyone here welcomed me back. Your father was one of the first. He invited me to stay with them when he found out I was sleeping in my office. I'm forever indebted to your parents."

English was surprised to hear about that. He had no idea his parents had been that close to Daniel. Or that he'd ever lived in their house. He wondered what else he didn't know about his parents and their life.

"I'm sure they don't feel the same. If they offered, I know they meant it as a kindness, not hoping you would repay the favor."

"Oh, I know. That's what makes it that much more important to me. Truth be told, my parents were not like that. I loved them, but my father had a mean streak."

English eyed the other man, wondering why he was sharing something so personal. "I'm sorry to hear it."

Daniel nodded, looking embarrassed to have said it. "Thank you. I probably shouldn't be telling you any of this, but I feel like those are my parents, too." He nodded to English's parents on the other side of the eight person table. "That makes us brothers. I always wanted siblings."

"Me, too," English told him honestly. He wouldn't confess he found a family in the Navy or that he built a company with the men he thought of as his brothers. For a week, he could be Daniel's brother. Maybe Daniel would have some information for him.

"So, I hear you were in the Navy but now are part owner of a task force or something?"

Guess that wasn't a secret. "Yeah. Some of my teammates from the Navy got together. Long story, but our former commanding officer kidnapped someone and tried to blow up Niagara Falls."

"And you stopped him?" Daniel asked, his brown eyes wide.

English nodded. "We all did. We stayed in the area after

and helped find him. And others who wanted to hurt or kill people."

"Wow. That's impressive. All I ever did was buy a company."

English chuckled with him. It was obvious how significant Daniel's investment in the factory was, and how much it meant to the people who lived in town. If he hadn't done what he did, English's parents and many others would have been forced to leave if someone didn't step in and buy the factory.

"You saved this town, Daniel. I hope you know that."

Daniel smiled sheepishly. "Thanks. It's home. Are you ever moving back?"

English glanced at his parents and shook his head. "No. It's not home for me anymore."

"Sorry to hear that. It would be nice to get to know you better."

"Maybe we can grab a drink while I'm in town."

Daniel smiled. "I'd like that. A lot."

English nodded and realized he would, too. Daniel might not be his actual brother, and they wouldn't ever be close, but having someone in town to kick back with a few times would be good. Especially someone who knew everyone in town and, hopefully, wanted to find Jeanine Waterford as much as English did.

AS THE NIGHT WORE ON, his patience wore thin. Dinner was done, plates were cleared, and it should be time to go. He wasn't willing to leave yet. Not when there was a chance people would talk. He had to keep up appearances.

He finished his drink and pushed away from the bar.

The DJ played music no one danced to, but the thought was interesting. Maybe he could find a new woman while he was there. Someone who would see what he had to offer. Someone who would love him the way he deserved to be loved.

Patty and William moved around the party, talking to people at all the tables. It was like a wedding reception for them. He smiled. That meant no one was watching him. Trying to figure out what he was doing.

Not that he was doing anything. And definitely not anything wrong. He was in control. Like always.

Exhaustion pulled at him, making him see things that weren't there. Like Jeanine talking to that fat bitch she was friends with. He knew she wasn't really there, but he had to look twice to make sure.

Caitlyn Powers was a thorn in his side. She carried trays and smiled at guests, but aside from when she manipulated that young server so she could deliver food to Liam Johnson, she hadn't approached him. There was no doubt she knew who Liam was and what he did for a living, but it wouldn't be too hard to convince him she was batshit crazy.

"Can I get you anything?" the pretty server asked him as she walked by.

He held up his drink and shook his head. He watched her as she walked away, shaking her ass. His cock hardened at the sight. It had been a while since he'd taken someone home. Almost ten days since he'd put his cock to good use.

"Actually," he called out, catching her attention before she was out of earshot.

She smiled as she walked back over. "What can I do for you?"

"We should meet up after this."

Her eyes widened. Her smile froze on her face, the edges

of it tilting down. "Um, I... I can't. I have...a boyfriend. We have plans later."

He nodded slowly, not buying the lie for a second. "Is that why you're shaking your ass like that? For your boyfriend?"

She gasped and drew back.

He shook his head. "I apologize. It's been a long day."

"It's...fine. I'm sorry I gave you the wrong impression."

He jerked his head in a nod and stared past her. She took the hint and hurried away from him. *Fucking whore.*

Just like Jeanine. When they met, he was sure she would see him for who he was. He loved her, and he was going to treat her like a queen. She would have had everything she ever wanted. But she didn't deserve him. She laughed when he proposed and said they weren't serious enough to even talk about marriage. Then she said her last words.

"Hell, we're nothing more than fuck buddies. My best friend doesn't know who you are, and you're not the only man I'm sleeping with. I don't know why you ever thought I'd marry you."

CAITLYN CHANGED out of the uniform she wore for the party and accepted her check. She walked to her car and slid the key in the lock, cursing to herself when it stuck and refused to turn. She jiggled the key, hoping it would let her in soon. She'd been more anxious than usual since Jeanine disappeared.

Footsteps echoed on the pavement behind her. Her heart pounded in her ears and tried to make a break for it. Caitlyn spun, stupidly unarmed in the dark parking lot alone.

"You okay?" Alec, one of the other servers for the night, asked.

"Yeah." Caitlyn tried to tell herself she was safe, but Alec had never worked the same party as her. She had only met him a few hours earlier.

"Car trouble?"

"Key trouble. It sticks."

"Want me to give it a try?"

"No," Caitlyn said quickly. "I'm fine."

Alec backed up, hands in the air like she'd pulled a gun on him. "Shit, I'm just trying to be nice. You don't have to be a bitch about it."

She thought about apologizing, but he was already gone. And really, she didn't care if he thought she was a bitch. She was a bitch. As a kid, she had to be if she was going to beat out the other girls for modeling jobs. As a teen, it was a rite of passage. And as an adult, it was the only thing she had.

Jeanine was the only person who saw through that shield and was willing to let her be a bitch and know it wasn't because that was all that was there.

The key turned in the lock, and Caitlyn finally got into her car. The fall evening was cooling off. She rolled down the window and turned up the radio for her drive home.

Her apartment was barely habitable, but it was the only thing she had. The last fifteen years had not been kind to Caitlyn. She thought she'd have a nest egg to live off of for a while, but instead, she was broke and homeless the day she turned eighteen.

Caitlyn tossed her keys on the small table by the door and dug her phone out of her pocket. She checked for messages that weren't ever there and sighed. As she did every night, she called Jeanine.

"Hey, girl. It's me. Hoping I'll catch you tonight. I haven't given up on you. I know they all say you left, but I know that isn't true. I'm going to keep looking until I find you. Stay strong."

Caitlyn fought the tears that always came when she thought of her best friend. Her only friend. Jeanine walked in the day she started working at the diner and introduced herself to Caitlyn. She told Caitlyn she had no idea why she thought moving to the tiny town was a good idea, but she was going to make the best of it. And that meant making a new friend. Caitlyn was the chosen one.

Caitlyn laughed and blew off the crazy woman she'd never seen before, but Jeanine didn't stop talking to her. Eventually, she wore Caitlyn down, and they became best friends.

Until Jeanine vanished. Four years of talking almost every day, and then she was gone. There was no way Caitlyn was going to believe it was because she left. She just needed one person to believe her.

Liam Johnson.

She stared at her phone and prayed it would ring. If he wasn't willing to meet her, she'd have to find another way to convince him. But he was her last hope. The police didn't care. The FBI hadn't done shit. But Liam...

Caitlyn carried her phone to the bathroom and made sure the ringer was on high. She stripped off her clothes and stepped into the shower, bracing herself was the not quite lukewarm water that ran through the pipes of her old building. She briefly considered sneaking into one of the locker rooms at the factory and taking a shower there, but she knew if she got caught, it would be worse than a hot shower was worth.

She showered and dried herself and, letting her hope get

the better of her, changed into a clean outfit. Just in case Liam called.

He was going to call. He had to.

ENGLISH WAS MORE than a little curious about the stunning, curvy server who left her number and nothing else for him. She reminded him of Caitlyn Powers, but he doubted she would still be in their minuscule hometown. She was a star before any of them knew what a star really was. There was no way she stuck around.

Whoever the woman was, she piqued English's curiosity enough that he made the call when the party was finally over. She answered on the first ring, and when he told her who he was, she eagerly agreed to meet him for a drink.

Which was why English was walking into the one and only dive bar in East Charlottesville, Vermont, ten minutes before midnight.

He looked around the dark interior of Sparky's for the woman and found himself a seat at the bar when he didn't see her.

"What can I get you?" the bored bartender asked.

"Beer. Whatever you have on tap."

The man nodded, giving English a cursory once-over and dismissing him as not a threat. English accepted the dismissal and passed a twenty over when the beer landed in front of him.

He sipped the beer and looked around, wondering if the woman was going to show. He wasn't normally reckless enough to meet a woman he didn't know out for a drink, but absolutely nothing dangerous ever happened in East Charlottesville.

His beer was half-gone when the door opened and the woman he was waiting for walked in. She locked her gaze on his and sauntered across the room toward him like she owned the place, and English. He couldn't explain why he was drawn to her, but he was. Maybe it was the memories that being home brought up, or maybe it was watching all his friends and teammates pair up and settle down, but the woman in the black leggings, black sweater, and the mess of black curls piled on top of her head made his pulse race.

She slid onto the stool next to him and grabbed his beer, taking a healthy sip of it before she took a deep breath. "Thanks for calling. And for meeting me here."

"Sure," English said, wondering how he could ask her name without making it obvious he didn't remember her.

"I need some help. And I'm sorry to hijack your weekend, but no one else believes me."

English's body went from tight with need to tight with awareness. The air in the bar shifted before he drew his next breath. Everything and everyone focused on them. The men at the pool table moved closer. The bartender walked into the back room, leaving the bar unattended. Even some of the patrons seemed to have vanished in the minute or two since his not-date showed up.

"No one believes you about what?" English asked, unsure if he wanted the answer.

"My best friend disappeared. Something happened to her. And I think something is going to happen to me, too."

"Why do you think that?" English asked. As the words left his mouth, the hair on the back of his neck stood up. His heart slammed against his chest.

A cue stick snapped on the bar next to him, right where his hand had been. The glass he was drinking from shattered, the shards spraying like champagne at a party.

English leaped to cover the woman with his body as someone else reached for her.

"We told you to stop this, Caitlyn."

"Caitlyn Powers?" he blurted.

Her gaze met his as the man yanked her ponytail.

"Believe me now?" she choked out.

4

———

CAITLYN FOUGHT AGAINST THE GUY HOLDING HER PONYTAIL, but the effort was useless. He was bigger and stronger. The only thing she had going for her was desperation. Mostly a desperate desire to get away from his rotten stench and beer-breath.

"Let go of me," she shouted, aware of the entire bar watching. The more of a scene she created, the more unlikely it was that she would vanish the way Jeanine did. If everyone knew who she was, her disappearance wouldn't be swept under the rug.

"You need to quit telling people something happened to Jeanine," the guy said, his mouth close enough to her ear that she could feel his breath on her neck.

"Something did happen to her," Caitlyn growled back.

Where the hell was Liam? She asked him to meet her there because it was where Jeanine was going the night she disappeared. But more than that, Caitlyn thought he would actually help her.

Caitlyn tried to turn her head, but her ponytail was

locked in the beer-breath guy's grip and her head unmovable.

"The woman asked you to let go," another voice said. It was similar to Liam's, but dangerous and deadly and not at all like the sweet guy she remembered.

"And what are you going to do about it?" the man holding her asked.

A whimper from behind her was followed by a yelp. Pain. A lot of it. Did they hurt Liam? Shit.

Caitlyn's head was released, the man stepping back. She finally sat up and looked at Liam. Fucking hell. He was...intoxicating. Her eyes went wide at the sight of him. His feet set apart, easily supporting the weight of the limp man in his arms. His tee stretched tight across his chest and showed off just how strong Liam Johnson was. His normally quiet persona was offset by this badass warrior she didn't know was under there. Sure, Caitlyn knew he was in the military, but this? If she wasn't so scared, she'd be trying to talk him into going home with her.

Caitlyn looked around the room at the rest of the men. They stood in a circle around her and Liam and his prisoner. Pool cues, mugs, and fists were their weapons of choice. She and Liam only had one of those, and there was no way they would win against half a dozen men.

"Now, we're going to walk out of here. And you're going to let us," Liam snarled at the room. He jerked his head toward Caitlyn for her to move closer to him. She didn't hesitate to do so, but she didn't get very far.

Someone stepped between them and grabbed Caitlyn's arm, yanking her toward the other men in the group. "Ow!"

"Let her go!"

"Fuck you."

A sickening snap echoed loudly through the mostly

silent bar. Before Caitlyn could see where it came from, a howl of pain followed the sound.

"You broke his fucking arm!" one of the men shouted.

"And I'm gonna do the same to you if you don't let her go."

Caitlyn's already racing heart thumped harder. Her palms dampened. She wasn't going to have to worry about disappearing because she was going to die, right there in that bar.

She kicked the man holding onto her, hoping it would be enough to catch him off guard. He was surprised, but he didn't go down. He squeezed her arm tighter as one of the other guys rushed past them toward Liam.

"You're going to stop making trouble around here, bitch."

Another guy stepped in front of Caitlyn. She lunged at him, intent on poking him in the eyes. He deflected her move, her fingers jabbing him in the cheek. Then he laughed.

"You think you're going to get out of this? You really think you have a shot?"

"One of you took Jeanine! I'm going to find out who."

The two men around her laughed. The guy holding her arm let go, and Caitlyn elbowed him.

"Oof," he said. "Bitch."

Caitlyn didn't stop to think, she just reacted. She kicked the knee of the guy in front of her, smiling when he dropped to the floor. She shifted her weight to kick him again when the other guy grabbed her around the waist and hoisted her in the air like she was still model-thin.

He slammed her onto the bar, knocking the wind out of her. Her head felt like it split wide open where it hit the edge of the bar. She saw stars, then darkness as her brain fought to keep her awake. She groaned from the pain, but she couldn't stop.

Someone hit the bar next to her, grunting before sliding down the front of it to the floor. Liam was fighting another guy, punching and kicking the man with ease. If she survived this, she needed to ask him how to do that.

Hands grabbed her shoulders and yanked her to her feet. She wobbled and tried to figure out if there were still two of them or if her dizziness was making her see double. She squeezed her eyes shut and opened them again, still unsure.

It didn't matter. She was going to fight until she got answers about Jeanine.

Caitlyn dove at the men. One easily sidestepped her telegraphed move, and she went flying to the floor, sliding across the disgusting wood in beer and peanut shells and God knew what else. The need to vomit tore through her. Then she was on her feet again, hands supporting her once more.

"You're a fun one, Caitlyn. Maybe after this, you can come home with me. I like it when they fight back." The first guy said, his voice low and for her ears only.

"Is that what happened to Jeanine? She fought back, and you killed her?"

The guy laughed and licked the shell of her ear. "Nah, it was nothing like that."

"Tell me where she is!"

Caitlyn barely got the words out when his hand wrapped tightly around her throat, cutting off words, breath, thoughts. Caitlyn clawed at his meaty hand, desperate for air. The pounding in her head grew stronger as the pounding in her heart slowed.

She was going to die. He was going to hold her throat

until she stopped breathing. And no one would care. Her one and only friend in the world was gone. Her father ran off before she was out of the womb. Her mother stole from her and disappeared. Caitlyn had no one. And she never would.

She stared up at the man whose fingers were around her throat. He wasn't going to beat her. He might kill her, but she wouldn't give him the satisfaction of knowing she wanted to beg for her life.

His eye twitched, unease slipping into his gaze. He stared back at her, his confident smirk fading at the edges. He was trying to figure her out. Could she use that? His fingers were still cutting off her air. She was likely seconds away from passing out.

A hand reached around the man's throat and squeezed. His eyes widened with surprise before he let Caitlyn go. She sank to the floor, gasping for much needed breath that made her lungs burn. Then he was on the ground next to her, holding his throat and wheezing.

"Let's go. Now!" The voice was a command, one Caitlyn wasn't sure about, but it was her only choice. She grabbed the offered hand and let him drag her to her feet and out of the bar into the cool night.

"Liam," she breathed, vaguely aware that he was the man getting her out of there. "How...?"

He pushed her into the backseat of a fancy SUV with leather seats and a new car smell. She curled onto her side as the door slammed near her feet. Within seconds, the vehicle purred to life, and she nearly fell off the seat as it lurched out of the parking lot and into the darkness of the night.

Caitlyn closed her eyes and focused on breathing. Liam

was her last and only hope. And she almost got him killed. What the hell was going on?

"I NEED INTEL," English barked. "We're missing something."

"I don't—" Caitlyn choked out from the backseat before she was interrupted.

"What are you talking about?" Dunn asked over the speaker in the vehicle.

"I just got jumped by six fuckers in a goddamn bar, Dunn. I was there to meet...someone I went to school with. She said she needed my help, and these guys surrounded us. They told her to let it go. I heard them mention Jeanine. What the hell am I in the middle of?"

"They're the ones who took my friend, Jeanine," Caitlyn groaned.

English looked in his mirror as much to see if they were being followed as to see Caitlyn as she sat up. She rubbed her throat gently and cleared it.

"Who the hell is that?" Dunn asked.

"Caitlyn Powers," she answered for herself. "I went to high school with Liam. My friend, Jeanine Waterford, is missing. The police said she left town, but I know that's not true. They won't let me into her apartment, but I saw inside when they were there and her stuff is still there. Plus, Jeanine wouldn't have left without telling me. Something happened to her. And those men at the bar are behind it."

"What makes you say that?" English asked. "And why the hell did you tell me to meet you there if you knew that?"

"It's the only bar in town. And I didn't think meeting you at The Bend would be a good idea."

English's cheek burned with his teenage fantasies of

doing exactly that. Caitlyn Powers was the girl every guy at school had a crush on. She was beautiful and funny and popular. She was also untouchable for guys like English who could barely speak when a pretty girl was around.

"What's The Bend?" Dunn asked.

"It's where everyone goes to make out," Caitlyn provided. "Would you mind telling me who you are?"

"This is Dunn. He's the leader of... He's my boss. We..."

"I know what you do, Liam. I know you were in the military and are part of some group that finds people or helps people or whatever. When I heard the rumor that you were home, I knew I needed to talk to you. Try to get you to help me. That's why I gave you my number. I need your help to find Jeanine."

The fire in English's face burned his cheeks. He was thankful for the darkness of night that hid it from her. He was foolish enough to think the beautiful, curvy server who asked him if he wanted to catch up was really looking to hook up instead. But nope, she just needed something from him. And not an orgasm.

"We're already on the case," Dunn answered when English didn't supply any information to Caitlyn.

"You are? What does that mean?"

"It means he's there to look for your friend. The file landed with us because there wasn't much of any evidence. The FBI think the local PD are right, so they asked us to take a look. Due diligence and all that."

"So, you're here to find her?" Caitlyn asked, her voice rising in volume.

"Not exactly," Dunn said. English could feel Caitlyn's disappointment. "English is there to visit his parents. While in town, he was supposed to ask around and see what he could find out. At some point, he would have reached out to you, since you're the one who reported her missing, but unless he finds a reason to believe something happened to Ms. Waterford, he won't be there long."

"But something did happen to her. And that fight proves it."

"What that fight proves is that you're reckless with my life and yours," English growled at her.

She froze, retreating from her position between the two front seats. She sat back, sinking into the leather and shutting her mouth.

"I'm sorry," Caitlyn whispered.

English grunted, but he wasn't ready to accept her apology. He felt like the same stupid kid he was in school. The kid who thought Caitlyn Powers would look at him one day. The kid who fooled himself into believing she might notice him or like him or even talk to him. Instead, she was the girl with all the power. The one who had him wrapped around her little finger.

And she did it again with ease. She knew exactly who he was when she approached him at dinner. She said his name, but never said her own. She flirted with him and made it seem as though she was interested in more than a drink. She used him.

"All of that is beside the point," Dunn said, snapping English back into the moment. "Ms. Powers, you've clearly picked a scab. The men you say are responsible for your friend's disappearance could very well be, but this stunt didn't do anything to help us out. We need to look into them and find out what we can. We need to know who they are and what connection she had to each of them. And we need to know who she was. Who did she spend time with? Boyfriends or girlfriends? Coworkers, family, acquaintances. Anyone who could have had something against her."

"My father said she slept with married men," English said, his voice flat and emotionless.

"She's a good person!" Caitlyn argued instantly. "She sleeps around, sure, but she doesn't seek out married men. You know how this town is, Liam. Nothing is secret here. And Jeanine wouldn't go after someone if she knew he was married."

"Are you sure about that?" Dunn asked.

"Yes. She's my best friend."

"Then you can give us a list of all the men she's slept with in the past six months or so?"

"Um, well, actually, no."

"Why not?" Dunn asked.

"Because she doesn't tell me who she's sleeping with. Not by name. She calls them all by a descriptor," Caitlyn mumbled.

"A descriptor? What does that mean?" English asked.

"It means she doesn't use their names at all but their anatomy, doesn't it?" Dunn asked.

"Yeah. I don't know who any of them are. There was one guy she was sleeping with fairly regularly, but she only called him Lengthy Lefty."

"What?" English blurted.

Dunn choked. "Fuck me."

"She said he was really long and curved to the left, so..."

"Dear fucking God," English mumbled. "How the hell did I get this assignment?"

"You volunteered," Dunn said.

"I quit."

"Too late for that. She needs protection. Sounds like you both need to be off the radar a little bit. Or at least away from that bar. Where are you going?" Dunn asked.

"Driving around right now. I have no idea what I need to do."

"First, you need to get into Ms. Waterford's place."

"The police have it locked." Caitlyn leaned forward again, grabbing the edge of English's seat. She pressed her body between the two front seats, her breast brushing against his arm and making his dick hard.

Fucking hell, was he so desperate for a little sex that a fully clothed side-boob was enough to get his rocks off?

"A locked door won't be a problem," Dunn said. "I think you should go now. Get there before any remaining evidence is gone. And before the men Caitlyn thinks are behind this show up."

"I agree. Her place isn't likely to be monitored. The police here don't have enough staff for that. Getting in and out unseen will be easier at night. I have a few hours before daylight hits."

"What are you going to do with your visitor?" Dunn asked.

English risked a glance at Caitlyn. She was hanging on their every word. When Dunn asked about her, she turned to him. Their faces were close. The darkness made it impossible to make out all her features, but when they passed under a streetlight, he saw hope in her eyes.

"I'm not sure I have a choice," English answered, dragging his gaze from Caitlyn back to the road.

"She'll be an asset. She knows what the apartment looked like before. And she'll know what items Ms. Waterford would have taken if she actually did disappear."

"So, you believe me? That something happened to her?" Caitlyn asked, her voice barely a whisper of relief and hope.

"We aren't sure yet, Caitlyn. Best case scenario, your friend left town. But English dug into her financials and she didn't withdraw any large sums of cash and none of her cards have been used since you reported her missing. If she left on her own, we should have seen some activity. Since there's none, it's suspicious."

"That isn't good, is it?"

English turned to look at her. She wasn't asking Dunn, she was asking him. She wanted to know what he thought. How he felt. And staring into her eyes, the red fingerprints on her throat and desire pulsing through his veins, he couldn't lie to her.

"No, Caitlyn, it isn't good."

5

___

CAITLYN WAS SILENT THE REST OF THE DRIVE TO JEANINE'S. She didn't ask how Liam knew exactly where her friend lived, and she didn't really want to know. Hearing he was in town to investigate Jeanine's disappearance was enough to scare Caitlyn into the harsh reality that she was right and something was wrong.

Liam parked around the side of Jeanine's apartment, tucking his SUV out of sight of anyone who drove by. The only noise when they got out was the crickets chirping. And the blood rushing through Caitlyn's ears.

Liam led the way, making impressively quick work of Jeanine's locked door before letting them into the apartment. Caitlyn reached for the light switch, but he stopped her with a gentle touch.

"Just in case." He turned on the flashlight on his phone and nodded for her to do the same.

Caitlyn followed orders as unease crawled up her spine. She'd broken into her best friend's apartment in the dead of night with a man who was more a stranger to her than anything else. She'd always been a little reckless, but this might shoot up to the top of her *WTF was I thinking?* list.

Liam moved carefully, shining his flashlight at the floor before each step he took. Caitlyn stuck close to him, stepping where he stepped and moving where he moved.

"Tell me the layout of this place," he said quietly. His tone was patient but anxious, as if he could feel the tension rolling off of her.

"It's a one bedroom," Caitlyn said. "Jeanine's room is over there. She has a bathroom in her room. Kitchen is in the back near the window. Obviously, this is her living room, and the dining room is right there." The space was small enough to see all of it. A soft light filtered through the bare window over the kitchen sink. There was another window in the bedroom on the same wall, casting a similar glow through the space they hadn't moved toward yet.

"Do you want to go into her bedroom?" Liam asked.

Caitlyn hesitated. Why was he asking her? Did he think they were going to find her body? What was in her bedroom?

"I only meant are you comfortable doing this, Caitlyn? A woman's bedroom is personal. If she weren't missing, I'd never go in there without her permission. I need to know what's in there, but she's your friend. If you don't want to go in, I'll understand."

"Do you think she's in there?" Caitlyn whispered.

"No," Liam said easily. His confident tone gave her the space to breathe for the first time since they walked in. She hadn't realized how terrified she was being there.

"I'll go. You said you need to know if something is missing, right?"

"Yes. If you're okay with that. It can help us prove she's truly missing. Get more help here."

Caitlyn nodded. Hope warred with fear inside her. If she could prove Jeanine was missing, the search would expand, but it also meant she proved her friend was missing. Caitlyn wasn't sure what she wanted to find.

Liam moved toward the bedroom, shining his light in both directions before pointing it into the room. Again, he left the light off, ramping up Caitlyn's heartbeat.

What if someone was there? What if they were hiding in the closet and waiting to jump them? What if...? God, so many terrifying options.

Liam went to Jeanine's bed and lifted the covers back. Caitlyn went straight to her vanity. Jeanine would sit in front of it and brush her hair, do her makeup, and pick out her jewelry. Jeanine was always wearing a delicate silver necklace with a blue crystal pendant. It matched her eyes. There was more to the story, but Caitlyn never got her to share what it was. All that mattered at the moment was it wasn't there.

Caitlyn looked through her friend's jewelry for pieces she knew Jeanine loved, but aside from the blue pendant, there was nothing she wore daily. Nothing Caitlyn could tell was missing, or not.

Liam walked into the bathroom. The shower curtain rings scraped the metal rod. Plastic rustled for a second, then stopped. Caitlyn ignored what he was doing and kept looking.

Jeanine's closet was its usual disaster of clothes dangling from hangers and piled on the floor. She complained constantly that her closet was too small for all her stuff so she left half of it on the floor. Jeanine was not the neatest person. Purses hung on the back of the closet door, shoes were kicked into the closet and spewing out, some buried and others on top.

Tears flooded Caitlyn's eyes. The boots Jeanine wore the last time they went out were still on top. They'd walked back to Jeanine's after their night out and crashed. The two of them giggled about the men they flirted with as Jeanine kicked off her boots and cracked the wall next to the closet. She joked about her landlord getting pissed at her for destroying the place.

Caitlyn told her he'd have to find out about it and promised to help Jeanine fix the wall. One of Caitlyn's many jobs over the years had been receptionist for a handyman. He taught her a few tips when she worked for him, including how to do a simple patch job on a wall. That one skill saved Caitlyn more than a few security deposits.

She stared at the cracked drywall and sank onto the overly soft mattress. Her right hip hit something, and she stood again to dig it out from under the comforter.

Jeanine's Columbia sweatshirt. The tears Caitlyn was keeping at bay overflowed and streamed down her cheeks. The sweatshirt was Jeanine's favorite thing in the world. She said it reminded her she was capable of great things. Jeanine was a Columbia grad, but it wasn't something she shared with a lot of people because she didn't use her theater degree.

Caitlyn pressed her cheek to Jeanine's sweatshirt and drew a deep breath. It smelled like her favorite perfume, the cheap one she bought monthly from the general store in town. Caitlyn teased her mercilessly about the two sides of her personality, but Jeanine said it was because she was a Gemini.

"Did you find something?" Liam hissed, bringing Caitlyn out of her memory and back to the present.

She held out the sweatshirt. "This was under the covers."

"And?"

"It's her favorite sweatshirt. She doesn't wear it out, but she wears it almost every day. As soon as she gets home, she changes into this. All the time. If she left, she never would have left this behind."

"A sweatshirt?"

Caitlyn sighed. "I know it doesn't seem like much, but yes. Her Columbia sweatshirt was important to her."

"Okay. Put it back where it was. We need to be able to tell the FBI to look for it. If it's not here, or if we take it, they won't be able to use it to prove something happened. Did you find anything else?"

Caitlyn stood and stuffed the sweatshirt back. She wanted to keep it, to keep a piece of Jeanine, but she knew he was right. "Her charger for her phone is still here. I didn't see her purse. It looks like she just left for work or something. Like nothing has changed. If she left town, wouldn't she have taken all of her stuff?"

"Not if she was running from someone," Liam said, bringing a whole new level of fear to Caitlyn.

"Running from someone? Someone could be after her?"

"We have no idea. What we're doing tonight is figuring out if we think she left on her own or if we think someone else had something to do with her disappearance." He looked around the room, either not caring or not realizing the effect his words had on Caitlyn. "Did she have a computer?"

"Coffee table," Caitlyn said, pointing to the living room.

Liam walked that way with the confidence of a man who dealt with these situations all the time. He knew what to look for and what would be important. Caitlyn floundered and got emotional, and Liam just moved on to the next thing.

Caitlyn scanned the room once more before following

Liam to the living room. He was on the couch with Jeanine's laptop open in front of him. The screen glowed with a password-protected page. Blue, again. Always blue for Jeanine.

"Do you know her password?" Liam asked.

His voice was distant, mechanical. Caitlyn was struggling to hold her shit together, and he was going through the motions. Sure, it was her friend, not his, but still.

"No. I've never had a reason to use her computer. I always have my phone with me."

Liam's fingers flew over the keys. The screen didn't change except to tell him the password was wrong over and over again. He kept trying, pausing briefly after the first few attempts before entering more.

Caitlyn left him to break into the computer and moved toward the door. Jeanine always left her purse on the small table. Caitlyn moved stuff around to see what else was there. No purse, no keys, no wallet. A small stack of mail that was unopened. A few sticky notes. A discarded tube of lipstick. Caitlyn laughed to herself when she saw a black heel.

A wisp of something out of place tickled her nose. A smell she knew, but one that didn't belong. Caitlyn sniffed the air. Was it coming from the kitchen? She turned, and the scent dissipated. No. The hallway? Maybe it was a neighbor. Cooking, no burning—

"Is that smoke?" she blurted.

"What?" English was on his feet in an instant. He crossed the room to her in three large steps. He pressed the back of his hand to the door and drew back instantly. "Fuck. We have to get out of here."

"What do you mean?"

English moved toward the couch and grabbed the laptop from the coffee table. He tucked it under his arm and looked around. Was there anything else he needed? Her toothbrush was still in the bathroom, as were the rest of her personal items. The sweatshirt in the bed was important, but it wasn't as big of a clue as the entire fucking apartment being torched with them inside.

"Liam?" Caitlyn whispered, her voice sounding farther away than a minute ago.

She was still standing by the door, her gaze locked on their escape route.

"We need to go out the window, Caitlyn. That door is too hot. We won't make it. We need to move. Now."

When she didn't budge, Liam grabbed her arm and dragged her toward the bedroom. His teenage fantasies of being in a bedroom with Caitlyn Powers mocked him as he shoved her past the bed and to the second story window that was their only hope.

"How are we going to get out of here?" Caitlyn was panicking. The high pitch shout and the unfocused movements told English he needed to get moving or she might have a panic attack or anxiety attack or any number of attacks that would lead to them being trapped in the apartment while it burned around them.

English didn't bother answering her. He shoved the laptop into her hands and grabbed the dresser under the window. He yanked it, grunting when the solid wood piece barely moved. He repositioned his feet and tried again, getting it to swing to the side and out of the way.

The lock on the window fought him when he turned it, but it finally moved. He looked down, hating that there was no easy way to get to the ground. Nothing like a trellis or an awning or a fucking tree they could grab hold of before dropping to the ground and praying they could get up again and run before the entire building went up in flames.

A crack echoed through the space as the front door splintered from the fire. The roar of the flames drew closer. Smoke filtered into the room in thick waves.

English pulled at the window, but it didn't budge. "Why won't this open?" he asked no one.

"It's painted shut," Caitlyn provided.

"What the fuck? Why? That's a violation of fire code."

Caitlyn snorted. "Gee, that's ironic."

English would have found it funny except it wasn't. Not even a little bit. Not just because it was ironic, but also because they were going to have to hold on to the windowsill and drop to the ground. It was going to be bad enough, but if the window was painted shut, he needed to break it.

He grabbed the lamp from the nightstand and wrapped the cord around the base. It was heavy, solid, and should do the trick. Caitlyn shouted at him as he swung.

The glass shattered, sucking fresh air into the room. The fire was as happy as English was, sucking in the oxygen happily. It was time to go.

English knocked as much of the glass away from the window as possible, trying to give them the best shot they could get at having a good grip. It was going to hurt like hell, but it was their best chance. Their only chance.

"Here," Caitlyn said, handing him two tees. "Wrap these around your hands."

English nodded his thanks, grateful she knew what they had to do and wasn't going to fight him on it. He glanced around, making sure the laptop was close by while he wrapped his hands. "You're going first."

"You should. If I don't make it out of here, find out what happened to Jeanine."

"We're both going to make it, Caitlyn." The smoke was starting to make him dizzy. He was already choking, but the fresh air that should have helped them only drew the fire closer. It licked at the bedroom doorframe, sneaking in and getting closer.

"You need to go first," she said. "I... I don't know if I can do this."

"It's going to hurt."

She nodded. "I know."

The fire caught on the bed, igniting it almost instantly. They didn't have long. "Caitlyn, go. Now. I'm not leaving you in here. Go out the window, and I'll toss the computer down to you."

She drew a breath and nodded. There was no graceful way to get out of the window. She brushed away more of the glass with her wrapped hands, then sat on the far right edge. She swung one foot out, then the other. Slowly, she eased herself forward until her butt was barely on the windowsill. She leaned back and turned her body, laying on her stomach.

She winced and closed her eyes.

"Caitlyn?"

"I'm fine."

He knew she wasn't, but she had no choice. She had to be. She lifted on her right side and moved herself back. Only her shoulders and head were visible.

The room cracked and popped, the fire consuming everything. The dresser English pushed away from the window was orange on one side. He snatched the computer from the top before it melted. Fire was trying on all of

Jeanine's clothes. Finding all her favorite things and claiming them.

English turned his focus back to Caitlyn in time to see her vanish. Her fingertips were there for a few more seconds, then they let go.

"Caitlyn!" he called out the window. Despite the fire inside, outside remained pitch black. She was gone. Invisible in her black outfit. Or maybe gone.

"Liam! I'm right here." She waved her hands, her t-shirt covered palms barely visible. "Toss the computer."

He didn't think before he dropped it toward her, hoping she would catch it.

"Got it. Now, get down here."

Sweat ran down his back and soaked into his jeans. Every inch of him burned. He had to go. He was out of time.

English moved to the window. Blood glistened in the firelight on the glass Caitlyn cut herself on. One shard, barely above the edge. But it was enough that she was hurt.

He tried to move the offending piece away, but it was stuck in the frame. He couldn't break it to make it smaller. It was just right there, in the middle of where he was going to put his body.

English put his hand over the glass shard and spun his legs out the window. He turned and lowered his body in one motion, using his arms to support his weight as stretched as close to the ground as possible. Just doing a pull-up, he told himself. On a bar of glass.

He extended his arms fully and let go of the window. He dropped, falling seconds longer than he expected to. Pain shot through his shins. He grunted and rolled away from the burning building. He pushed to a stand and looked up at the flames shooting out of the window he'd just freed himself from.

"Are you all right?" Caitlyn asked.

"Yeah. How are you? Where are you cut?"

"I'm fine. I think I hear sirens, though. Should we go?"

"Fuck. Yeah, we need to get the hell out of here. I'm sorry about all this."

"It's not your fault. I'm the one who brought you into it. I should be apologizing to you. And I understand if you don't want to help me anymore. This was... This was a lot."

"Caitlyn—"

"Stop! Put your hands up! You're under arrest!"

Are you fucking kidding me?

6

─────────

Caitlyn winced when the arresting officer snapped the cuffs on her wrists. Blood trickled from the wound on her side, but she didn't bother complaining. Officer Henry wouldn't care. He'd probably tighten the cuffs even more if he knew it might make her night worse.

"We get a phone call," Liam argued. To his credit, he didn't sound angry, but his harsh tone definitely left no room for the officer to think Liam was happy about the situation.

"You'll get a call when I say you get a call. Right now, you're going to sit in the back of my car."

"She's injured. You need to take her to get treatment."

Caitlyn closed her eyes and tried not to hate Liam. He was trying to help. He thought it would get things moving. He was dead wrong, but he was trying.

"I'm fine," Caitlyn hurried to say.

Officer Henry gave her a slow once-over. His dark eyes lingered on her oversized breasts. She tried to hunch her shoulders and hide her size from him, but he was a class one creep.

He'd hit on her more than once over the last handful of years, always making sure she knew he was doing her a favor. Because he was God's gift to women, of course. Such a conceited ass.

"You could at least loosen her cuffs," Liam snarled.

Officer Henry's gaze traveled back to Liam for a second. Long enough that Caitlyn could shoot him a *shut the fuck up* look that she hoped he understood.

"Do you need me to loosen your cuffs?" Officer Henry asked.

"I'm fine," Caitlyn said. She stiffened her shoulders and tightened her jaw, glaring at the man before he had a chance to move closer to her.

"She said she's fine. Let's get you two in the backseat before you run off." Officer Henry grabbed Caitlyn's wrists and shoved her forward, nearly sending her flying into the dirt. He caught her, wrenching her shoulder.

Pain so intense she nearly threw up sliced through her side. She stumbled, trying not to pass out. Officer Henry pushed her again, not giving her a second to stop and breathe.

He opened the door and shoved Caitlyn's head down before pushing her into the back of the car, then walked Liam around to the other door and put him in the back with her. He slammed the door and walked away.

"Are you okay?" Liam asked.

"I'm fine," Caitlyn lied.

"Why didn't you tell him you were hurt? He would have been forced to take you to get medical attention."

"He's a disgusting pig. If he knew I was hurt, he would do whatever he could to make it worse."

"Like forcing you to walk fast so you'd stumble. Fucking asshole."

"Yeah, well, I'm used to it. It's not the first run-in I've had with Officer Henry."

"What does that mean?"

Caitlyn hated the way her cheeks burned with the memory of their last encounter.

"What did he do to you?"

"Nothing," Caitlyn said. She wasn't interested in reliving it, or in telling Liam about it. The tables had turned since high school. She was the girl who had it all back then. She was beautiful and thin and popular. She had her entire future ahead of her. She thought her life was perfect, and she almost felt bad for guys like Liam. Guys who were skinny and nerdy and loners. Guys who didn't get a date any time they wanted.

But Liam wasn't that guy anymore. If she had to guess, he had women lined up to date him. He was gorgeous. And she was the woman men like Officer Henry hit on out of some misguided sense of pity. They expected her to put out whenever a guy showed the slightest interest because she should be grateful that a man even looked at her, let alone was willing to fuck her.

Well, fuck him. Fuck them. Fuck all of them. Caitlyn knew who she was. She was trying to be a better person. After her mother left, she was bitter and angry. She still was, but she refused to take it out on everyone around her. Now, she just wanted to live her life.

"Caitlyn," Liam said, his voice gentle like he knew something bad had happened.

It had been a long time since someone acted like they cared about her. Jeanine did, but Jeanine wasn't gentle. She was brash and funny and aggressive. If she knew what happened with Officer Henry, she would have flirted with him just so she could make him look like an ass. But Caitlyn never told her. She never told anyone.

"I'm going to fucking kill him," Liam growled.

"Who?"

"Officer Henry. For whatever he did to you that made you feel the way you're feeling right now."

"I—"

The car door opened, and Officer Henry slid into the driver's seat. "All right, lovebirds. You two are getting a free ride to the police station. Someone needs a word." Officer Henry smiled at them in the mirror before he took off into the night.

Liam shifted in the seat, but Caitlyn sat perfectly still. She knew the roads well enough to anticipate turns so she didn't lose her balance. When they stopped in front of the station, she waited while another officer came out and opened her door.

"I'll take her in. You get him," Officer Henry said.

Caitlyn drew a deep breath and prepared herself. He grabbed her shoulder and forced her forward, again sending pain through her side. The cut, still bleeding, and his jerky movements were doing the job and making her hurt. She bit the inside of her lip and refused to let him see the effect.

He guided her into the station with his hand wrapped firmly around her bicep, his fingers brushing the outside of her breast. He opened his hand and let the backs of his fingers caress her more openly when they turned down the hallway toward the interrogation rooms.

Caitlyn wanted to hit him, but it would only make things worse for her so she held back the tears and the words and the hatred and tried to pretend she was anywhere but there.

He led her into a room and uncuffed one hand. He swung both around and shoved her onto a chair, then resecured the cuffs in front of her and to the table in the middle of the room.

"Sit tight. Someone will be in to speak with you shortly," Officer Henry said in a sickeningly sweet voice.

The door slammed shut and made Caitlyn jump, but at least she was alone. She didn't have to deal with him touching her or Liam watching her. She knew someone was watching her, but it was someone who thought she burned down her best friend's apartment, not someone who was going to try to protect her or take care of her.

She snorted. Liam wasn't taking that role either. She was stupid for even considering it. Story of her life.

Caitlyn sat in the room for what felt like hours. There was no clock to tell her just how long it had been. Her side ached, and she had to pee. Her neck beaded with sweat from the overly warm room. It was all a tactic to make her talk when they finally joined her. One she wasn't going to fall for.

The door creaked open before slamming shut again with another man inside with her. He looked up from a file folder with a pretend smile and tsked. "Oh, they shouldn't have cuffed you to the table. I'm sorry about that. Let me get you out of those."

Caitlyn watched him, cataloguing everything about him as he withdrew a key from his cheap gray suit and approached. He set the folder on the table, open, nearly inviting her to read it, but she didn't look at it. She focused on the man she knew to be the one and only detective in the northern part of the state. He didn't live in East Char-lottesville, but he was called in when they needed help.

He was older than her, probably in his late-forties. His dark hair was receding on top and graying on the sides, possibly making him look older than he was. Faint wrinkles lined his face. His eyes were light brown, a few shades lighter than his hair. His tan was definitely not natural in Northern Vermont fall, meaning he either frequented a tanning salon, went on vacation recently, or got it out of a bottle. The faint orange tone around his jawline suggested bottle.

"That's better," the man said, as though his wrists were the ones locked to a table for hours. "So, how about we talk for a minute?"

Caitlyn leaned back in her chair and refused to rub her aching wrists. Or her aching side. Or give him any emotion. She just stared at him.

"What were you doing at Jeanine Waterford's apartment tonight?"

Caitlyn stared at him. She crossed her arms and tilted her head to the side.

He narrowed his eyes. The edge of his mouth quirked up. He nodded. "How about why did you take her computer?"

Fuck. Caitlyn had forgotten about the computer. She was sure there was something on it that would be helpful, especially since Liam wanted to take it. But now the cops had it. The useless cops who told her Jeanine had left town.

"Not answering that one either. Maybe you'll tell me why you burned the building down. Two people were treated for burns, and three more residents are in the hospital for smoke inhalation. That's attempted murder, Ms. Powers. Six counts."

"You said five," Caitlyn blurted. She tucked her slick palms under her sweaty armpits and tried not to panic. Liam would get her out of this. He was with her. And he was a local hero. They would believe him.

"Liam Johnson. You jumped out of the window first,

leaving Mr. Johnson to die. At least, that's what he told us. So, six counts."

Tears stung her eyes and fear swelled her throat. Caitlyn was going to jail. For something she didn't do.

She wanted to demand he let her call someone, but she had no one to call. She knew she could ask for a lawyer, but she couldn't afford a good one. Not only was she not going to get answers about Jeanine, she was going to spend years in jail for something she didn't do.

She nibbled the inside of her lip and willed her tears to stop. She refused to cry or ask for anything. Eventually, they would have to give her a break, but until then, she had to wait them out.

"Nothing to say for yourself, Ms. Powers?"

Caitlyn glared back at the man.

He smirked and stood. "Nice to meet you."

The words *fuck you* were on the tip of her tongue, but she bit them back and held her shit together until he walked out and let the door slam behind him. She was definitely screwed.

ENGLISH REFUSED to answer any questions the cops had for him until he was given his phone call and had his attorney present. Of course, his attorney wasn't local, but he had other options. Like his cousin.

Adam answered on the first ring, sounding less than pleased with a middle of the night call. "What?"

"Adam, it's Liam. I need your help. Caitlyn Powers and I were at Jeanine Waterford's apartment when it went up in flames. We're at the police station."

"I'm on my way," Adam said, hanging up before English could say anything else.

English was escorted back to the holding room where a guy in a gray suit, who never introduced himself, tried to question him. English almost laughed at the shitty tactics the guy used. Did he learn interrogation from TV? He clearly had no idea who English was or the training he'd been through if he thought empty threats and manipulation would get him to admit to anything.

Halfway through the guy's questioning, someone pounded on the door. Gray Suit tossed a glare toward English before letting in whoever interrupted them.

"This case is no longer your jurisdiction," Adam said loudly, his voice echoing through the metal box English was stashed in. "I'm not sure why these two individuals were brought into this station, or what in the hell made you think you had any right to question them at all, but—"

"They set fire to—"

"Did I tell you to speak? Because you have no authority here. Let them go. Now."

"I need to see some credentials," Gray Suit said. He straightened to his full height, as though that made a damn bit of difference.

Another second and Gray Suit was backing out of the way to let Adam by. Adam tucked his badge back into his pocket. "Let's go."

English stood and followed his cousin out of the room. Gray Suit glared at him, but English just winked at the other man. Fucking worthless. If they put in half this effort to finding Jeanine Waterford, English wouldn't have been in her apartment when it was torched.

"Where's the woman he was brought in with? Caitlyn Powers?" Adam demanded of the closest officer.

"Um, she's in that room," the guy stumbled over himself to say.

Adam went to the room the guy pointed to and opened the door. "Caitlyn Powers?"

"Yeah?" she said, her voice hollow and small.

"Come with me, please."

"Who are you?"

Adam glanced back at English before stepping into the room. "I'm an FBI agent. We've looking into the disappearance of Jeanine Waterford. My understanding is you were at her place tonight."

"I didn't do anything," Caitlyn said. Her voice was shaky and scared. Small. Nothing like the Caitlyn English knew.

"Ms. Powers, please come with me. The FBI wants to help. We have no reason to believe you or your friend are at fault for anything."

"Really?"

"Liam's right behind me," Adam said softly. He couldn't tell the police he wasn't taking them into custody or he'd risk the cops holding them. Which meant he needed Caitlyn to go on her own.

"Liam said I left him there to die. I didn't do it. He's lying."

What? Adam glared at him, and English shook his head.

"Ms. Powers, we'll clear everything up. If you'll please come with me."

English waited a painfully long moment before her chair scraped across the vinyl floor. Her footsteps were sluggish. Adam reached for her and held her arm lightly as she walked out of the room.

Caitlyn met English's gaze with a harsh one of her own. She believed what the cops told her. That he blamed her for everything and was willing to let her take the fall for it.

What explanation would he have possibly had for being there? If he said it was her fault, he still had no right to be in a missing woman's apartment.

But the cops don't always play fair, and these cops didn't seem to be concerned with that in the slightest.

"There was a computer," English whispered to Adam. If they left without it, they'd never see it again.

Adam stopped. "The things they had when they were brought in. I need them. Now. Including the computer."

Adam in full agent mode was not someone the rinky-dink cops would mess with. It was only a few seconds before someone handed over the laptop and they were on their way.

English followed Caitlyn and Adam outside to his SUV. English wanted to be the one helping her, but she leaned into Adam like he was saving her. He was the hero.

Adam opened the door and helped Caitlyn up into the front seat. English climbed in the back with the laptop. Adam jogged around and started the engine.

"Start talking," he barked.

"Caitlyn and I met at Sparky's earlier tonight. Some guys attacked us and told her she needed to stop asking questions about Jeanine's disappearance. We barely got out of there, and I called Dunn to talk about it. He agreed that there's more going on than a woman skipped town and suggested we go to her apartment while it was dark and before the thugs at the bar got there and did something. We were looking around when Caitlyn smelled smoke. The hallway was on fire, so we had to smash the bedroom window and drop out from there. The cops were there in seconds. Like they were waiting for us or knew we would be there."

"You think it was a setup?" Adam asked.

"Absolutely."

"Fucking hell. This got a lot more complicated than we thought it might be. Is your vehicle still at the apartment?"

"It should be, but who knows if they towed it. Caitlyn's is at the bar." English looked at Caitlyn. She hadn't said a word since they got in the car. Her eyes were closed and her face was pale. "Adam, she cut her side on some glass when we climbed out of the window."

"Shit," he hissed. "I'm guessing they didn't rush to give her any medical attention."

"She told them she was fine. She thought they'd take longer or make it worse. The guy who picked us up... The way he treated her should never have happened."

"What are you saying?"

"I'm saying she was right, and there's no doubt in my mind the cops in this town are dirty. Quite possibly all of them. And my list of suspects keeps growing."

"So much for an easy case." He glanced at Caitlyn again. "She needs a doctor. Now."

English nodded. "Know any open this late?"

Adam chuckled. "I just might."

7

———

CAITLYN ROLLED OVER AND CRIED OUT. HER SIDE HURT LIKE hell. She stretched her hand along the sheet. Soft, smooth, expensive? What the hell?

Her eyes popped open, the rest of her body completely still. Where was she? The room wasn't familiar. A tall red dresser was across from the bed. An open closet held clothes that weren't familiar. Women's clothes.

Not Jeanine's, though.

Jeanine!

Everything came back to Caitlyn in a flash, like it had all been a dream, but it wasn't. She sat up, the cool rush of air from her movement drawing her attention to her bare torso. Thank God she still wore her bra, but her shirt was gone. Her leggings were still on. What the hell was going on?

Caitlyn stood, holding her breath when the pain in her —*what the hell?*—freshly stitched side sliced through her. It wasn't as bad as the night before. In jail.

She was fairly sure Liam and his cousin, or a guy she thought was his cousin, got her out of there, but her mind was fuzzy.

Caitlyn used the edge of the bed to get her close to the closet, then let go and took a few tentative steps on her own. All the clothes were way too small for her. Small and medium tops and pants. Even the jackets were smalls. She turned to the dresser. One drawer after another held the same. Small and medium. Small and medium. Mocking her plus size figure.

Caitlyn came to terms with her size years ago, loving the way she felt in her body. Growing up as a model, she lived on salad and water. Breakfast, lunch, and dinner were monitored carefully so she didn't gain weight. She was proud of her tiny waist, because her mother told her she should be.

But when the modeling jobs stopped and the money disappeared with her mother, Caitlyn tried all the things she hadn't been allowed to have. Ice cream, cheeseburgers, chocolate. It was amazing. She didn't know food could be so good.

She promised herself she'd never go back to obsessing over every calorie. There were days she longed to walk into a clothing store and buy whatever she wanted instead of being forced to look through the meager selection of plus-size options, but even that wasn't enough to get her to give up grilled cheese sandwiches.

Maybe if she had a few less of them, she could fit into something in the bedroom she slept in.

"Hey," a male voice said from behind her.

Caitlyn jumped and spun, finding Liam hovering near the door.

"I, um, I brought you your sweater. I washed it for you. It's still, um, there's a cut in it from the glass. Holly tried to fix it, but she's better with skin." His gaze drifted to her side and lingered. His cheeks reddened before he tore his gaze away and focused on her face again.

"Thanks," Caitlyn said. She resisted the urge to cover her body with her hands and took the sweater from him. She reached to pull it over her head and stopped when her skin stretched and her breath vanished.

"Are you okay?" Liam asked. His voice was closer. Anxious.

"I'm fine," Caitlyn insisted even though she was nothing close.

"Your stitches—"

"Hurt. A lot."

"Can I... Let me help you. I won't touch you. Just..."

Tears of shame stung Caitlyn's eyes. She had been on her own since she turned eighteen. She'd never asked anyone for help. She didn't like knowing she owed someone something. But the simple act of putting on her sweater was beyond her capabilities with a two-inch line of stitches on her belly. "Okay."

Caitlyn didn't look at Liam as she handed her sweater back to him. She kept her eyes averted when he bunched it up and lifted it over her head. He touched the hand on her uninjured side and guided it through the sleeve first, covering part of her embarrassed body.

"Go slow," he murmured.

He pulled the top as low as he could, making it easier for her to get her hand through the sleeve. When it tugged, she stopped and took a shaky breath.

"I never told the cops you left me in the apartment. They lied to try to get you to turn on me."

Caitlyn nodded. "Okay." Something about the way he said it had her believing him. He wouldn't have taken care of her if he thought she was willing to let him die. And he wouldn't have brought it up if it wasn't bothering him.

He didn't say anything else, just waited for her to be

ready to continue dressing. Liam was patient and kept his eyes focused on her face instead of her bare skin.

The pain subsided enough for Caitlyn to try again. She got her arm through the sleeve, and Liam helped her to pull the sweater down to cover her belly. She looked up at him. A five o'clock shadow coated his jawline, blond like his hair and only visible up close. His blue eyes were dark, almost navy, as he watched her. She reached her hand up and touched his face. He closed his eyes and leaned into her.

"Thank you," she said, knowing the words weren't nearly enough to tell him how much she appreciated him. Not only did he meet her to talk, but he stayed with her and protected her, got her out of jail and took her someplace safe so she could heal. No one had ever done any of that for her, let alone all of it in one night. "Thank you for helping me."

Liam stiffened at her words. His gaze darted away, and he took a step back, letting her hand fall between them. "You're welcome. Um, there's food downstairs if you're hungry. Then I can take you home."

Caitlyn wondered what she said that made him pull back so quickly. Normally, it wouldn't bother her when a guy flipped a switch, but they'd been through hell in the last twenty-four hours. Hell, barely twelve hours. And he was done.

She didn't bother asking him anything because he was already walking away from her. His retreating back was bunched up tight, his shoulders inching closer to his ears. He was like every other man. Not interested in her.

Well, fine. She wasn't interested in him either.

ENGLISH CLOSED and locked the bathroom door behind himself and took a deep, mind-clearing breath. What was he thinking touching her? He should have known better. Caitlyn Powers was so far out of his league they weren't playing the same game.

She reminded him of that quickly. It might not have been her intention to throw it in his face that she wasn't interested, but her thanking him was a sharp reminder that the whole thing started because her friend disappeared and she wanted his help finding her.

He was the one who was wishing it was more.

English splashed water on his face and tried to wake up. It wasn't the first time he'd pulled an all-nighter and wouldn't be the last. But it was the first time he'd sat up all night watching a woman sleep. When he carried Caitlyn into Holly's house the night before, she was weak and mumbling incoherently. She passed out in Adam's SUV on the drive and fought Holly and Adam when they got to her house, but Caitlyn settled when English spoke to her. He whispered words of encouragement while Holly put in an IV and gave her fluids, and again when Holly stitched up the wound on her side.

Holly assured him Caitlyn would be okay, but whenever he tried to leave the room, Caitlyn would make a noise. So, he stayed. With the door open so there was no risk of anyone thinking he took advantage of her.

All night, English prayed she'd be okay. And when he wasn't praying, he was trying to figure out what was going on that led him straight into a bar fight and attempted murder.

A thud outside the bathroom caught his attention. He opened the door and found Caitlyn sitting on the top step. "Did you fall?"

She shook her head. "No. I'm fine. I was going to walk downstairs."

"Do you need help?"

"No. I'm fine," she repeated.

She pushed herself to stand and grabbed the railing. Her white knuckles gave away her unsteadiness, even though her tone said she wasn't willing to take his help.

English moved next to her and slid his arm around her waist. She flinched at the touch, then sighed and wrapped her arm around his neck. She didn't let go of the railing as they took the stairs one step at a time, stopping when she shifted more of her weight to him.

"I'm sorry I'm so heavy," she mumbled.

"You're not."

She snorted. "I'm just glad I was able to walk up the stairs. I don't remember it, but it wouldn't have been easy to carry me up."

"I carried you just fine," English growled. It wasn't just that she wasn't attracted to him, she thought he was weak. Unable to support the weight of another person. He spent all four years in college lifting weights and increasing his body mass to get stronger. When he joined the Navy, part of training was learning how and being able to carry someone else. Dead weight wasn't just an expression to anyone who served in the military.

"You carried me?" Caitlyn asked.

"You were passed out. And you wouldn't let Adam touch you. You're not that heavy."

She stared up at him, her eyes taking him in. "I wouldn't have survived the night without you. Thank you, Liam. No one..." She ducked her chin.

"No one what?"

"No one's ever taken care of me," she whispered. She lifted her head and gave him a small smile. "Thank you."

"You're welcome," English choked out.

Her gaze scanned his face before settling on his lips. She licked hers, leaving a glossy sheen on them. Her fingertips tickled the back of his neck, teasing him. Torturing him.

Pulling him closer.

English turned toward her, taking a step down so they were eye-to-eye. She whispered his name, a breath between them as she leaned forward and closed her eyes.

Her lips brushed against his, and everything within him stilled. There was no nervous energy trying to escape. No hum of unease. No buzz of busyness. Just silence and Caitlyn.

She pulled back quickly, far too quickly for English. He hadn't gotten a chance to taste her or touch her or do anything more than press his lips to hers.

"I, um—"

"I'm going to see if Liam and Caitlyn are up," Adam said loudly, interrupting Caitlyn's words.

English turned in time to see his cousin come around the corner of the stairs and draw back in feigned shock.

"Oh, hey, guys. You are up. Holly has breakfast ready. If you're hungry."

"We were just on our way down. I'm moving kind of slowly," Caitlyn said. She sounded like it was an ordinary day to wake up in a stranger's house and have breakfast with people she didn't know.

English stepped to the side again and let Caitlyn lean on him. Adam stepped back with raised brows and a smirk. Son of a bitch.

"You're up," Holly said when she saw Caitlyn. "How are you feeling?"

"Better. I'm guessing a lot better than when we met. I'm sorry I don't remember it. Of course, I know who you are, though. Thank you for helping me."

"Any time. Liam didn't tell me a lot, but it looks like your cut wasn't too deep. It obviously bled a lot, but it should heal okay. If you have any issues, let me know, and I'm happy to write you a prescription or refer you to a plastic surgeon if you need it." Holly reached out for Caitlyn's hand and squeezed it.

When Adam said he knew a doctor, English was not expecting them to end up on Adam's sister's doorstep. Holly didn't hesitate to let them in and help out. As a general surgeon, she had supplies with her at all times, just in case she had to do a house call. English knew the night would have been much different if Holly wasn't available.

"I really appreciate it." Caitlyn chuckled. "This all feels very surreal."

"What do you mean?" Adam asked.

Caitlyn shrugged. "I know who you two are, but I don't really know either of you. And Liam I haven't seen since high school. And now I'm in your dining room eating breakfast you cooked with stitches in my side you put there and all of you have seen me in my bra."

"Well, when you put it that way, I feel like I should have bought you dinner first," Adam teased.

Caitlyn and Holly laughed, but English just stood back. Adam was younger, but English always looked up to him. Smart and strong and easygoing. He was fearless, and that extended to women. English could barely carry a conversation with a woman, and Adam had them eating out of the palm of his hand in seconds.

Case in point. Two minutes ago, Caitlyn was kissing English, and now she was flirting with Adam.

"Maybe next time," Caitlyn said. "Although, I really hope there's not a next time for all of this. Getting arrested after almost dying was not a fun experience."

"We need to find out who's behind this," English growled. He wanted to hit something. Maybe two somethings.

"We will," Adam said calmly. "Let's eat, then we'll talk to your team and mine. We'll get some answers."

English didn't like Adam calling the shots, but he wasn't clearheaded enough to do it himself. He settled onto a chair next to Holly and ate his breakfast while Adam and Caitlyn chatted like long-lost best friends.

When English was finished, he cleared the plates from the table and washed the dishes Holly used to cook. He was buying himself time, and avoiding watching Adam and Caitlyn together.

"You know he's a flirt, right?" Holly asked, joining him in the kitchen.

English nodded.

"Hey," Holly said, her hand on his arm and drawing his attention to her. Her blonde hair was so light it was almost silver. Her fair skin and blue eyes were near identical matches to his own. She was almost five years younger than he was, but they still spent time together growing up. Holly never wanted to leave East Charlottesville, which separated them, but Holly was always supportive of both English and Adam leaving.

"I know."

"He's trying to get her to let down her guard. After the way she reacted to him when you guys got here last night, he thinks she's hiding something. Especially since before that, she accused you of turning on her."

"That was all bullshit."

"I know. And you know. And he knows. But he's trying to see if she knows. Did she tell you how much she remembers from last night?"

"I didn't ask her. I did tell her it was a lie."

"Let him talk to her. I know you like her, but that means you're not objective."

"I don't like her. I barely know her."

"That doesn't always matter."

"What are you trying to say?" English crossed his arms and studied his cousin closely.

Her cheeks pinked under his appraisal. She fiddled with the edge of her flannel shirt. She shuffled her bare feet and studied the floor.

"Holly? Are you seeing someone?"

"It's early."

"Who is it? Anyone I know?"

"Her name is Mallory. She works at the clinic with me."

"Is she another doctor?"

"Yes. She's also a few years older than me."

"How many years?"

"Five."

English tilted his head to the side. He only knew one woman named Mallory. "Are you talking about Mallory Bennett?"

Holly bit her lip and nodded.

"She's awesome. She was valedictorian of my class. She beat me by one-one-hundredth of a point."

"I know. She told me. She thought I wouldn't be interested in dating her because of it."

English snorted. "This town. I swear."

"It's not that bad."

"Maybe, but I've been here less than twenty-four hours

and I've been in a bar fight, in a house fire, arrested, and my cousin almost didn't get a date because of fifteen year old history between me and the woman she likes. I hope you understand why I don't visit often."

Holly snorted and shook her head. "When you put it like that, I don't know why you'd ever come back."

English laughed with her. If it hadn't been for his cousins, he wouldn't have survived growing up. They kept him sane when his dad was going on and on about not needing more out of life than what East Charlottesville offered. He never understood why English wanted to leave.

"Maybe you and Mallory can come visit me sometime. I have a guest room and live about ten minutes from Niagara Falls. It's beautiful there."

Holly smiled. "If we're still together in the spring, we'll talk about it."

"Good plan. And I'm happy for you, Hol. It can't be easy to find someone you connect with when your dating pool is so small."

"It's been more my schedule is so crazy than how small my dating pool is. But I know what you mean. How about you? Anyone special back in New York?"

"Nope. I've dated a little, but my job isn't always easy for women to accept."

"And what exactly is your job?"

"He does the things I can't do," Adam provided before English could answer. "And he does them well. Speaking of which, do you want to power up this computer? See what we can find out about Ms. Waterford?"

English nodded. "Any word from the Bureau?"

"Nope. Since I'm not on the team, they're not real interested in returning my calls, but I've got my boss on it. He should be able to get some answers about why the cops said she disappeared and the FBI went along with that lie."

"Good. That's the first question we need answered."

"And the second?"

"Who tried to kill us last night? And why?"

8

Caitlyn chewed on her nail and felt useless while the others dug through her best friend's life. Liam was able to get into Jeanine's computer without a lot of resistance once he had time, and no fires burning. And Adam finally got a call from his boss.

"So, the FBI never even came here?" Liam asked.

"Apparently not. One agent talked to the captain and asked a bunch of questions. When they got answers that seemed to check out, they turned the case over to your team. We're overworked. All departments are."

"That's not a good enough excuse," Liam growled at his cousin.

"No, it's not. But it's all I can say."

"My team is overworked, too. We have other cases. Cases that have actually been investigated before they were handed over to us. Cases that were done the right way."

Adam sighed. He looked down, his blond hair falling over his forehead and blocking his eyes from view. He was attractive in a boy next door kind of way, but he did absolutely nothing for Caitlyn. Not the way Liam did when his angry gaze brushed over her.

"I'm sorry," Liam said to her. "Jeanine never should have been missing for this long. By the time my team gets cases like these, especially ones without much information, we don't have much hope. I expected to come here, find nothing, and turn the case back over as a cold case. That's clearly not what happened, but after almost two weeks, it's less likely we're going to get any good information."

"You're giving up," Caitlyn said. Resigned but pissed.

"No. I'm not. My team won't either. But my team isn't here. I don't know when I can get them here."

"Are you leaving?"

"No. I'm staying until we find some answers."

Caitlyn breathed a sigh of relief. She'd been the only one fighting for Jeanine, and she wasn't alone anymore. She had help. Help that wasn't deciding women like Jeanine, like Caitlyn, weren't worth the trouble.

"Is there anything you can tell us about her? Anything we should know?" Adam asked.

Caitlyn nibbled her nail and pretended to think. So far, they weren't judging Jeanine, but they would if they knew the full truth about her.

"Her computer isn't very helpful," Liam said as though Adam hadn't asked Caitlyn a question. "Her email account is mostly full of spam, her social media is essentially empty. I know she had a phone, but I can't find where it was backed up anywhere."

"Has a phone," Caitlyn said. "She has a phone."

"Caitlyn..."

"No. I can't start thinking she'd dead. Being told she left was hard enough, but her being dead is just..."

Liam stared at her while she tried to regain what was left

of her composure. Adam quietly slipped out of the room. Caitlyn swallowed roughly, her throat fighting her. Jeanine couldn't be dead. She just couldn't be.

If she was, it was Caitlyn's fault. She should have gone out with her that night. She should have asked who she was going to see. Instead, she told Jeanine she wasn't in the mood to go anywhere. Left her friend to go out alone.

She should have been safe. She wasn't.

"Caitlyn," Liam said again. Softer, more gentle. Like she was going to bite his head off.

"Liam, I can't. If you tell me there's no chance of finding her alive... I can't. Please."

"There's always a chance, Caite. Always."

"Then I'm going to hold on to that."

"You do that. It's good. Don't ever give up hope." He paused and smiled tentatively at her. "Can you tell me more about her? What is she like?"

Caitlyn smiled. "She's funny. Sarcastic. Swears like it's her job and isn't afraid to tell people what she thinks."

Liam snorted. "I can't imagine that wins her a lot of friends around here."

"Oh, no, it definitely doesn't."

"How did you two meet?"

"She came to work at the diner. She walked up to me on her first day and told me we were going to be friends." Caitlyn chuckled at the memory.

"Just like that?" Liam's brows lifted in surprise.

"Just like that. She told me later I was the only person there who was even close to her age, but she recognized a kindred spirit in me. She made me want to be better."

"In what way?"

Caitlyn looked up at Liam. He was sweet. Innocent. Kind and strong and smart. He was the good influence in his world. The one who probably made everyone else want to be better. He had no idea what it was like to be the bad seed.

"The day I turned eighteen, my mom left. With all the money I earned modeling as a kid. She was my manager and my mother, so she had access to everything. I planned to leave. To get the hell out of here like you did. But she stole everything from me. I was bitter and blamed everyone else, especially her, but I blamed this town and these people and everything. I couldn't see where any of it could have been my fault, so I blamed everyone else."

"It sounds like it wasn't your fault," Liam said.

Caitlyn shook her head. "It wasn't anyone else's either. Except my mother. But it wasn't the town's fault. I had alienated everyone here because I blamed them for her decisions. Meeting Jeanine was enlightening. She showed me that I'm in control of my life, and I could wallow in self-pity or I could change. I decided to change."

"She sounds like a great friend."

Caitlyn sniffed and nodded. "She is. The best one I've ever had. That's why I have to find her. She'd be looking for me if I disappeared."

"I understand. I have friends who are the same. We watch out for each other."

"You're really going to help me?"

Liam nodded. "We'll find her."

He didn't add dead or alive, but Caitlyn felt the words in her chest. Jeanine was out there. She might be dead already, but she was out there. Caitlyn wasn't giving up until she found Jeanine. She just had to keep Liam looking and not let him know about Jeanine's secret.

HE SIPPED his coffee at the counter, watching the rest of the diner in the mirror. Not many people approached him, but the ones who did always hurried to say hello and leave. A man like him was not a man you interrupted to chat with.

"Did you hear about the fire last night?" a woman at the table behind him asked her friend. "That woman who left town, Jeanine, her apartment burned. The police are scrambling now. They had suspects, but they got out because it's William and Patty's son. I can't imagine how they're feeling knowing their son is a criminal."

He smiled to himself. It was only a matter of time before people would start talking about the fire. It was why he was there. His only regret was that they made it out alive.

"Do you think they set it? I heard they barely made it out of there."

The first woman snorted. She worked at the school. He couldn't place her name, but she'd been there forever. "Messed up is what it sounds like to me. Tried to burn the evidence."

"What evidence?"

"I don't know. Maybe there was something they left behind when they kidnapped her."

"I thought she left town."

"Well, that's what everyone said, but why would they burn down her place?"

"Patty's boy just came back yesterday. The woman's been gone for almost two weeks."

"Maybe she did run away. Maybe she was having an affair with him and left to go be with him."

The second lady shook her head. "I don't understand young women these days. In our day, you got married, had some kids, and turned the other way if your husband stepped out on you. Now, these girls are skipping marriage and just sleeping with everyone's husbands."

"Was she sleeping with your husband?"

"George? God no. He can barely get it up once a week. He's not going to pay for it and waste a pill."

Both women cackled, but he was no longer paying attention to them.

How did those women know Jeanine was sleeping with other men? He didn't know. Not until she threw it in his face. She was supposed to be his. Only his. She wasn't supposed to be with anyone else.

When she said it, he thought she might be lying, but those women...

He drew a breath and straightened his shoulders. He unclenched his fist and smoothed his hand over his shirt. He looked up at the mirror, making sure no part of him was out of place.

Perfection. As always. He was still in control. He was always in control. He had no choice. Men were in control. If they weren't, women would think they could do things.

Things like sleep with other men. And get paid for it.

No. His Jeanine didn't do that. Those fucking women were liars. They didn't know what they were talking about.

He grabbed his knife and held it tightly. It wouldn't take much to shut them up. One quick slice or a sharp stab and they'd stop spewing their filth about his Jeanine.

No one was going to say anything else bad about her. People didn't talk ill of the dead. It wasn't polite. And the people in East Charlottesville were always polite.

But they didn't know Jeanine was dead. He was the only one who knew that. And he couldn't tell anyone. Not yet. Not until he set everything up so Caitlyn, and now her boyfriend, were the only suspects.

"WHAT IS WRONG WITH YOU? Why did you get involved with that girl? She was no good when you were in high school, and she's no good now," English's mom said through the phone. He was sure Caitlyn could hear every word from across the room, but she didn't flinch.

"Mom. I will be home later tonight."

"I'm not going to jail for you. Don't you dare come here when you're running from the police. I'll turn you in!"

"I'm not running from the police."

"That's not what I heard. You're a fugitive."

"This fucking town," English murmured. He pinched the bridge of his nose and hung his head.

"You can stay with me," Caitlyn said quietly, confirming his suspicion that she heard everything his mother said.

"Okay, I won't come home. I'll keep you and dad out of this."

"You better. When he gets home, he's going to be livid. He already has a hard enough time with a son who left town. Now, you finally come back and you're burning down apartment buildings and evading the police. Oh, God, Liam, who have you become?"

"I need to go, Mom. The cops are coming. I'll try to call you later. If you get a call from a Canadian number, make sure you answer."

"Liam! I am not helping you!"

"Then this might be goodbye, Mom. I love you. Tell Dad I love him, too."

"Oh, Liam. This is all that Caitlyn's fault. You never should have talked to her."

"Yep. You're right. Sorry, Mom. I really do have to go. Bye."

"Bye, Liam. Call when you're safe."

English hung up the phone and tried to roll the tension out of his shoulders. It was useless, but he tried.

They were still at Holly's house, using it as a workspace for the day. She was going about her business and ignoring them, and Caitlyn, English, and Adam were camped out in the dining room trying to make sense of Jeanine Waterford's life.

"I'm sorry about what she said," English told Caitlyn.

She shrugged. "I'm used to it. No one wants their son involved with the biggest bitch in town, let alone the biggest bitch in town who's also a man-stealing, woman-hating, broke, fat whore. I'm a real catch."

"You're none of those things," English said.

Caitlyn shook her head. "See, you don't live here. So, you're impressionable. I'm trapping you like I do all my victims. I ensnare them with my feminine whiles and then I devour them with my excessive fat and bitchiness."

"Caitlyn..."

She pressed her lips into a smile. It was fake. As fake as the rumors about her. "I earned some of it. Probably all of it over the years."

"You're not any of those things."

"I know who I am. I'm not perfect, but I've never knowingly slept with a married man. The only reason I don't get along with other women is because they all think I'm trying to steal their husbands. And the rest..."

"The rest is just people being nasty," Holly said.

"She's right. People spend too much time focused on what everyone else does instead of being good themselves. Even if you were all those things, it wouldn't stop me from wanting to help you. Or Jeanine." English crossed his arms and glared at Caitlyn, needing her to understand that he didn't give a shit what his parents, or anyone else in town, said.

Caitlyn snorted. "I doubt that."

"Why do you say that?"

"You're a boy scout. You were perfect in high school, and you went into the military. Now, you own a company that saves people for a living. I mean, you have to judge people. Think poorly of the ones who put themselves in shitty situations."

English's spine tingled. He rarely ignored his instincts, and they were telling him to tread carefully.

"I don't think anyone ever deserves to be hurt or threatened or have anything bad happen to them. Do people make poor choices sometimes? Sure. We all do. That doesn't mean someone should be hurt. I broke the law last night. I broke into Jeanine's apartment. I justified it, but it was still illegal. Do I think we deserved to have the place burned down around us because of that? No, I don't."

"Yeah, but that was something small. What if someone does something really bad? Really big?"

English shrugged. "Like what? Kill someone? I've killed people. In combat. I've been involved in taking down some very dangerous people, and while I think what they've done is disgusting, I know their victims were victims."

"Not everyone is a victim." Caitlyn picked at her nail and looked at the computer. It was still open, still active.

English knew what he found on Jeanine's computer wasn't the whole story about who she was, but he also knew most people didn't spend as much time on computers as he did. If he had her phone, he was sure there would be a different picture. Adam put in the request, and so had Dunn, for her complete phone records and an online backup of her phone to be provided to them, but so far, it hadn't been approved.

Time was running out for Jeanine. If she was still alive, she wouldn't be for much longer. They needed a lead, one that was more solid than she told Caitlyn she was going to Sparky's that night and was never heard from again.

Her car was never found. Her phone was off. Her charger was left at home, which could explain why her phone was off, but it didn't explain why she left the way she did.

There was more to it. And English was fairly sure Caitlyn knew some of it.

"Was Jeanine a victim? Did someone hurt her?" Adam asked.

Caitlyn looked at him as if she'd forgotten he was there. She blinked, her eyes focusing again. Just that quickly, whatever she was about to say was gone.

"No. Of course not. If I knew something like that, I would have told the police. Or you guys. I don't know about anything."

"She's your best friend, Caitlyn. If you know something that could help us find her, we need to know," Adam pushed.

"Do you really think I would hide something that could help you find her? Like you said, she's my best friend. She's the only person in the entire damn world who has ever cared about me. And she's gone. Vanished. Just like my mother. Except Jeanine didn't steal all my money when she left, she just left."

Adam and English exchanged a look. Adam's expression said he knew they lost the chance to learn something important, but he couldn't roll it back. If they were lucky, whatever Caitlyn was about to share would come up again, and she'd tell them the truth. Until then, they had to keep digging with what they had.

Which, in all reality, was shit. English needed Caitlyn to hold on to the hope they might find Jeanine alive because he had none. And he didn't think Caitlyn could handle that.

9

———

English forced his gaze away from Caitlyn for the hundredth time that day. He was starting to worry himself with how much he was staring at her. The case was too slow to hold his focus, and Caitlyn was.... Well, she was Caitlyn.

Adam walked back into the living room, staring at his phone.

Liam jumped on the distraction from Caitlyn. "Did you get something?"

Adam shook his head. "My orders."

"What does that mean?"

"It means I can't stay. I requested an extension to my leave, or to be put on this case, but my boss didn't approve either. We have a big case of our own, and he can't spare the manpower. I report back Monday morning."

"Shit," English said.

"You're leaving?" Caitlyn asked.

"Tomorrow, yes. But you're in good hands with Liam." Adam winked at her.

Caitlyn wrapped her arms around her waist and chewed on her lower lip.

English wanted to offer her some kind of reassurance that he was capable of handling the case, but he wasn't sure what to say. Other than promising her he wasn't leaving, he knew the job would be harder without any backup.

"Thank you for your help," Caitlyn said to Adam.

"I'm sorry I wasn't able to do more. We have one more day. And once I'm back in the office, we'll dig a little deeper."

"We?" Caitlyn asked.

"Lorelei and I. My partner. I called her and told her what was going on. She offered to come up here to help, but our boss wouldn't let me stay so we know he won't let her come here. But Lorelei is willing to help however she can. If we find anything, I'll be in touch."

"Thanks, man," English said.

"Until then, let's see what else we can figure out."

"I want to get back into Jeanine's apartment," English said.

"The place they set on fire last night?" Caitlyn asked.

"Exactly. I want to see it. See if there's anything left." English looked at Adam.

Adam nodded slowly. "I think that's a good play. We need to know if it was a total loss or if anything was salvageable. And we need the report from it."

"You want to take a ride?" English asked.

"Yep." Adam turned to the kitchen and shouted for his sister.

"You can't just walk into the other room like a normal person?" Holly asked as she joined them in the living room.

"Nope. That's no fun. Liam and I need to go out. You two stay here." Adam pointed at the two of them.

"Where are you going?" Holly asked.

"To get the report on the fire from last night."

Holly nodded and hugged them both. "Be careful."

English squeezed Caitlyn's shoulder and followed Adam out the front door. There was no reason to think they wouldn't be okay, but leaving them alone made English tense.

"They'll be fine," Adam said, reading English's mind.

"Hope so. Let's make this quick, just in case."

Adam nodded and turned back toward town. Five minutes later, they were parked in front of Jeanine's apartment building. What was left of it.

Adam whistled as he turned off the engine and got out of the SUV. "Damn."

"Yeah," English agreed. The building was little more than a shell. The entire top floor was gone. The roof sagged on the side, exposing the beams that held part of it up. The front door and staircase weren't there. A metal mailbox and charred pieces of the building were all that were left.

"Glad you two got out of there," Adam said.

English nodded. He knew the fire was hot, but for it to have burned the entire building like that, there had to have been an accelerant. That meant someone definitely set the fire on purpose. Most likely the same someone who called it in.

"We need the call log. Any chance we can get it?"

Adam shrugged. "If it exists."

"You don't think it does?"

"I wouldn't be surprised if it was misplaced. Let's go to the station and see what we can find."

The police station was an old cinderblock building in the center of town. It hadn't been upgraded since English was a kid. He didn't take much time to get the layout of it when he was dragged inside in cuffs, but walking in on his own was easier to see things. Like who thought they were in charge.

"We need a copy of the report on the fire from last night," Adam told the guy at the desk.

The guy turned to the bullpen behind him and motioned for one of the other cops to come over.

English was sure he knew the guy, but like so many others, he couldn't place him. The less than happy look on his face said he knew exactly who English was, though.

"We aren't at liberty to share reports for active cases. Especially with one of the suspects," the cop said. He hitched his thumbs in his belt and leaned back like he was the boss on an old TV show.

It took everything in English not to laugh at the guy. He couldn't have been much older, if any, than English and Caitlyn, but his attitude said he thought he was a badass.

Adam stepped forward, blocking English from glaring at the cop, and said, "Except the apartment belonged to a woman whose disappearance is being investigated by the FBI. That means you have to give me whatever evidence you've found, and provide all the details of your report to me. Including the call log."

English loved watching the smug smirk melt off the asshole's face. The cops he worked with back in Niagara Falls were always willing to help out. They wanted to put away bad guys and stop more from stepping up. But these cops, they were happy to do as little as possible and get away with it.

The cop snarled and snapped at the guy at the desk to give them whatever they wanted, then stomped back to his desk like a toddler having a tantrum. He glared at them the entire time they were there, arms crossed and scowling.

English smiled and waved at him when they collected

the report and the handful of items that survived the fire and were deemed important enough by the officers to bring into the station. As expected, they couldn't provide the call log.

"Friend of yours?" Adam asked when they walked outside again.

English snorted. "The best."

Adam chuckled. He loaded the box into the back of his SUV. Their quick excursion already over, they headed back to Holly's to dig into their new evidence.

Holly and Caitlyn were sitting in the living room talking when English and Adam walked in. Their conversation stopped immediately, which made English's cheeks heat. Especially when both women looked at him.

"Everything okay while we were gone?" Adam asked, oblivious to tension English was feeling.

"Yep. Just chatting." Holly got up from the couch and walked over to them. "Find anything?"

Adam shrugged and set the box down on the table. "We'll see. This is what's left from the fire. No clue if any of it will be helpful."

"It looks like burnt...everything. How can you tell what any of these things are?" Holly asked. She picked up something square and black, but all bets were off if it started out black.

"We have the report. With any luck, we'll get something out of that," Adam told her. He pulled the report from the box and set it to the side so they could all read it.

Caitlyn stood from the couch and stretched, drawing English's attention. The move exposed a sliver of skin. No different than the skin he sat up watching all night, but it felt different. When she was sleeping, she hadn't given him permission to see her. She didn't know he was there. But now...

She caught him looking at her and smiled. She tugged the edge of her sweater down and moved toward him. "Is it okay if I see it?"

English nodded. "Of course. We're not keeping secrets from each other."

She grimaced. It wasn't long before she fixed the look with a smile, but it made him wonder if it was his words or something else that caused it. His gut said it was the same something else he thought she was hiding earlier when they talked. He needed her to open up.

Caitlyn moved to stand next to English. Adam read a page, then slid it in front of them. With each word in the report, English felt his rage tightening in on him. The report was as helpful as the one about Jeanine's disappearance had been.

"This is fucking useless," Adam said when he was done reading. "There's nothing in here."

"They never once asked us what actually happened. They immediately considered us guilty and started questioning us that way. They never tried to get a depiction of the events." English was pissed. It usually took a lot to make him so angry, but he was beyond furious.

"We need to talk to the fire investigator or something," Adam said.

"There isn't one," Holly told him. "I mean, there is, but he works on the other side of the county and rarely comes in. I heard they'll only call him in if there's a fatality."

"Fucking hell. This is no good. There's nothing in here about the cause of the fire, what accelerant was used, or any actual police work that could point to a suspect. Except you two," Adam said. He ran a hand through his hair and stared into the box of charred odds and ends. "Why bother if this is the best they're going to do? That's what I told my boss when I asked about the report on Jeanine. Why did we even bother to rubber stamp it? I asked for the agents who passed Jeanine's case on to you guys to be questioned about their lack of an investigation."

"What did they say?" Caitlyn breathed, leaning closer to English.

"It'll probably be Monday, but I'm guessing they are going to say they're overworked and didn't have time to look into it. The police report is a joke, but unless you've been here, you don't see all of that."

"Who wrote the police report?" English asked.

Adam crossed the room to where the other files were. "It's signed...Pattinson."

Caitlyn snorted.

Both men turned to her. "Do you know him?" English asked.

She quirked an eyebrow at him. "You don't remember him? Nickolas Pattinson? We graduated with him. He was a douchebag in high school, but now he has a little bit of power. He hates me."

"Do you think he falsified the report?" Adam asked.

"I do," English answered. "But I thought that before. He was the cop who didn't want to give us these files." English pointed at the fire report. "I didn't recognize him, but I remember him now. He used to try to copy off my tests. He always tried to get a seat next to me. Even back then he wasn't willing to actually do any work."

"Did he sign the fire report?" Adam asked.

English checked. "Yep."

"Is he on our suspects list?"

"He is now," English said.

CAITLYN HELPED Holly clean up after dinner while Liam and Adam went back to work. Holly was talking about her new girlfriend when the men came back with the evidence from the police station, so Caitlyn picked the conversation back up where they were.

Holly said they met at work, and even though they'd both always lived in East Charlottesville, they didn't know each other until they started working together. The way her eyes lit up made Caitlyn more than a little jealous.

"Anyone special for you?" Holly asked.

Caitlyn shook her head. "No. I was a pretty big bitch when I was growing up. I thought I was better than everyone else, and I got knocked down more than a few pegs afterward. No one really wants to date the fat former model who's still not a good person."

Holly chuckled with Caitlyn and shook her head. "I don't think that's true. For one thing, you're not fat. You have fat, like everyone else on the planet. And being a bitch in high school is normal. But you are a good person, Caitlyn. Not everyone would be going through all of this to find someone."

"She's my friend. The way those guys at the bar reacted, I know they know more than they're admitting. That's why I keep going back there." Caitlyn rubbed her throat and winced at the bruises.

"I still think you're a good person for doing all of this. I know I consider myself lucky to call you a friend."

Caitlyn smiled at Holly. She was the lucky one. "Thank you."

They went back into the living room where Adam and Liam were working. Caitlyn was getting tired, but they were all working to find her friend, so she took a seat on the couch near Liam and tried to think of anything she could do to help.

"Dammit," Liam muttered.

"What happened?" Adam asked.

"I want answers. And everywhere I think I might get some, I'm shit out of luck."

"Like what?"

Liam shook his head and sat back on the couch. He rubbed his hands over his face, then let them fall. One landed on Caitlyn's foot. "Sorry."

Caitlyn moved her foot, surprised at the spark that shot up her leg at the brief touch. Her cheeks heated. She pressed her lips together and nodded.

Liam wasn't fazed by it. He stared at the computer and ignored her. "I'm trying to find the men from the bar, but I can't get anything without a warrant. I'm trying to dig into Pattinson, but I can't without a warrant. I'm trying to get Jeanine's records... Doing things by the book sucks."

Adam chuckled. "Not all of us can work behind the scenes."

"Yeah, well, it's easier that way. A woman is fucking missing. And because these fucktards didn't do their job in the first place, I have nothing to go on."

"I know," Adam agreed. His smile faded. "I'm sorry."

Liam sighed heavily. "I know this isn't on you. And it's not on the agents who are so overworked they couldn't get here. But it pisses me off. We shouldn't have this much red tape to go through. We're trying to find someone."

"I agree. It makes my life a living hell most of the time. But I know it's there for a reason."

Liam nodded but didn't say anything else. He stared at the computer like it would give him answers.

"Maybe we should get some sleep," Adam said.

Caitlyn's entire body flashed hot. She forgot about sleep. She was in a stranger's house, and there were four of them. Holly's house only had two beds. Caitlyn slept in one of them the night before, but she was injured. She spent the entire day relaxing and healing. It wasn't fair to take the bed again.

"That's probably a good idea," Liam said. He scrubbed his hands over his face again and closed his eyes.

Caitlyn studied him for the first time. Dark circles hung under his eyes. The day old stubble she liked the look of added to his worn out appearance. His wrinkled clothes were the same ones he was wearing when they met at Sparky's the night before.

She could barely believe it had only been one night. One night since she stopped feeling like the only one who cared that Jeanine was gone. One night since she saw Liam Johnson again.

"Caitlyn, you need to be in the bed," Adam said.

"No, I—"

"He's right," Liam said. "You lost a lot of blood and you need as much rest as you can get."

"I'm fine. You two are doing all the work," Caitlyn argued.

"We're not debating this. Liam can help you up the stairs. You're on my bed," Adam said.

Caitlyn could tell she wasn't going to win against either of them. She accepted defeat and stood. She swayed a little but caught herself and started toward the stairs.

Liam was right behind Caitlyn on her walk up the narrow stairs. It'd only been a few hours since she kissed him right there. Feeling him behind her, his footsteps soft on the carpet, she wanted to turn around and do it again.

She didn't. She kept walking, turning at the top of the stairs and going into the bedroom she woke up in that morning. Caitlyn went to the bed and sat on the edge.

"Are you okay?" Liam asked after a minute.

Caitlyn shrugged. The entire day was surreal. Before Liam arrived, a part of Caitlyn thought maybe Jeanine did leave town like the police said. Maybe she was done being friends with Caitlyn and just left. But after the last twenty-four hours, Caitlyn knew that wasn't true. Jeanine was gone, but it wasn't because she left on her own. Something happened. And that made Caitlyn feel both better and worse.

"Today has been a lot. Do you want me to stay until you get settled in the bed? Holly has an extra toothbrush in the bathroom that you can use. I can wait here in case you need something."

Caitlyn nodded, having a hard time finding the words she wanted to say to him. Instead, she went to the bathroom and closed the door. She brushed her teeth and used the bathroom, then washed her hands and went back to the bedroom.

Liam smiled at her when she walked in. "I'm sorry we didn't get you any clothes. We should have gone to your apartment today to get you something else to wear."

"It's fine."

Liam looked closely at her. Caitlyn avoided his gaze. She didn't want him to see the truth.

"Caitlyn?"

"I'm fine, Liam."

"You don't look fine."

She huffed a breath. "Okay, I'm not fine. The one and only person in the world who cared about me is gone. She's missing. And after eleven days of looking for her alone, I finally have people who believe me. Except that means she really is missing. Someone tried to kill me, twice. And I'm sleeping in a stranger's guest room and every noise makes me jump. I'm terrified. I'm just..."

Liam crossed the room to her and wrapped her in his arms. He held her tight and close, not letting go when tears rolled down her cheeks and soaked through his tee.

Caitlyn clung to him, afraid to let go and afraid to hold on. She hadn't needed anyone her entire life, but she needed Liam Johnson. And more than that, she wanted him. She wanted someone like him in her life. He was good and kind and decent. Caitlyn hadn't ever known a man like him.

"Do you want me to sleep in here?" Liam asked quietly.

Caitlyn wanted to be brave and tell him she would be fine, but it would be a lie. She wanted him to stay with her. She just didn't want him to feel like he had to. "I would feel better, yes."

"Okay. Let's get you into the bed."

Caitlyn nodded and let him guide her to the mattress. He pulled the covers back and waited until she slid under them to let them fall over her body again. Caitlyn followed him with her gaze as he walked around the bed toward the chair in the corner. "What are you doing?"

"I said I'd sleep here, Caitlyn." Liam looked at her like she lost her mind.

"Don't be dumb, Liam. Just sleep in the bed with me."

"Caitlyn."

She shook her head. "No. I'm not going to make you sleep in that chair again. It can't possibly be comfortable. And we can share a bed without it being weird."

Liam looked like he wanted to argue that point, but he nodded. He turned off the light and closed the door partway, then walked over to the bed. Caitlyn pulled the covers back on his side. He hesitated, then crawled in next to her.

Caitlyn laid facing Liam. He was on his back, his hands tucked under his head. She stared at his profile and swallowed roughly. She hadn't ever shared a bed with a man. Not for a full night. The few men she'd been involved with never stayed over, and she never spent the night with them. She never wanted to.

But lying next to Liam, Caitlyn couldn't think of anywhere else she'd rather be. Until Liam stretched his arm out toward her. He nudged the back of her head. Caitlyn closed the distance between them, resting her head in the crook of his shoulder. His heart beat steadily beneath her ear. His hand settled on her side. And Caitlyn knew she was safe. Liam would never let anything happen to her.

10

Morning came far too early for English. He could have laid there forever holding Caitlyn in his arms.

She stirred, her hand sliding over his stomach, and stilled. English felt her tense up, then relax when she realized where she was. She snuggled in tighter to him and pressed her nose to his neck. English didn't stir, letting her think he was still asleep.

Caitlyn looked at him, her head on his chest but tilted up to see his face. She kissed the edge of his jaw, her lips barely brushing his skin. She did it again, his neck that time.

English hardened, unable to stop the reaction to Caitlyn kissing him. When she licked his throat, he groaned and tightened his hold on her.

She settled against his side again, pretending to be asleep. English wasn't going to call her on it. He just held her close and acted like he was waking up.

Caitlyn didn't move when English opened his eyes. He pressed his nose into her hair and kissed the top of her head. He rubbed his hand up and down her back. Only then did she stir.

"Good morning," she said, her voice soft and sleepy.

"Morning. How did you sleep?"

"Better than I expected. Thank you for staying with me."

English nodded. "You're welcome."

Neither of them made a move to get out of bed. Her hand held tight to his waist, and his hand drifted up and down her back. They laid there like it was normal to wake up holding each other. Like they'd done it before.

Caitlyn finally lifted her head and met his gaze. She nibbled her lip and dropped her gaze to his mouth. "Liam," she whispered.

He leaned toward her, encouraging her to meet him in the middle with a hand in her hair. She didn't hesitate to close the rest of the distance between them.

English groaned when their lips touched. When she kissed him the day before, he was surprised and his brain stalled out. This time, he was in full control of his faculties and he wasn't going to miss out on the full Caitlyn Powers kissing experience.

English tugged her hair just enough to tilt her head to the side. He licked her lips. She opened for him, giving him his first real taste of her. He pressed his tongue into her mouth, thick and sure and desperate. She sighed and slid her tongue alongside his.

Caitlyn's fingers wound tighter around his waist, pulling herself closer. English used his free hand to encourage her ever closer, bringing her body on top of his. She spread her thighs and straddled him, giving him all her weight.

English growled in approval. One hand stayed in her hair, the silky curls tickling his fingers. The other roamed her back, sliding under her sweater to the soft skin below.

Caitlyn shifted, lifting herself up, and whimpered.

English immediately stopped his assault on her, pulling back and releasing her from his aggressive hold.

"Ow," she choked out. "I forgot about the stitches."

Fucking hell. English did, too. He was pushing her around and ready to fuck her and she was injured. "Let me see."

"It's fine."

"Caitlyn, please let me see. I don't want to hurt you."

She sighed and gently moved off of him. She laid on her back on the bed and let him lift her sweater.

The stitches were still intact, but the skin around them was red and puffy. Not infected, just raw. English kissed her stomach and pulled her sweater back down.

"I'm sorry," he said. "I got carried away."

"I am not going to complain about a sexy man kissing me," Caitlyn said with a smirk.

English grinned back at her. He wanted nothing more than to lose himself in Caitlyn for the day, but he was no longer there on vacation. He had work to do.

Reluctantly, English pulled back. Caitlyn's gaze matched the way he felt as they took turns using the bathroom before they headed downstairs together.

The first half of the day was a repeat of the one before. The four of them had breakfast together, then went to work. English was able to get Jeanine's phone records and online backup, but neither gave him any new information.

English was getting frustrated with the way the case was going. He knew there was something he was missing, something that could help him solve the case, but he didn't know what it was. Caitlyn said Jeanine mentioned a man she was seeing, but there was no record of him in her phone. Her contacts were limited. She didn't have many texts or emails. If she wasn't the one missing, Jeanine would be a suspect.

After lunch, Adam announced he was heading out.

"Already?" English asked.

Adam nodded. "I know you've got this."

They clapped hands and hugged, smacking each other on the back.

"Any time." Adam turned to Caitlyn. "Take care of this one."

She walked into his open arms and nodded. "I'll do my best."

"Are you leaving?" Holly asked. She was drying her hands on a kitchen towel and watching the three of them.

"Yeah. I don't want to be driving too late. I'll keep an eye on things from home." Adam met Holly and pulled her in for a hug.

"Be careful out there."

"I always am. Let me know if you need anything."

Holly nodded and released her brother. Adam didn't delay grabbing his things and leaving, waving goodbye to them as he walked out the door.

English understood. When your boss said go, you said yes, sir. Especially when your boss was the US Government. But losing the only other person with training from their search party was not going to be easy.

"What are your plans for tonight?" Holly asked. Her gaze bounced between English and Caitlyn.

Caitlyn looked at him and shrugged.

"We haven't gotten that far."

"Are you going back to your parents' house?"

English shook his head. "Mom made it pretty clear she's not willing to let me stay there."

"Did you need to stay here?"

"What are you getting at, Hol?" English asked.

Holly's cheeks flushed. She fidgeted with the dishtowel. "I just had plans for tonight. But I can cancel them. I was just wondering what you were doing."

"Don't cancel your plans. I don't want to mess up your life. We can get a hotel room or something."

"We?" Caitlyn blurted.

English met her gaze. "I'm not leaving you alone. We can get a room with two beds, but someone tried to kill you. Twice."

"Not just me. Us."

"I know."

Caitlyn clenched her hands into fists and tucked them under her arms to hide the way they shook. English didn't mean to scare her, but he wanted her to understand that she wasn't safe. He wasn't going to let anything happen to her. And that meant keeping her in his sight.

"If you want to leave town, I can give you some names and numbers of people you can trust. You can go stay in a safe house. We will protect you."

"I'm not leaving," she said firmly. "Not until we find Jeanine."

"Then I want to stay close. So I know you're safe."

"You can... We can stay at my apartment. I meant it when I offered yesterday. If you want."

"Are you sure?"

She nodded. "I don't really have money for a hotel, anyway."

"I was going to pay. Let's get out of Holly's way and go see your place. Make sure no one's been in there."

"You think they'd go to my place?" Caitlyn's face turned white. She reached for a chair to support herself before she sank onto it.

"I don't know. I don't know who we're dealing with. That's the issue. But we will find out."

Caitlyn nodded. Her eyes were unfocused and glazed. Terrified.

"I need to stop by my parents' house and get my things. Then we'll pick up some dinner and go to your place. Is that okay?"

Caitlyn nodded again. English exchanged a glance with Holly. She shook her head. Good old fashioned fear was not something a doctor could treat. Caitlyn had to deal with it on her own.

English just hoped he could help her.

CAITLYN STOOD on the porch outside Liam's parents' house and tried not to listen to their conversation. More like shouting match, but she wasn't one to judge. That was how she and her mom used to communicate, too. Super healthy.

The shouting finally stopped, and the silence made her ears ring. The shouting made her cheeks burn, so it was a relief. It was also nice to know exactly how little people thought of her. Words like *white trash* and *waste of time* and *floozy* were so much fun to hear coming from the mouths of people she saw on a regular basis.

Why hadn't she left town yet?

Oh, yeah, Jeanine.

Caitlyn was thinking about it when Jeanine moved to town. She knew what people said about her and was sick of it. Even though she had no money, she figured she could pack up her crap in her car and go somewhere. She couldn't get far, but anywhere had to be better than the town that didn't care if she existed or not.

Then Jeanine showed up. Having a friend made the bull-shit tolerable. Caitlyn still thought about leaving, but she didn't want to until Jeanine was ready.

That was the plan. But now…

Caitlyn couldn't think that far ahead. She had to find her friend, and then they'd make a new plan.

The screen door swung open. Liam stepped out onto the porch and nodded toward his SUV without a word. Caitlyn followed him, keeping quiet as he tossed his bag in the back and started up the monster of a vehicle.

Neither of them spoke until Liam stopped in front of the diner. It was the only place open on a Sunday evening, and their only option for food.

"Do you want to stay here or walk in?"

Caitlyn wanted to bury herself under her covers and never come out, but that wasn't an option. She was tired and dirty and sore. But she was hungry, and she hadn't skipped a meal in more than a decade.

"I'll come in."

Liam waited for her to get out of the SUV, then put his hand on her back and guided her into the diner. Every single person turned to watch them as they moved toward the counter.

Heather was working, and not looking too happy about it. She sneered at Caitlyn before smiling up at Liam. "Hey, honey. What can I get you?"

Liam nodded to Caitlyn to order first. Heather rolled her eyes and wrote down the order before pouring the sugar on for Liam. He ignored her, bless him, and guided Caitlyn to a booth to wait for their food to be ready.

"Fan of yours?" Liam asked with a smirk.

"They all are," Caitlyn told him, nodding toward the nosy onlookers.

Liam picked up her hand and brought it to his lips before settling their joined hands on the table. "They need lives of their own. I wonder how quickly this will get back to my parents?"

Caitlyn snorted.

"I'm sorry for the things they said about you."

"Why?"

"Because they weren't true."

"You don't know me, Liam. Not really."

"No, but I don't like people being judged for something outside their control. It's not on you that your mom stole from you. That doesn't make you trash."

"Just a waste of time?"

Liam swore under his breath. "No. None of it. Listen, I don't have a great relationship with my parents. I haven't since the day I told them I wanted to leave here. They didn't get it. My dad thinks I ruined my life, and my mom is only worried about appearances and making my dad happy. Neither of them cared what I wanted. So, a lot of what they said has nothing to do with you and everything to do with me being a disappointment."

Caitlyn breathed a laugh and shook her head. "I admired you when we were in high school."

Liam threw his head back and laughed at that. Caitlyn bit her lip as she stared at his throat. His Adam's apple bobbed, the golden shadow from the last two days making his skin glow. His black tee, the same one he'd been wearing since they met at Sparky's two nights ago was tight over his chest. He was incredibly attractive. And insanely out of her league.

"I mean it," she said when he stopped laughing so hard. "I wanted to be as sure of myself as you were. You never let anyone bother you. You didn't care when they called you a nerd or tried to copy your homework. You just went on about your business and ignored all the assholes I desperately wanted approval from."

"That's not entirely true," Liam said. "I wanted approval, but I knew I'd never get it. Those guys needed someone like me to make them feel better about themselves. I was weird, so I was a good target. I still am weird, but I've learned to embrace it. My team works well because we all have our role. If all of us were the same, we'd never get anything done. But I had to learn the value in my obsession with computers. It took me a while."

"I bet you have women all over you," Caitlyn said. She was totally fishing. She hated herself for it, but she wanted to know if he was single.

"I—"

"Food's ready," Heather snapped, dropping a bag between them on the table. "Have a great night."

Caitlyn rolled her eyes and pulled back from the grip Liam had on her hand.

Liam grabbed the food in one hand, and his other hand resumed its position on Caitlyn's back. He opened her door and set the food at her feet before jogging around the front and getting in beside her. He took off toward her house, again without needing directions.

"Can I ask you something?"

"Sure," he said.

"How do you know where I live? And you knew where Jeanine lived. Are you a stalker or something?"

Liam chuckled and shook his head. "Jeanine's address was part of the file we were given on her. Your address was one I had to get the old-fashioned way."

"What's that?"

"Online search."

Caitlyn laughed with him. She couldn't remember the last time she'd enjoyed time with a man as much. It had been a while since she'd had sex, but it was more than that. Liam was funny and smart and sarcastic. He was different than what she always imagined he'd be like.

Liam parked in front of her apartment building next to her car. Holly and Adam retrieved both vehicles while Caitlyn was sleeping and refusing to let Liam leave her side. She was surprised her windows weren't smashed and her tires weren't sliced. Maybe she had a little luck left.

Caitlyn led the way to her third floor unit. She let them in and turned on the lights, thankful she was a fairly neat person. Liam walked in right behind her and locked the door. He tossed his bag on the floor and marched through her apartment.

"What are you doing?" Caitlyn called after him. She didn't mind him looking around, but most people would have asked first.

"I'm making sure no one is here."

"Seriously?" Caitlyn froze, drawing the bag of food tight to her chest like it could protect her.

"Just a precaution. Until we figure out what's going on..."

The implication was crystal clear. Someone could be after her, too.

Caitlyn put the food on the coffee table and dropped onto the couch. She stared at it while Liam unpacked their dinner. When she didn't take her food right away, he asked, "Are you okay?"

Caitlyn breathed a laugh. She shook her head. The last forty-eight hours were almost her last. She'd been in a bar fight, in a burning apartment, arrested, stitched up by a virtual stranger, and was being protected by a man she barely knew because her best friend went missing and she had the nerve to ask questions.

"There's a lot more going on, isn't there?"

Liam took her hand but didn't say anything. Caitlyn swallowed roughly and looked up at him. His eyes held pity, sorrow, and a little bit of fear. It was the last one that worried her the most.

"I don't know what's going on yet, Caitlyn. That's the truth. I'm not giving up on finding Jeanine, but there are a lot of unknowns. I don't know who Jeanine really was. I don't know who the men in the bar were or why they attacked us. I don't know where Jeanine is. I don't know why her place was burned down. I don't know why the cops and the FBI didn't investigate her disappearance. I want to find all the answers, but I don't know if I can do it alone. I'm used to having a team. Other people helping me, making sense of what we find. My team can't come. Not right now. And Adam couldn't stay. So, I'm on my own. I wish I could make you feel better, but right now, I have more questions than answers."

Caitlyn took a breath and let it out slowly. "I never should have gotten you involved. You could have visited with your parents and asked a few people about Jeanine and gone home. Instead, I dragged you into the middle of this and almost got you killed."

Liam laughed. "Not the first time that's happened. And you have nothing to apologize for. If I decided the case was nothing more than a woman who ran off, then found out I was wrong, I would've had a hard time with that. Something is wrong, and I'm going to find out what it is."

Caitlyn smiled at him. "One more thing."

"Yeah?"

"You're not alone in this. I don't have any education or skills, but I'll do whatever you tell me to do to help find my friend."

Liam smiled back at her. "That's good to hear."

11

———

ENGLISH CLEANED UP THEIR TRASH WHEN DINNER WAS
finished. He felt awkward in Caitlyn's apartment. When his
teammates were watching over people, they made themselves at home, but English struggled with the idea. At
home, he'd be on his computer playing a game or doing
research or watching a movie. At Caitlyn's, he wanted to be
with her.

It felt like a lifetime had passed since he woke up with
her in his arms, but it had only been a few hours. It had
been two days since he saw her at his parents' anniversary
party, and less than that since he stayed up all night
watching her sleep. He was exhausted, but he didn't want to
miss a moment with her. Eventually, he would go back to
Niagara Falls, and she would go wherever she wanted, and
he'd probably never see her again. But for the moment, they
were in the same state, same town, same apartment, and
English was going to soak it all in.

"Is it okay if I take a shower?" she asked.

"Yeah. The bandage should keep your stitches dry, but I

have more of them so I can replace it for you. I'm not a medic, but I have basic first aid knowledge."

"Okay, thanks. Um, when I'm done. You can use the shower if you need to. Or anything else. I...I know being here with me is..."

"Being here is exactly where I want to be, Caitlyn. Go clean up. You'll feel better after that."

She nodded and went into her bedroom. She closed the door, but no lock clicked into place. Smart, but also tempting. English wasn't the kind of man who would barge in on a woman, but he couldn't help but think of her wet and naked just a few feet away when the shower turned on.

English walked around her apartment and tried to let his brain work out whatever he felt like he was missing. Dex and Dunn were usually the ones who figured out the missing pieces of a case. English just knew where to look for confirmation. Without his team, he felt like he was operating at less than full capacity.

The door to Caitlyn's bedroom opened. She walked out in dark sweats and a loose tank top that, if he had to guess, was not covering up a bra. Her breasts swayed gently under the fabric. Her black curls hung in wet chunks down her back, the ends twisting and curling as they dried.

She moved toward him and lifted her shirt. "I tried to keep it dry."

English swallowed roughly and focused on the stitches instead of the soft, creamy skin they were holding together. He nodded. "Do you want me to change it?"

"Probably, right? I don't know. I've never had stitches before."

"I think I should. These can stay on for up to forty-eight hours, but since it was wet, we should change it. Do you want to lie down?"

She nodded and moved to the couch. She lifted her shirt again when she was stretched out.

English kneeled in front of her with the new bandage on the couch next to her. He met her gaze and said, "This might sting, but I'm going to try not to pull at your stitches when I peel this off. If it hurts, tell me."

Caitlyn sucked in a breath and nodded.

English lifted one edge of the clear plastic bandage and pulled slowly. He flipped his gaze between her stomach and her face, doing his best to not hurt her.

Caitlyn closed her eyes the entire time, breathing slowly while English worked. When the bandage was off, he wiped the wound with a clean cloth, then pressed the new bandage into place.

"All set."

"That wasn't as bad as I expected," Caitlyn said. She let English help her sit up.

"That's good. I don't want to hurt you."

"Thanks. Um, did you want to use my shower?"

English nodded. He didn't want to let her out of his sight, but he needed to clean himself up. And a few minutes away from Caitlyn was probably in order to clear his head.

He grabbed his duffle and went into her room. He dug through and found some clothes he could sleep in, then left the bedroom door open and went to the shower.

The warm-ish water felt good, not as good as hot water would have, but it was the best he got. English hadn't realized how sore his muscles were until the mediocre warmth seeped into them and started to relax him. He ducked his head under the spray and let it beat on his shoulders.

He groaned, knowing he couldn't stay there long. If someone broke in, Caitlyn was at risk. Until he could figure out what was going on, he needed to stay as close to her as possible.

He reached for a bottle of shampoo and squirted some into his hand. As he washed his hair, her scent filled his nose and soaked into him. His cock rose at the thought of her being in the same space just a few minutes earlier. Naked. Wet. Slippery skin.

Guilt pulsed through him, but desire was stronger. He reached for himself, wrapping his hand around his erection and stroking. He closed his eyes and let his body take over as he quickly brought himself to orgasm.

It was over far too soon. He stood under the spray as his body quivered and protested being alone. It had been a while since he'd shared his bed with a woman, especially a woman who made him hard without being in the same room.

English finished washing himself and got out, drying and dressing and heading back to the living room with Caitlyn. He just hoped she didn't know what he did in her shower.

"Do you want to watch a movie?" Caitlyn asked softly.

English nodded and resumed his seat on the couch. The apartment was locked up, and they were as safe as they could be inside. A movie might settle him. The way her eyes were drooping, he was sure it would help Caitlyn sleep.

She picked a romantic comedy, one he'd seen when Lily insisted they all go to the movies together. English liked it as much as he could like a movie about two people falling in love. He preferred something with action usually, but when someone was trying to kill you, he understood the desire to push that from your mind.

Caitlyn snuggled into the cushions of the couch and covered herself with a blanket. She glanced at English and lifted the edge. Using the blanket meant moving closer to her. It meant sitting right next to her. Her thigh against his. Her arm against his.

English shifted over until he could pull the blanket over his lap. Caitlyn twisted and her leg rubbed over his. She pulled back, and English immediately missed her touch.

The movie played on the screen, but English barely noticed it. Every thought in his head was of Caitlyn, and every bit of his focus was on not pulling her into his arms. She wasn't the same girl she was in high school, but that only made him want her more. Back then, she was popular and beautiful and untouchable. Now, she was even more beautiful, but she was savvy and creative and funny. She gave him hope that he might not be the nerdy, dorky kid he still thought of himself as.

Caitlyn shifted again, bringing her side in contact with his. English moved over so he wasn't crowding her. A minute later, she adjusted herself again, once more touching him.

English didn't move that time. He tried to look at her, but she was watching the screen and ignoring him. Her scent drifted up to him, making him hard again. She used the same shampoo he did.

Through the rest of the movie, Caitlyn repositioned herself closer and closer to English. If it was intentional, he was sure it was only because she was scared. Her life was threatened, and he was there to protect her. She wasn't interested in him. Not really.

The credits finally rolled, the couple in love and their issues resolved. English didn't move, giving Caitlyn a chance to get up first.

Instead, she leaned her head on his shoulder.

English tensed. The blanket covered his lap, but with

her body pressed against his, he wasn't sure it would hide his growing erection.

"Thank you for protecting me," she whispered.

"You're welcome," English croaked.

She was silent for another minute. Then she said, "Can I ask you a favor?"

"Anything."

"Will you... I mean, are you willing... Shit, this isn't easy."

"What is it, Caitlyn?"

She took a breath and sat up. She crossed her legs and looked at him, straightening her shoulders and meeting his gaze. "I wondered if you wanted to have sex."

English drew back. "Excuse me?"

Caitlyn huffed a breath and shook her head. She unfolded herself from the couch and took the blanket with her. "Never mind. I shouldn't have asked. I know you're here because of Jeanine and I'm not exactly a catch. I'm just stressed and anxious and usually sex helps when I feel like this. But it was stupid."

"Yes," English said. His brain skidded to a halt at her question, but once it started working again, that was the only thing he could say.

"Wow, that was mean. I didn't think you'd agree that it was stupid of me to ask you."

"No, I... I was saying yes to sex. Not to you being stupid. You're not stupid. You're amazing. You're smart and beautiful and—"

Her snort interrupted him. "You don't need to butter me up. I know I'm nothing special. I've been reminded of that my entire life. And I know this is basically a pity-fuck, but—"

"Fucking hell, Caitlyn. Just stop talking. It's not pity and you're definitely special. You were the girl every guy fantasized about in high school. Maybe that's creepy, but it's true. You were always out of my league, but I still imagined one day you'd notice me. I'm not the guy women want. I know I'm just the guy who's here, but I'd never say no to you."

"You make me seem like a catch."

"Because you are." He stood and walked over to her. He tucked her dark curls behind her ear and let his fingers glide over her jawline. He tilted her chin back and forced her to meet his gaze. "When you kissed me yesterday morning, I nearly swallowed my tongue. When you did it again today, and crawled on top of me, I almost came in my pants. I'm sorry you don't see yourself the way others do, but you're stunning. If you need a few orgasms to relax, and you're asking me to help you out with them, I'm at your service, Ms. Powers."

She smirked and breathed a laugh. "I like that. Ms. Powers."

"You have the power here. I'm just your humble servant, making sure you're safe and serviced."

She snorted. "I was a fool for not getting to know you better in high school."

"Nah, I was a dork. I definitely wouldn't have been able to make you come so hard you see stars back then."

"Are you saying you can do that now?"

"Why don't you go get naked and let me show you, Ms. Powers?"

Her body trembled with his words. She licked her lips and nodded, then turned and hurried to her room.

English wasn't sure whose ass he had to kiss for this one, but he was not going to waste the opportunity he was given. Not one second of it.

CAITLYN'S HANDS trembled as she took off her clothes. Sex was not an emotional event for her. It never had been. From the first time she had sex with a guy, she knew sex was a tool. Sometimes a tool to get what she wanted, sometimes a tool to feel good, sometimes a tool to scratch an itch. She enjoyed sex, but she also enjoyed movie nights on the couch with ice cream and wine for dinner, so her standards were not high.

But when Liam stalked into the bedroom and his gaze raked over her body, she wasn't sure sex with him was going to be just a tool. He had the look of a man on a mission. And she was his target.

Heat pooled in her belly. She'd removed her tank and sweatpants but hadn't gotten to her panties yet.

"Fucking hell," Liam breathed. "Get on the bed."

She did as he asked, leaving her panties on while she positioned herself on the pillows. She stared at him, mesmerized, as he stripped out of the black tee and sweats he put on after his shower. His erection pressed against the boxer briefs he wore, making her mouth water.

Liam dug through his bag before pulling out a strip of condoms. He tore one off and tossed the rest back into his bag. He set it on the nightstand, then climbed onto the bed with Caitlyn.

She looked up at him. In the two days since she pushed her phone number into his hand, she hadn't given much thought to how attractive he was. His eyes were a stormy blue color that darkened when she reached up and ran a nail over his stubbled cheek. The blond hair prickled her finger and excited her. She wondered if she'd get to feel that between her thighs. She asked for sex, not foreplay, but she could dream.

Caitlyn ran her hands down his arms, caressing his muscles. She brought them back up, then moved to his chest. He kept himself still, supporting his weight over her like he was doing a plank. She ran a fingertip around his nipple, and he faltered for a second.

"Be careful, Ms. Powers," he warned.

She smirked up at him and did it again.

He growled and lowered his bottom half. She spread her legs and made room for him to settle against her. His erection was thick and strong between her thighs, and she ached to have him thrust inside and show her some stars.

"I think I might like watching you lose control a little bit," Caitlyn admitted.

"You might get more than you bargained for."

"You mean I might get two orgasms that make me see stars?" she asked innocently.

He chuckled and looked down at her body. His attention snagged on her breasts. He scooted lower and sucked one into his mouth hard.

"Damn, there are those stars I keep hearing about."

"That's nothing, sweetheart. Stick with me, and you'll be out of your mind."

"I'm not going anywhere," she said, holding his head in place. She threaded her fingers into his hair and pressed her breast into his mouth.

He opened wider and took more of her inside. He rolled her nipple between his tongue and the roof of his mouth the same moment he pinched the other nipple.

"Oh, God," she moaned, the pleasure and pain slamming her eyes closed.

Liam groaned against her chest. She released his head,

unable to keep the pressure there as her body tingled in anticipation of what he was going to do next.

Liam licked his way to her other nipple and teased it, gently blowing on it after he licked it. Her nipple beaded tight under his treatment.

"I think you like that," he said against her skin.

"Uh huh."

"Let's see what else you like, Ms. Powers." He kissed and licked his way down, nipping at her ribs and slurping at her belly button. When he reached the barrier of her panties, he caught them with his teeth and tugged.

Caitlyn lifted her hips and pushed at the sides, helping him pull them off. She'd already been mostly naked, but without her panties on, she felt exposed. She was the one who asked for sex, and he agreed, but what if it wasn't good enough for him? Caitlyn hadn't worried about her capabilities in years. What if she was one and done because she wasn't the only one not interested in a second time?

"Spread your thighs for me," Liam said, his voice growly.

Shivers raced up her spine. She did as he asked and watched his face as he stared at her.

"You're already dripping, Caitlyn. Can you feel it?"

She nodded.

"Are you going to let me taste you?"

"You don't have to."

"Does that mean you don't like it?"

She shook her head.

"Can you come like that?"

She nodded.

"Good, because I'm sending you to space to see some stars."

She smiled at his cheesy line. The other men she'd been with were worried about performance and the way they looked. Liam was only worried about making her feel good. She didn't deserve him. But she couldn't resist him.

Liam pressed her thighs wider and stretched out on the bed with his face between her legs. His forearms brushed her thighs, making her tingle. More wetness dripped from her, and he touched one finger to it. He dragged the wetness through her folds and around her clit before going back to her entrance for more.

"Liam," she whispered.

He looked up at her, his face barely visible over her round belly. Their gazes locked and held for a long moment before he lowered his head and licked her.

"Oh, God," Caitlyn cried out.

He licked her clit first but pulled back quickly. He tasted her, exploring all her folds with his tongue before filling her with it. He pulsed in and out of her gently, his nose pressing against her clit. She shifted against him, her body coiled tight and in need of a release.

Liam pulled back and blew gently on her skin. He replaced his tongue with a finger and dragged his lips back to her clit. He pulsed his finger inside her and teased her clit with quick swipes of his tongue.

She went from teetering on the edge to desperate to fall in less than a minute. Her body tightened, signaling to him that she was ready. She couldn't speak, or breathe properly, but when he sucked her clit hard, she knew he understood everything she couldn't say.

And then she saw those stars he mentioned.

She splintered like a fallen tree. Her body took over, forcing breath into her lungs. The stars exploded and reformed over and over again while Liam licked and sucked and fucked her with his fingers and tongue.

As fast as one orgasm ended, another one built up right

behind it. Caitlyn knew she could have multiple orgasms, but it had never happened with another person. Her former lovers were proud of themselves when they got her to cry out, then focused on their own pleasure.

Liam was not like anyone else she'd ever known.

Caitlyn begged Liam to stop at one point, sure she wouldn't survive another orgasm. Her head was fuzzy and her throat was raw. Her entire body tingled. She'd never felt so good in her entire life.

"You okay?" Liam asked.

Caitlyn's eyes refused to open, so she just nodded and reached for him.

He guided her hand to his face and kissed her palm. "Can I kiss you?"

"Yes. Please," she said. She wanted to taste herself on his lips. To feel his body on top of hers.

He leaned over her side and gently pecked her lips. Caitlyn grabbed his face and deepened their kiss, thrusting her tongue into his mouth. He growled and grabbed her breast, kneading it as he pressed his erection to her hip.

"Inside me," she breathed, barely breaking their kiss. "Now, Liam. Please."

He rolled off the bed, and Caitlyn finally found the strength to open her eyes. He stripped off his boxer briefs and rolled on the condom. Her gaze was glued to his erection the entire time, her mouth watering at the sight of it. Long and thick with a slight curve. The nest of hair at his base was a darker blond than she expected. When he turned back to her and caught her looking, she couldn't bother with embarrassment.

"You're beautiful."

"That's my line."

"It's true."

He smiled and crawled over her. He kneeled between her thighs before he lined them up. His gaze snagged hers and held as he pressed inside her with one quick move.

"Oh, fuck, that feels good," she breathed.

"Yeah, you do."

Caitlyn looked up at him as he started to move. His eyes were closed at first, but after a few strokes, he opened them and watched her, too.

Each slide of his body into hers had Caitlyn letting go more and more. She wanted sex, an orgasm, but she got something much more. Much better. She got a man who put her pleasure first and, even when it was his turn, was focused on her.

Caitlyn cried out when Liam thrust hard into her, hitting that spot deep inside that most men missed. He did it again, and again, until Caitlyn couldn't stop the orgasm chasing her down.

"Liam," she breathed as she went flying once more.

"Fuck. Caitlyn. God, Caitlyn." He grunted and groaned and followed her over the edge.

Everything inside and out of Caitlyn shook. She'd never known sex could be a full body experience, but with Liam Johnson, it was.

With Liam Johnson, she was quickly realizing everything was different. And she liked it more than a little bit.

12

English rolled to the side so he didn't crush Caitlyn. Her bare skin was against his side, their bodies cooling together while they fought to catch their breath.

Inside his head, his teenage self high-fived him for sleeping with Caitlyn Powers. His lips lifted in a satisfied smirk, but sex with Caitlyn was definitely not about fulfilling some teenage fantasy. It was all about fulfilling her adult need. And based on the way she lost control, he was quite confident he'd succeeded.

Before his heart slowed, English crawled over Caitlyn, kissing her on the nose, then went to the bathroom to take care of the condom. He washed his hands and went back to her. She hadn't moved, which made him smile.

"Get that smirk off your face," she said. "It's been a while."

"Doesn't mean I can't smirk," English said. "If it was bad, you wouldn't be laid out right now."

"I might need a refresher in a few hours. Just to make sure it wasn't bad."

English laughed loudly. He appreciated her sense of

humor. And her. In high school, he worshipped her, but he didn't really know her. Spending the last forty-eight hours with her was giving him a sense of who she was. And he liked her.

"Until then, I need some sleep." Caitlyn rolled over and tugged the covers out from under her body. She turned toward the wall, letting the blankets fall over her.

English wasn't sure what he was supposed to do. Did he crawl into bed with her, or did he go out to the couch? Did he—

"Are you coming?" she asked, looking over her shoulder to where he stood in the middle of her room. Her gaze drifted lower and lingered.

He was definitely coming. Again.

English lifted the blankets and laid down behind her. She snuggled against him and was asleep within minutes.

English was not so lucky. He laid there and listened to her breathing. He tried not to grind his erection against her backside while she slept. And his mind raced with everything he knew, and everything he didn't know.

He didn't know if it was ten minutes or an hour, but English finally accepted he wasn't getting any sleep. Not until he figured a few things out. He slowly extricated himself from Caitlyn's bed. He grabbed his boxer briefs and tiptoed out of the bedroom.

The lights were still on in the living room, giving him plenty of light to work from. He opened Jeanine's laptop once more, but after an hour of searching, he was still unable to find anything new.

He knew there was something Caitlyn wasn't telling him about Jeanine, but English had no idea what it could be. If it was important, he assumed Caitlyn would have told him. She was the one who reported Jeanine missing, and from what he could tell, she was the only one who cared about her being found.

English felt guilty that Jeanine didn't matter to him. She was a job, a task, not really a person. Sure, he wondered about the woman she was, but not in a way that made him really care about her. He learned early on in his military career that if he cared, he couldn't do his job. Having an emotional connection meant putting himself and his team at risk, and he couldn't do that.

It was easier to keep his distance. From the victim, their family and friends, and from everyone.

Caitlyn was the only person he'd ever struggled to follow that rule for. She was the woman he'd always put on a pedestal. The one he looked back at and knew was everything he wanted a woman to be.

She had changed, but so had he. He wasn't the scrawny, nerdy kid he used to be. And she wasn't the untouchable model she used to be. What happened between them was amazing, but English knew it was just sex. It was two consenting adults letting off some steam. It was spectacular, but it was just sex.

English forced himself to stop thinking about Caitlyn and to focus on Jeanine again. He wanted to call Dex and talk things through, but Dex and the others were neck deep in another assignment. One that English should have been on.

No, he shouldn't have. If he was there with them, no one would be looking for Jeanine. No one except Caitlyn.

English pulled out his own computer and started a file. It wasn't much, but he needed to collect his thoughts. He had the case file from the police and the FBI about Jeanine's disappearance, both of which were essentially useless. He had his own account of Jeanine's apartment before it burned down. He had Caitlyn's insistence that Jeanine was at Sparky's before she disappeared. And he had the events that happened since he arrived in town.

What was he missing?

Aside from everything there was to know about Jeanine, he didn't know. They had her financials. Her online history. Her personal history. But there wasn't much about her as a person. English knew where she grew up, who her parents were, and what grades she got in school, but he didn't know if she wanted to be a server for the rest of her life, why she moved to East Charlottesville, or what she was doing at a bar alone the night she disappeared.

He finished his notes and stared at the screen. It was never good when he had more questions than answers about a case. He'd asked Caitlyn about Jeanine, but she didn't provide a lot of insight. English was starting to wonder if his personal feelings about East Charlottesville were clouding his ability to see what was going on. He couldn't fathom staying in town after graduation. Why would a woman with zero attachments ever want to move there? It was the question that plagued him the most.

English stood and paced the room. He tried to let his mind work things out. Get out of his own head and into Jeanine's. Stop letting his feelings interfere with—

"I need to tell you something," Caitlyn said quietly.

English hadn't even noticed her standing in the doorway to the bedroom. She had a robe tied tight around her waist. She chewed on a fingernail. Her curls tumbled around her shoulders, messy from his hands just hours earlier.

His body immediately responded to her. His gaze dipped to the neckline of her robe where it looked like she wore nothing underneath. Her legs were bare from above her knees all the way to her toes. He wanted her again. But she was standing there to tell him something.

"What is it?" he asked, resisting the urge to cross his arms.

"Jeanine had a second phone."

His brows tugged together. "What do you mean?"

"She had two. One is the number I gave you. The other one she used for work."

"Work? Why would she need a second phone as a server at the diner or working at the church?"

"Those weren't her only jobs. And those weren't the ones that paid the most. Jeanine was... for lack of a better term, a prostitute."

English stared at Caitlyn for a long moment, wondering how he was supposed to respond to that. A part of him wanted to laugh, but he was fairly sure Caitlyn was being serious.

"I know I should have told you, but I didn't want you to stop looking for her if you knew. Jeanine was a good person. Is a good person. And I know what she does is not that great, but she's still been a good friend to me. I care about her, and—"

"Caitlyn," English growled, getting her to stop. His fists were clenched tight at his sides, his entire body taut.

"I'm sorry," she breathed. She moved toward him, disappointment in her gaze. "Please don't stop looking for her."

"I'm not going to stop. What she did for a living or in her spare time has nothing to do with whether or not I'm going to try to find her." He loosened his fists, trying to calm himself down. People were dismissed too easily. It wasn't fair.

"I told her she was going to get hurt one day. She liked sex. A lot. She said the men she slept with were fun. Some were a little crazy, but she promised me she was always safe."

"Caitlyn, no one deserves to be hurt. A woman has every right to enjoy sex. I don't care if Jeanine was walking naked down Main Street and offering herself to anyone who saw her, she should never have been hurt because of it. But knowing this, it gives me a new place to look. I need to know the other phone number and anything else you know about her job. Who she was with, how often, where she met them, everything."

Caitlyn nodded and tugged her robe tighter around her neck. She folded herself into a ball on the couch and looked up at him with wide, sorrowful eyes. "I should have told you, but no one else cared. They knew what she did, and they ignored me. I thought you'd be the same."

"I understand. But I'm not, so you need to tell me everything, Caitlyn. Now."

CAITLYN NODDED AND STARTED TALKING. She gave Liam Jeanine's phone number and told him everything she knew about her friend's job.

"So, you're telling me she would meet men at Sparky's. They would set up dates with her ahead of time, and she would arrange to meet them there. The night she disappeared, she was supposed to be meeting someone?"

"That's what she told me. She asked if I wanted to come. Sometimes I went with her so she didn't have to worry about getting her car back. But I didn't want to go out that night."

"Do you know who her regular customers were?"

Caitlyn shook her head. "She used nicknames for all of them."

"But you went with her before. Didn't you see her with anyone?"

"No. I stayed outside. She told me she didn't know if all the men were single. She didn't care as long as they were paying her, but she knew how I felt about cheating."

Liam sighed and stood from the couch. He paced across the room and stood at the window. A faint glow highlighted his profile. "Was she dating anyone?"

"Just the one guy she mentioned. Lengthy Lefty. I'm not sure if they were really dating or if he was just a regular she had a soft spot for. She said he liked to buy her things. Presents. She felt bad charging him when he was paying for other stuff."

"What kind of stuff?"

"I'm not sure. They went out to dinner a few times, but I know they left town. It sounded like he had money."

"There aren't a lot of people here who have money," Liam said.

"It also doesn't take much to have money around here. Your parents fit that category."

Liam's brows shot up. "You think she was sleeping with my father? I thought you said she didn't sleep with married men."

Caitlyn shrugged. "I honestly don't know who she was with. And what I said was she doesn't go after married men. If they approach her, that's on them. And anyone who can afford their mortgage, buy a new vehicle every five years or so, and has two good paying jobs in one household is like royalty around here. Your parents are Gold Standard."

Liam rubbed his jaw, the stubble of his beard rasping against his fingertips.

Caitlyn clenched her thighs together, remembering how the stubble felt between them. Her panties, the only clothes she put on beneath the robe, grew wet. Sex was the last thing she should have been thinking about, but Liam Johnson was spectacular in bed. She was a fool if she didn't try to get him in there again. And Caitlyn was not a fool.

"I need to find that phone," Liam said, almost to himself.

Caitlyn knew she'd upset him when she mentioned his parents. She was fairly sure Jeanine was not sleeping with his dad, but she also didn't know who Jeanine was sleeping with. She could have been sleeping with anyone. Which was why Caitlyn went to Sparky's after Jeanine disappeared. She knew someone there had to have been with Jeanine. Or knew something. But none of them were willing to talk to her.

Liam stared at his computer screen and ignored Caitlyn. She admired his focus and determination. She felt guilty for doubting him, but she couldn't help it. He was a stranger, and after what his father said about Jeanine not being worth his time to find, Caitlyn had to assume Liam felt the same way.

"Shit," Liam breathed, leaning back on the couch. "Holy fucking shit."

"What is it?"

"Her phone. I found it. It hadn't been backed up in a while, but it's there. There isn't a lot on it. A few apps and some contacts. Text messages are deleted regularly from what I can see."

"Can't you get them even after they've been deleted?"

He shook his head. "I can see the number a text was sent to if I can get her phone records, but I can't see the content of the text."

"I thought you had her phone records."

"Not for this phone."

Caitlyn's cheeks warmed. She was to blame for that. She never told anyone about the secret phone Jeanine carried. Caitlyn only knew about it because she saw it once. They were finishing up a shift at the diner and it fell out of her bag. Caitlyn asked about it, and Jeanine brushed it off. She pressed later, worried her friend was in trouble, and Jeanine admitted the truth.

Caitlyn didn't know what name it was under, but she knew it wasn't Jeanine's. No one would have found it unless she told Liam.

"I'm sorry I didn't tell you."

Liam shook his head. "I don't blame you. But I'm glad I know now. I can see some of the people she was in touch with. It looks like she had plans to meet up with someone that night, but she canceled at the last minute. Why would she do that?"

Caitlyn shook her head slowly. She tried to think back to the last time she talked to Jeanine. Jeanine asked Caitlyn to go with her. She said she was meeting someone but wouldn't say who. Caitlyn brushed her off after a double shift that left her feeling more anxious to get the hell out of town.

"Why were you so sure about her being at the bar?"

"That's where she told me she was going to be. She wanted to pick me up on the way there so I could drive her car back. Since I'm closer, she sometimes would come here after she was with someone."

"So, whoever she was supposed to meet lives walking distance to here?"

"Everyone in town lives walking distance to here."

Liam exhaled heavily. "Fuck. Okay, what else. Did she say anything else?"

"I told her I was tired. That I just wanted to stay in. She pushed, which wasn't unusual, but it felt different. Like she didn't want to meet this guy."

"But you don't know who he was?"

"No. She never told me details about any of them." Caitlyn wished she'd asked more about her friend's life. About who she was seeing.

"Is there any chance the guy who bought her things didn't know about her job?"

Caitlyn snorted. "Not likely. Jeanine was discreet, but she wasn't subtle. She didn't tell me who she was with, but she never hid that she was with someone almost every night."

"Dammit," Liam breathed.

"Why?"

He shrugged and shook his head. "Basically, the entire town are suspects. If she was sleeping with married men, their wives are suspects. The men could have gotten jealous, so they're suspects. Until we can figure out who all the men she was with are, we have a few hundred people who might have done something to her."

"And how are we going to figure that out?"

Liam rubbed his jaw and stared at the screen again. "I have no idea."

Caitlyn chewed on her nail and stood. "There's one more thing."

"What is it?"

"I have a file. It's not a lot, but it's stuff I've collected over the last week. Some articles, a few things I remembered her saying, mostly small stuff, but maybe it would help."

"Where is it?"

"I'll get it," Caitlyn said. She went to her room and retrieved the folder from under her mattress. She worried someone would break into her apartment and try to steal it.

Liam took the folder from her and opened it up. His eyes scanned the pages quickly, flipping from one to the next. The longer he read, the more Caitlyn's cheeks heated. Her file was dumb. It wasn't helpful. And she never should have shown it to him.

"This is good info," Liam said after a minute.

"Yeah?"

He nodded. "It's a decent timeline of the last few weeks. I want to fill in a few missing pieces, but this is a good start. Can we spread this all out? Table?"

Caitlyn nodded and moved ahead of him to clear her dining room table. She grabbed the discarded mail and her purse, depositing both on the kitchen counter. Liam followed behind her with the candle and paper towels, then started setting articles and notes on the table in order.

When he was done, he stepped back and rubbed his jaw. "All we need now is her work schedule and a few names and we have a chance at finding her."

"Really?"

Liam nodded slowly. "Thanks to you, yeah."

Caitlyn took a deep breath for the first time in almost two weeks and let hope filter in. Someone finally believed her. And they were going to find Jeanine.

13

———

Caitlyn napped on the couch while English kept digging. The information she gave him helped. It painted a picture of Jeanine in a way only a friend could. Caitlyn picked out things English never would have thought to notice. Like the mention of someone filing for divorce. If Jeanine had something to do with that, the husband and wife were definitely suspects.

Jeanine's full phone records came through sometime around five am. English was going through them and searching for names attached to the numbers she contacted most frequently, especially leading up to her disappearance. He narrowed it down to six numbers he was going to investigate first.

English didn't have the same legal rights to get information that the police or FBI had, but he could do some general searches and see what he came up with. Two of the numbers weren't available publicly. One was for a woman. One for a man English didn't know. But two were for men he remembered from the bar fight. The two men who started the bar fight.

Guilty people usually acted in a guilty way, so English focused his efforts on the two men from the bar. If they were willing to attack Caitlyn and him, it was reasonable to assume they could have hurt or killed Jeanine.

Caitlyn never said why she was so sure those men had anything to do with Jeanine's disappearance. Aside from Jeanine saying she would be at Sparky's, there was no reason for Caitlyn to be so adamant. Was there something else she wasn't telling him?

English stood from the couch and went back to the table. He looked over the timeline he created from Caitlyn's files. It was more information than he had before, but there was still a lot missing. The most important pieces were who she was sleeping with. If any of the men were angry that she was with others, it would have been easy for them to take advantage of the situation when they got together.

But it still didn't explain where her car was or why a body hadn't turned up. A crime of passion was one thing, but that usually led to regret. Someone who didn't mean to hurt someone else. It meant they would mess up. Get caught.

Jeanine had been missing for thirteen days. In thirteen days, nothing was found to give any indication of where she was. At least, nothing English was aware of.

His phone buzzed, the vibration tickling his leg. He dug it out and moved to the bedroom. He closed the door so his voice didn't wake Caitlyn.

"Yeah?"

"Any update? Did you find anything at the apartment?" Dunn asked.

English chuckled to himself. It felt like a lifetime since he talked to his boss. "What used to be the apartment had a whole lot of stuff left behind for a woman who supposedly disappeared. I grabbed her laptop before the place went up in flames."

"What?"

"Yeah. While we were in there, someone torched it. We got out, but the cops were there and thought we did it. My cousin got us released."

"Fucking hell. This case is not an easy one. Do you need backup?"

"I didn't think there was any to spare."

Dunn exhaled loudly. "There's not, but we're not going to leave you alone. You should have someone watching your back."

"Caitlyn's here."

"The woman from high school? Can you trust her?"

English shrugged. "Do I have a choice? She has a lot of intel. Our missing person had a secret life as a prostitute."

"You're shitting me," Dunn replied, his tone flat.

"Nope. Secret phone and everything. I met a few of her clients at the bar the other night."

"Your new friends?"

"Yep." English chuckled. "I'm looking into them. There are more, but not all of them have public info. I'll need a warrant to get some of the information."

"The local PD really fucked this up, didn't they?"

English sighed. "It appears that way. The FBI didn't help much. I get that they're overworked, but to not even show up is pretty sad."

"It is. Do you think the PD there is in on whatever is going on? That someone is responsible and they're covering it up?"

"I've been wondering the same. The bad thing is, with her job, there's no shortage of suspects. If the captain had ever been with her, she could have threatened him or he could have just gotten out of hand. Anyone could have. Instead of narrowing the pool, I keep expanding it."

"So, at this point, I'm assuming you're no longer considering she might have actually just skipped town."

"No, I'm not. Her cards haven't been used. There haven't been any cash withdrawals. Her place looked as though she could be back at any time. Her phone charger and favorite sweatshirt were still there."

"Favorite sweatshirt?"

"That's what Caitlyn said. The place wasn't tossed, but it also wasn't cleared out. I don't know how any officer could walk in there and say it looked like she left town."

"What about another option? What if something did happen to her, but the cops aren't interested in finding her because they think it's better for her to be gone?"

English nodded to himself. "That's where I'm leaning right now. The cop who did the report is someone I graduated with. A real tool. But he's not the only one who isn't a fan of hers. My dad didn't have anything nice to say about her, but—"

"That doesn't mean she deserved to die or disappear."

"Exactly what I said," English agreed.

Dunn sighed heavily. "All right. It sounds like you have things as under control as possible. What's next for you?"

"I'm going to get in touch with the FBI and get some information about Jeanine's work schedules. I'm building a timeline, with Caitlyn's help, of the events leading up to the disappearance. Once I have that, I need the names of the people on my short list that I can't get. While I'm waiting on the FBI, I'm going to pay a visit to the men who jumped us in the bar."

"Be careful with them."

"I will. I did some digging, and they work at the same

place my dad does. I was thinking of paying them a visit at work, where they won't be drinking and will get fired if they get violent."

"That sounds like a good plan."

"I hope so. I'm going to find out everything I can about them before I head over there."

"Good. Keep us posted. If you need someone, we'll make it work."

"Thanks. Talk soon."

"Yep."

English tucked his phone away and left the bedroom. Caitlyn wasn't on the couch anymore. A second of panic hit him square in the chest until he smelled coffee in the air.

Caitlyn was in the kitchen with her back to him. English took a moment to appreciate her figure. Her curves were full and lush and gave him something to sink into. His teammates were all with women who were extra curvy. Most of the women English had slept with over the years were thin, but the few he'd actually felt a connection to were curvy. Thick thighs and a love of food drew him in, and Caitlyn had both.

The sizzle of bacon wafted through the air and pushed him closer to her. She turned and flashed him an uneasy smile before looking back at the bacon in the frying pan.

"I can't go long without food. I'm guessing you don't eat bacon, but I made enough in case you do."

"I love bacon. What kind of person doesn't?"

"A vegetarian?" Caitlyn said.

English snorted. "They don't know what they're missing."

"True. My mom had me on a vegetarian diet once. It wasn't bad, but I always felt hungry. Of course, I never ate enough no matter what diet I was on."

"That's child abuse," English growled.

Caitlyn shook her head, her curls bouncing with the gentle movement. "It's how she was. If I gained weight, I couldn't get the good modeling jobs. I shouldn't complain because I loved it. I'd probably still be modeling if she hadn't run off with my money."

"You can find her and sue her. You really should."

Caitlyn shook her head again. "I don't have the money to do that. And at this point, I doubt any of it is left."

"Still, she never should have been able to get access to it."

"I was a minor."

"And she was your mother."

Caitlyn sighed. She poked at the bacon with her fork and ignored English. It wasn't until she sniffed that he realized he'd pushed too far.

"Caitlyn," he said softly.

"I'm fine."

"You say that a lot."

"What am I supposed to say, Liam? I'm nobody. I'm trash. I was a bitch growing up because I thought I was at the top of the food chain, but I was that girl who peaked in high school. I've done nothing useful with my life since then. I have a tiny apartment that I can barely afford. I haven't left the state since my mom skipped town. I have no friends, no family, and no one. I'm just taking up space." She drew a breath and let it out slowly. "You should just go. Get away from me before something happens. Everyone I get close to vanishes eventually, one way or another."

"Caitlyn," he tried again.

She waved her hand in his general direction.

English caught her hand and tugged on it until she turned to glare at him. "I'm sorry I pushed about your mom.

She was horrible for doing that to you, but it wasn't your fault."

"Yeah, I know, but it still happened to me."

"And it sucks. I promise not to bring it up again if you promise not to call yourself trash."

She rolled her eyes and tried to pull away from him. He held tight, not letting her. "Why do you care? As soon as you find Jeanine, you're gone. Back to your life saving people. I'm not important."

English stepped closer to her, keeping her wrist in his grip. He brought it to his chest and tucked a lock of her hair behind her ear. "You are important to me. I'm a blip in your life, but you matter. Last night mattered to me. I know you just wanted sex, and I'm not asking you for more, but I don't sleep with just anyone. You're beautiful and smart and funny and have no idea that you're all of those things. Trust me when I say being here with you is not a hardship for me."

"Why? Why do you think any of that? I'm not the woman men fight over to talk to in a bar—"

"That's because you're too good for them. Caitlyn, nothing I say is going to change your mind, but I'm going to try anyway. You're the most beautiful woman I've ever seen. You always have been. Gaining weight doesn't change that. I don't care what size clothes you wear, just that you're a good person. And you are."

She snorted.

"I mean that. You're fighting to save a woman no one else seems to want to save. You're not giving up."

"She's my friend."

"Sure, but there are plenty of people who would never have gone back to Sparky's. Who never would have continued after everything we've been through. But you're not giving up. You're willing to risk your own life to find her. And that makes you a good person in my world."

"She's my friend."

"I know. And we're going to find her. Together. But first, we're going to eat that bacon because it smells really good."

She cracked a smile and nodded. She turned off the oven and pulled out a small casserole dish.

English leaned over and groaned at the baked French toast. "You keep feeding me like this and I might never leave."

Caitlyn smiled up at him without a word.

AFTER BREAKFAST, Caitlyn took a shower and changed into clean clothes she could lounge around in. She didn't have to work that day, but she was supposed to be at the diner the next day. That meant she needed to do some laundry and get groceries because she worked six straight days after that.

When Caitlyn finished in her room, Liam went in to take his shower. Caitlyn walked over to the table and studied the timeline he had. He'd added text messages from some of Jeanine's clients, but Caitlyn didn't know if they were men Jeanine had ever talked about.

When the water turned off in the bathroom, she went to the kitchen to clean up and found Liam had already done it. She smiled. If feeding him was the only requirement for him staying, she would make sure she cooked something every night.

Liam walked back into the living room with his hair still wet as he tugged his tee on. Caitlyn did not shy away from getting another look at his body before it was covered up again. She was already hoping she could talk him into sex that night.

Liam chuckled, drawing her attention to his face. "You okay?"

"Yeah, why?"

"You're looking at me like I'm your next meal."

Caitlyn's cheeks warmed. Her first instinct was to play it off, but she stopped herself. She found Liam incredibly attractive, and he made it clear the feeling was mutual. "I can't help but appreciate everything you have to offer."

"Is that so?"

Caitlyn nodded and held his gaze as he abandoned his path to the couch and approached her in the dining room.

"And what exactly am I offering?"

"A whole lot more without this shirt on."

He looked down at her tee and nodded. "I couldn't agree more."

His hands rose under her shirt before she could react. He stripped it off her and let it hang from his fingertip.

"Much better."

He reached behind his neck and yanked his own shirt off, folding them together and setting them on one of the dining room chairs. He smirked at her, then went to the couch and sat in front of his computer like it was the most natural thing in the world.

Caitlyn stared at the muscles on his back as he moved and twisted, grabbing a notebook he was using to record things from his computer.

"Do you have a printer?"

"Um, yeah. In the bedroom."

"Is it wireless?"

"Yeah."

"Mind if I connect to it?"

Caitlyn just stared at him. How was he not affected at all by this? She was about to combust, and he was going about work like they weren't both topless.

When Caitlyn didn't answer, Liam turned to her. His gaze dipped to her breasts before looking up at her face. "Caitlyn?"

"How are you acting normal?"

"We have work to do."

"And you normally work without a shirt on?"

"If I were more clever I'd say I do some of my best work without a shirt on."

"But you're not clever?"

He breathed a laugh. "It's just not the truth. I'm a computer nerd. I always have been. My first love was a computer. Women have always taken second place for me. No woman has ever been willing to understand or accept that I find computers relaxing. That I like figuring out what's wrong with a computer. That they have answers."

"Okay?"

Liam sighed heavily. "If I focus on a computer, I'm not focused on a woman. They don't like that. They want to be the center of attention, at least some of the time. It's not... I'm not like that. Which is why I'm still single, and why I can sit here and forget that you're standing behind me without a shirt on. I have a one-track mind, and when I'm staring at a computer screen and solving a problem, that's the only thing I think about."

"Not all women find that quality to be a negative one."

Liam chuckled. "I've heard that before."

"We all get in our heads. We all have moments when nothing else matters more than what we're focused on. I don't think it's a bad thing."

"Maybe not short term, but long term, it's never worked out for me."

"I can honestly say I was not complaining last night."

That got a small smirk out of him.

"And right now, you're trying to help find my friend, so I'm not going to complain. But I'm not as good at it as you are, so if I disappear for a few minutes and close the door, don't be shocked if you hear a buzzing noise."

"Fuck, Caitlyn," he breathed.

She shrugged. "Just being honest."

Liam scrubbed a hand over his face. "One hour. Give me one hour to contact the FBI and get Jeanine's work schedule from her bosses, and then I'll show you how focused I can be."

Caitlyn's entire body flashed with heat. His gaze rubbed her skin raw, desire flickering in the air around them. She wasn't sure she'd survive an hour, but the look in his eyes said she'd be very, very happy if she did.

She nodded once. Liam dragged his gaze away and stared at the computer again. Caitlyn watched him and fantasized about what that focus would do for her in an hour.

Fifty-nine minutes.

Fifty-eight.

14

ENGLISH HAD NEVER STRUGGLED TO FOCUS WHEN THERE WAS A computer in front of him. It was as basic as breathing. But he'd never known the magnetic pull of Caitlyn Powers either. Every few minutes, he glanced up at her.

She sat across the room, reading a book from the over-stuffed shelf next to the TV. She hadn't bothered to put her shirt back on, so English had a fantastic view of her breasts. He couldn't remember ever having such a distracting view when he was working.

"Thirty-seven," Caitlyn said without looking up.

English smirked. He was counting down, too. Which meant he needed to stay focused so he had time to devote just to Caitlyn.

Jeanine's bosses were curious when he asked for her work schedule, but neither argued with him. They both knew his name, and his parents, so they didn't hesitate to agree to send over the information. As soon as the schedules arrived, he could add them to the timeline and confirm her movements for those days.

The FBI contacts were a lot less helpful.

"Listen, the case didn't seem like there was much to look into," Agent Weaver said. "The cops told us her apartment wasn't tossed, her car wasn't there. There were a lot of indications she'd just left and didn't bother to take everything."

"I'm sure that's exactly what whoever took her wanted you to think. But now that you see what's going on, are you sending a team?"

Agent Weaver sighed. "We don't have anyone who can go. There's a nationwide manhunt going on right now and it's focused in the northeast. We're all pulled tight."

English sighed heavily, letting his frustration travel through the phone. He knew it wasn't entirely Agent Weaver's fault, but if someone had bothered to look into Jeanine's disappearance when it was first reported, they might have found her by now.

"If something changes, will you let me know? I'm on my own here. Even under the FBI umbrella, I don't have the same clearance."

"We'll be in touch. If we can get a jump on the guy we're tracking down, I'll send backup for you. And I'll get everything I can about the phone number you gave me."

"Thanks. I'll keep you posted on what I find."

"Thanks. Talk soon."

English hung up the phone and leaned back on the couch. He rubbed his temples and tried to clear the migraine starting to build.

"How long has it been?" Caitlyn asked. Her voice was close, not across the room.

English shook his head. "I don't know. But I'm stuck. I'm just waiting for information to come in."

"Then I think that means the hour is up. Let me distract you." She crawled onto his lap, straddling him with her hips.

English opened his eyes enough to see Caitlyn. His hands went to her hips without thought, instinct taking over with a woman on his lap. She slid her hands up his chest and around his neck. His erection thickened.

She dug her fingertips into his shoulders. He groaned, his eyes slipping closed again. She pressed harder, moving them around to massage the muscles of his neck.

"Fucking hell, that feels good."

"You haven't slept. And you're stressed."

"And I made you a promise."

She snorted. "Do you really think I'm the kind of woman who's going to get upset about something like that?"

He opened one eye and looked at her.

She chuckled. "Okay, fine. Fair enough. You don't know me well, and high school Caitlyn definitely would have. But I'm not like that. I told you I was a bitch. I still am, but I'm a more reasonable bitch now."

English laughed with her. "You're not a bitch. You might be a goddess, though. Jesus, that feels good."

"Lie down," she said, shifting her weight to get up.

English tightened his hold on her hips.

She laughed and pushed away from him. "You still have twenty-one minutes. Lie down, on your stomach, for ten minutes. Then you can check your computer and ignore me for however long you need to."

"Caitlyn," he whispered.

"Just do it."

He shook his head and stretched out. She crawled onto him again, her hips spread wide around his. Her fingers tiptoed up his back, kneading and massaging the muscles around his spine. He groaned.

She slid her hands around, urging him to relax with every move. She worked knots out of his shoulders he was sure he'd die with and eased discomfort in his lower back from years of hunching over a keyboard. He had a massage once, years ago, but it didn't do as much for him. He needed Caitlyn in his life.

The thought made him tense, and Caitlyn's hands stilled. "Did I hurt you?"

English shook his head. "No, sorry. I'm fine." He consciously relaxed his body. She resumed her massage, and English tried not to let the thought dig in deeper.

He did not need Caitlyn in his life. He just meant someone as skilled at massage. Not Caitlyn herself. She would never be interested in someone like him. Not for the long term. And English wasn't sure he could handle getting more involved with her and letting her walk away. It was best to keep whatever was going on between them casual and friendly.

Far too soon, Caitlyn was climbing off his back. English was almost asleep. He didn't want to move and let the anxiety of his life back in. He wanted to stay there for another minute. Or a hundred.

"Are you asleep?" she whispered.

"Yes."

Caitlyn laughed. "I can do that again later."

"What else can you do?" He turned his head to see her reaction. A flush rose up her chest to her cheeks. She bit her lip and sat in the chair with her book.

"I think you're going to have to wait to find out."

English nodded and pushed himself to a sitting position. He woke up his laptop and refreshed his email. "Good. Everything is here."

"What's everything?"

"Jeanine's work schedules are in, the location tracking for her phone is there, and the phone records for the two guys from the bar. My friend also got me information about a crazy woman who used to work at the church. I forgot about that."

"Do you mean Monica Beasley?"

"Yeah, did you know her? Someone at the church said she lost it a few years ago."

"She did. She insisted she saw someone the night the Wests were killed."

"The Wests? Like Daniel West's parents?"

"Yeah. Monica swore someone was at the house. She was leaving work, locking up at the church. She heard something next door at the Wests and looked. It was dark, and she wasn't close enough to see details, but she insisted someone walked in. The police only found Mr. and Mrs. West, asleep in their bed. Monica said maybe the third person got out, but no one ever came forward. Daniel was at college, and no one else had a key. After that, for years, Monica said she saw people at the church. People who weren't actually there. It was super creepy."

"What happened to her?" English asked.

Caitlyn shrugged. "No clue. She left one day, never came back."

"Left like Jeanine left?"

Caitlyn shook her head. "She quit her job. Told the church she couldn't stay there anymore. She packed up a moving truck and left. A lot of people saw her leave."

"Interesting," English said. He opened the report from Dex. Everything Caitlyn said was in the report, along with her current location. There was nothing included about a mental health issue or any strange sightings where she lived in Massachusetts. She had an electronic toll service that showed her vehicle was still in Massachusetts the night Jeanine went missing. Just because she worked at the same location as Jeanine didn't mean she had anything to do with her disappearance. She was definitely feeling like a dead end.

The next thing English opened was the FBI report of Jeanine's location. The phone he knew about was home when she wasn't at work, but that didn't mean both phones were. He knew he could hack into the system and get the data, but asking the FBI meant if he found anything useful, they could act on it.

And damn if he didn't find something useful. "You said Jeanine went to the bar the night she disappeared, right?"

"Yeah, that's what she told me. Why?"

"She was only there for a few minutes. Her phone pinged the tower near there at nine-thirty-two, but at nine-thirty-nine, she was at the church."

"What?" Caitlyn asked, moving across the room to join him on the couch.

"Right there. Her phone was there for a while, then it went off. That's where she was when she disappeared."

"Maybe she had to get something from work?"

"No matter why she went there, what we need to figure out is what happened to her after."

"And where she is now."

THE HOUR CAME and went with Liam staring at his computer. He wasn't kidding when he said he'd focus on something and forget about the rest of the world.

Caitlyn wanted to help, but she felt useless. She didn't have any training on how to find people. If she did, she would have already found her friend.

When her stomach rumbled, Caitlyn fixed sandwiches

for lunch. She forced one into Liam's hand so he'd at least eat. He hadn't gotten up from the couch except to pace to the table where their timeline was laid out, then went right back to his spot on the couch.

It was almost funny to Caitlyn to see him so focused and intent on finding Jeanine and piecing together her life. She wasn't hurt or offended at all that Liam was ignoring her, despite his assurance that every other woman he'd known was. Caitlyn found his determination sexy.

Caitlyn finished the book she was reading and put it back on her shelf. She thought about picking up another, but her mind wasn't on the story. Any story. She wanted to find her friend.

Caitlyn went to the table and looked at the puzzle Liam had put together. He had everything from the two weeks before Jeanine disappeared. Caitlyn's articles were there, but he'd also added sticky notes that showed when Jeanine worked, when she was home, and when she was unaccounted for.

It was a little scary how much information he was able to collect in just a few days. Caitlyn wasn't sure if there was anything else she could add, but she opened her phone to see.

She scrolled through text messages she traded with Jeanine and added some notes on days when Jeanine said she had a client meeting and nights when Caitlyn and Jeanine were together. Caitlyn made a list of the clients Jeanine mentioned in texts also, just in case that helped. When she finished those, she stepped back to see the whole thing.

"I missed our hour," Liam said, walking up behind her.

"It's okay," Caitlyn assured him. The heat from his body soaked into hers. She wasn't cold, but him being close made her warm. She hadn't bothered with a shirt all day, something that was freeing in many ways.

"I told you I'm not a good bet."

"Then it's a good thing we live in different states."

Liam was quiet for a minute. "Yep," he finally said.

Caitlyn turned to look at him. He pressed his lips up into a smile, but there was nothing in his eyes that said he felt it. It was all for show. "I was just kidding."

He nodded.

Caitlyn stepped closer to him and wrapped her arms around his waist. He returned the embrace and put his chin on top of her head. She listened to the steady beat of his heart.

"I'm not upset with you."

"I still feel bad for forgetting."

"I don't want you to. I'm the one who asked for sex yesterday. I'm not looking for anything. You're staying here, and I'm attracted to you, but I know you'll leave when this case is over."

"Still, that doesn't mean I should be an ass."

"You're working. Tomorrow, I need to do the same. In fact, I should go to the store today. I was planning to and just haven't bothered to put a shirt back on."

He chuckled, her head shifting with his movement. "Are you up for a field trip while we're out?"

Caitlyn shrugged. "Sure. What kind of field trip?"

"I was going to swing by West Textiles and try to catch our sparring partners from Friday night."

"I'm sure they'll be happy to see us."

"That's my guess. But I doubt they'll take swings at us if they're at work. Even if they're on their way out."

"We could always go to the dinner tonight."

"What dinner?" Liam pulled back and met her gaze.

"The tenth anniversary dinner is tonight. They're having events all week. Some are during the day just for employees, but some are in the evening for the families and the entire community. I figured your dad would have told you."

Liam shook his head. "We don't talk much."

"Oh. Sorry. Well, um, tonight is the dinner. It's open to the public. A thank you for supporting East Charlottesville's favorite son. I heard Daniel wasn't going to do anything for the anniversary, but his assistant insisted they celebrate because none of them would have jobs if it hadn't been for him. He tries to pretend he's humble."

"Tries? I don't think being humble is a bad quality."

"No, it's not."

"But you think it's an act?"

Caitlyn shrugged, wishing she hadn't said anything.

"Why don't you like him?"

"I don't know. There's something about him that's always sat wrong with me. Jeanine defended him all the time. He would sit in her section when he came into the diner, but he never sat in mine. Even before that, he looked at me like I'm not worth of touching his food. I shouldn't really be bothered by it since everyone else treats me the same, but it just gets to me sometimes. Especially someone like him."

"We talked about getting together for a drink sometime this week. I'll see if I can find out why he doesn't like you."

"Please don't say anything. I know you're trying to be nice, but it's not a big deal. But you should meet him. Everyone else likes him. You probably will, too."

"I'm not sure if that's a compliment or not. Really, I wanted to get together with him because he might know something. He's very well connected. He also might be able to help us. And I'm hoping he knows the two guys we want to talk to."

"You can talk to him tonight about them. If he can help you, I'm sure he will."

"I'll do that. But right now, I have something more pressing to take care of."

"Take care of?"

"Oh, yes. Definitely take care of. I promised you orgasms and didn't deliver. And I've been staring at those amazing breasts of yours all day. I might not last long."

"I don't need you to last long. I've been about to explode all day, too."

"Is that so?"

Caitlyn nodded against his chest. His heart beat louder, the steady thump of it speeding up.

Liam's hands slid between them and cupped her heavy breasts. He rolled her nipples in his fingertips, tugging slightly.

Caitlyn moaned. Her body flashed hot and trembled. Moisture pooled between her thighs. She didn't need a lot of foreplay this time. She just needed Liam. Now.

"Liam," she whimpered.

"Fuck," he groaned. He spun her in his arms, her back to his front. He cupped her breast with one hand and slid the other into her shorts. His fingertips teased her belly, then sank into her curls. He kicked her feet to get her to spread her thighs.

Caitlyn obeyed his unspoken request and tried not to pass out. Blood roared in her ears. There was no other sound in the apartment besides their heavy breathing. Liam's fingers found her center and pressed inside, making her moan loudly.

"Jesus, you're wet. I shouldn't have waited so long."

"So good," she replied. Caitlyn didn't care how long it took.

Liam pressed the heel of his hand to her clit, rubbing it as he fucked her with his fingers.

Caitlyn's knees weakened. She was already close. So close.

Liam nudged the side of her head. She tilted away from him, drawing her hair over the opposite shoulder. He licked her skin, then bit her. Caitlyn cried out, the pain sending sparks of awareness through her entire body. Liam licked her again, soothing the bite with his tongue, then dug his teeth in once more.

Caitlyn couldn't hold back her orgasm. The pain of the bite and the pleasure from his fingers sent her flying. She bucked against him, his hand on her breast the only thing keeping her from collapsing.

"So beautiful. Let go. Come for me. Fuck yes, Caitlyn," Liam whispered in her ear. He was a man of few words at times, but they were damn good words when he said them.

Caitlyn stumbled to the couch, holding on to the back and trying to catch her breath. Liam came up behind her and licked her spine.

"You're so beautiful," he said against her ear. He folded his body around hers and bracketed her in with hands on either side of hers.

Caitlyn pressed her backside against him. "Here."

Liam groaned and licked her shoulder. His hands skimmed her sides and hooked in the edge of her shorts and panties, drawing them down until they fell the rest of the way on their own.

He tapped her inner thighs, and she spread them wide. She leaned over the couch, crossing her arms on the back and supporting her weight.

Liam moved behind her again, his shorts gone. He lined up and eased himself into her with one hand on her hip.

Caitlyn tipped her hips up to give him better access, and they both moaned when he slid all the way inside. Liam stayed there for a minute, both of them panting. Caitlyn was desperate to move, but she waited.

Liam withdrew, then slammed hard into her. She gasped and moaned, sparks tingling throughout her body. His fingers dug into her hips, and Liam took what he needed from her. Claiming her body in a way she'd never been claimed before. Demanding of her, pushing her to the edge of everything she ever thought she knew and then pulling back just enough for her to think she still didn't know a damn thing about sex. Especially not sex with a man like Liam Johnson.

"Caite. Touch yourself, Caite. Let me feel you come," Liam grunted.

Caitlyn was halfway out of her mind from the feel of him deep inside her. She could tell from the demand that he was going to get there before her. But he wanted them to go together. He was trying to wait for her.

She reached down and pressed her fingertips to her clit. She instantly spasmed, her body still sensitive from the way he touched her earlier.

"Fuck, yes," Liam groaned. His fingers dug into her hips harder. He was close. Too close.

Caitlyn rubbed hard on her clit, pushing aside the embarrassment of having a man in the room when she touched herself. He grunted and groaned, mumbling words of encouragement as she raced to catch up to him.

"Caite," he choked. He swelled inside her, erupting before she got there.

Caitlyn slowed her race, leaving her hand between her thighs as Liam pulsed and twitched within her body. She wanted to finish, but it was too late for that, so she just lazily stroked herself.

"Don't stop," Liam grunted. "Finish."

"It's okay," Caitlyn told him, heat rising on her cheeks.

Liam followed her arm with his hand and wound his fingers through hers. "Finish, Caite. I want to feel you."

"But you already came."

"Please."

She couldn't resist him when he asked please. She pressed her fingers to her clit again, the intimacy of his fingers between hers making the moment stronger. Together, they rubbed over her clit.

Slowly, Liam withdrew from within her and pressed back inside. Over and over again, he dragged his cock against her inner walls, adding to the feeling that built up and up while he was fucking her.

Caitlyn whimpered, her orgasm just out of reach. Her body was wearing down, struggling to keep going. But she had to. She needed to.

Liam pinched her nipple and took over rubbing her clit. Caitlyn cried out, the pressure building inside her with each swipe he made. Up and up and up until she screamed out.

"Yes, Caite. Fuck me, yes," he grunted, holding her tight and letting her ride the entire thing out.

Caitlyn collapsed to the ground, almost hitting the floor before Liam caught her. He folding her onto his lap and held her close, his racing heart pounding against her ear. Happy. Satisfied. Safe.

15

He stared out the window with his back to the door. He was making plans in his head, but listening. Always listening. He learned long ago to be aware of his surroundings. When he wasn't, he got hurt.

Getting hurt wasn't an option anymore. He was a man now. The sniveling child he once was died a fiery death. In that child's place was a man everyone respected.

"Are you ready to go?" the woman asked from behind him.

He heard her coming. He knew what she was going to ask. He nodded. "Yes, I'll be right there."

"Is there anything I can do for you before I go?"

"No, but thank you. Just reflecting."

"Okay. I'll see you later."

"Enjoy."

Her soft steps faded away on the carpeted floor. He waited, ensuring he was alone before he retrieved the keys from his desk.

A blue lanyard was coiled in the top drawer. Five keys were on the ring. A car key, two keys for the apartment, one for the church, and the last one he hoped was for her friend's apartment. When she laughed in his face, she mentioned her best friend. In the months they were together, she talked about her best friend and the time they spent together. He was fairly sure the key would let him into Caitlyn's apartment.

He just had to choose the right time. He planned to go when she was at work, but with Liam Johnson staying there, he didn't think that was an option. Bringing in someone else wasn't possible. He had to handle the situation himself. He was the man. He had to deal with it.

He put the keys in his bag and slung the bag over his shoulder. First, he needed to put it in his car. Then, he was headed to the party. And later he'd use the key to find out what Caitlyn knew.

There was no way he was getting caught.

THE PARKING LOT at West Textiles was full. People were parked on the grass around the edges and along the long road in and out of the facility. English tightened his fingers on the steering wheel. He hated crowds. Especially crowds of people who were going to get into his business.

He found a spot close to the edge of the lot. He waited for Caitlyn to come around the vehicle and put his hand on her lower back as they walked toward the oversized tent near the guard shack.

Music played and people talked, but English and Caitlyn were there on a mission. It wasn't fun for them. It was work. They needed—

"Liam!"

English turned toward the voice. His parents were at a

table a few feet away, surrounded by friends English recognized from his childhood. "Hi, Mom."

"Come say hello," his mom said. She didn't get up from her seat, just waved him closer.

English turned toward them. The moment his mom saw Caitlyn with him, her face soured. "You remember Caitlyn Powers."

"Nice to see you again, Mrs. Johnson," Caitlyn gushed.

English fought to keep a smile off his face. His parents wouldn't dare speak poorly of someone in public. That sort of behavior was reserved for the privacy of their own home. But there wasn't a person there who didn't know exactly what the Johnsons thought of Caitlyn.

"You as well, Ms. Powers," Mrs. Johnson said carefully. She didn't sneer, but she did reach for her husband's hand.

"Mr. Powers," Caitlyn said, her gaze lingering just a little too long on him.

English pressed Caitlyn forward, leading her away from his parents. "We'll say goodbye before we leave."

Caitlyn snickered.

English didn't wait for his parents to reply. He nudged Caitlyn away and dropped his hand from her back, moving ahead of her into the crowd. If she wanted to follow him, she could, but he wasn't going to push it.

"What's wrong with you?" she hissed.

English stopped in the middle of the crowd. People moved around them, ignoring them entirely. Or at least pretending to. "Why did you do that?"

Caitlyn huffed a laugh. "I heard what your mother said about me. What was I supposed to do?"

English closed his eyes for a moment. This was why he hated being in East Charlottesville. He felt like a child all over again. His parents were disappointed in him, and the most popular girl in school was just toying with him. "I'm sorry for what she said, Caitlyn. I can't make excuses for her. But pissing them off is only going to make things harder."

"Why would it make things harder?" Caitlyn stepped back and crossed her arms over her middle.

"Because they know people. The best way to get information is for people to not know you're trying to get information. They stop talking when they know you're looking for something. And us being together and antagonizing them is not going to help anything."

"I wasn't trying to..."

English raised a brow.

She sighed. "Fine. I was trying to piss your mom off. I'm sorry. I'll go apologize."

English shook his head. "Leave it alone. Just stay away from them, and anyone else, for now. Let's see if we can find out anything about our friends from Sparky's and get out of here."

Caitlyn nodded. She let English lead her through the crowd to the far side of the tent.

"I didn't see them. Did you?" he asked.

Caitlyn shook her head.

"What's wrong?"

"You told me not to talk."

"I said to stay away from people who are going to be nosy and bitchy and make finding your best friend more difficult. My dad already told me not to worry about Jeanine. They're not going to say anything in public to tarnish their own image, but if no one likes Jeanine, they aren't going to think twice about telling people I'm helping you look for her."

Caitlyn averted her eyes. "I don't want to mess things up, but I have a hard time caring what people think of me. I've only survived this long here because I don't care. If people like your mom could upset me, I would have left a long time ago."

"But you planned to leave, didn't you?"

"Yeah, but that changed when I met Jeanine. I still want to get out of here, but not because of them. I want to leave because of me. This town doesn't fit me anymore. I want more out of life than to stay somewhere I know I'm not welcome. But I refuse to let any of them think they have the power to run me off. Fuck them."

"Caitlyn..."

"No, Liam, no. You don't get to feel bad for me. I've survived. I've never once stopped trying to figure out who I'm supposed to be. And I'm better than the person I am. So, if me being a bitch to people who treat me like shit is going to be a problem, maybe we shouldn't keep working together on this. Maybe I should go back to figuring things out on my own. Maybe—"

English stepped forward and yanked her against him in one motion. He captured her lips mid-sentence. She fought him for a second, her anger palpable between them. Then she sank into him and let him in. His hand speared through her curls and tilted her head, giving him access to her mouth to taste her exactly how he wanted.

Caitlyn's hands tentatively crawled up his back before finding a spot to hold on to his shirt. She sighed happily, and English finally pulled back.

"Fucking hell, you drive me insane," he breathed. Their foreheads rested together and all he could see was Caitlyn. Her hair was a curtain around them, blocking out the rest of the party. The rest of the world.

"I'm sorry I'm a pain in the ass."

English snorted. "No, you're not."

She laughed with him. "No, I'm really not sorry. But I do want to find Jeanine."

"We will."

"Glad you could join us," a voice said from behind English.

He kept his hand in Caitlyn's hair and turned. "Daniel. Nice to see you again."

Daniel nodded to them both. "You as well. I didn't realize you two were involved."

"We connected at my parents' party. We graduated together."

"East Charlottesville brings a lot of people together. Does that mean you might consider moving back to town?"

English opened his mouth to reply but stopped himself with a look at Caitlyn. He'd never considered returning. Not even once. Returning for Caitlyn wasn't something he was willing to think about. Especially not when she wasn't sure she wanted to stay there either.

"Forgive me," Daniel hurried to say. "I shouldn't be getting involved in other people's business. It's a bad habit of mine. I know how much your parents would love to have you back in town. If it's ever a consideration, please know you'd have a job here."

"Thank you, Daniel. I appreciate that." English knew he'd never take him up on it, but the thought was nice. "Hey, maybe you can help us. We were actually hoping to catch up with two of your employees."

"Oh, of course. I assumed you were here with your parents."

English shook his head and tightened his grip on Caitlyn. "No. They're not really happy with us being involved."

Daniel tilted his head to the side and shook it. "I'm sorry to hear that."

"Thanks. Anyway, John Valentine and Mickey Donnelly. Have you seen them?"

Daniel's eyes narrowed, and he looked down at them with a raised chin. "Why are you looking for them?"

English and Caitlyn exchanged a look. "Um, we had a drink with them the other day and wanted to get together again. Why do you ask?"

Daniel regarded them closely. "They're in the hospital, Liam."

"Both of them?"

Daniel nodded. "Yes. Their wives reported them missing on Saturday, but the police couldn't do anything for twenty-four hours. No one had seen them since Friday night at Sparky's, and on Sunday morning, people went looking."

"What?" Caitlyn breathed.

"I'm sorry. I didn't realize you were friends with them. Of course, there's obviously a lot I don't know about. They were in a car accident. Mickey was driving, but they'd both been drinking. The police think they might have swerved to avoid an animal in the road. Drove off the side and hit one of the big oaks along Anderson Street."

"Are they going to be okay?" English asked.

Daniel shrugged. He held up a finger to someone else. "I don't know. They're both in comas, and the doctors are doing everything they can. I apologize, but I need to speak to some others."

English and Caitlyn nodded absently as Daniel clapped them on their shoulders and walked away. They stood there for a long moment, processing what he said.

"They're in comas?" Caitlyn whispered.

"They tried to kill us, Caitlyn."

"I know. And karma is a bitch, but do you think it's a coincidence?"

"No. I think we need to talk to the bartender. He was suspiciously absent when those guys attacked us. He knew something was going to happen before we did. We need answers."

"Okay," Caitlyn said.

"Let's get out of here. I need to check in with my team and find out everything I can about John and Mickey."

Caitlyn nodded and didn't argue when English pushed her away from the crowd and to his SUV.

LIAM STOPPED by the grocery store on the way back to Caitlyn's. She picked up the bare minimum of things she needed, feeling exposed and vulnerable the entire time.

It wasn't until they were carrying groceries up to her apartment that she felt better. "What if it wasn't an animal?" Caitlyn finally asked Liam.

"I don't think it was," Liam admitted. "That's why I want to talk to the bartender. Maybe he can tell us if they had any altercations with anyone else."

Caitlyn wasn't sure if she felt better or worse knowing he agreed with her. They got into a fight with two men and days later, the men were in the hospital. It was too close for her. If someone was trying to help Caitlyn and Liam, why wouldn't they come forward? But if it was someone who wasn't...

Caitlyn unlocked her door and led the way inside. She went straight to her kitchen with the bags and stopped short at the clean table in her dining room.

"What?"

"Did you put all of that somewhere before we left?" Caitlyn asked Liam.

"All of—Fuck! Our timeline, our research. Shit!"

"Someone was in here?" Caitlyn breathed.

"Yes, someone was in here. And they took everything." He rushed to the couch and swore again. "They took the laptops, too. I need to call this in."

"The cops won't believe you," Caitlyn argued.

"I'm not calling the cops," Liam said. "Dunn. Yeah. Change all the passwords now. On everything. Stolen. Right out of Caitlyn's living room. We were out trying to get information and someone broke in. No sign of forced entry. I don't know." Liam turned to her. "Who has a key to your apartment?"

Caitlyn shook her head. "No one. Except Jeanine."

Liam's eyes widened for a second, quickly enough that Caitlyn wouldn't have noticed if she weren't watching him. "Our missing person. Yeah, that's what I'm thinking, too. Okay. That's next. I'll try to track it, but... I know. Hey, there are a few more things I need, but I'll call you back in a little while. Or I can call Dex. All right. Bye."

"How did someone get in here?" Caitlyn asked.

"Either Jeanine let herself in and is trying to cover up how she disappeared, or whoever had a hand in her disappearance has her keys and made themselves at home."

"Oh, God. That is... What if I'd been home?"

"I don't think they're after you. I think they're trying to keep you from figuring out where Jeanine is."

Caitlyn sat on the couch and wrapped her arms around her legs. She didn't want to be there. She wouldn't be able to sleep knowing someone else could get into her home. Could get to her. And had. They took everything.

"We're never going to find her now, are we?"

Liam joined her on the couch and put his hands on her knees. "Don't say that. We're not giving up. I'm going to figure this out. I promise you." He kissed her forehead. "Stay here."

"Where are you going?"

"I'm going to look for bugs."

"Why are you looking for bugs?"

"The listening kind."

An icy chill swept over her skin, making her shiver. Caitlyn nibbled the inside of her lip. She stared straight ahead while Liam moved around the apartment. She didn't know how long he took, but when he came back and sat down, he put his hands on her knees again. She looked up at him.

"I didn't find anything. I will change the locks tomorrow."

"What about tonight?" Her gut tightened. Her palms were sweaty. She wanted to run, leave the apartment and East Charlottesville and never look back.

"They won't come back. They have everything they need."

"Why did they do this?"

"To scare us and to find out what we know."

"They were good."

"Yes, they were, but they were also not the two men from Sparky's. Not if what Daniel said is true and they're in the hospital."

Caitlyn shook her head. "I was sure they were the ones who took her. I've seen her with both of them. I called them out one of the first times I went in there to ask questions. They lied to me. Said they didn't know Jeanine. I kept going back and they got more and more aggressive with me. I just wanted information, but they refused to talk to me. Kept saying I was lying. I thought if I kept pushing they'd tell me something."

"What happened to them is not your fault."

Caitlyn nodded. "I know. They were drinking, and if they got into it with someone else, I had nothing to do with it."

"I know that."

"Daniel West doesn't. You saw the way he looked at me when we asked where they were."

English shook his head. "He was worried about his employees. They might not have any information about the accident."

"I guess. I should be used to it, though. That's the way he always looks at me. It's the same look your mother gives me, and all her friends, and everyone else in town. Like I'm not good enough."

"I think you're more than good enough," Liam said. "I couldn't have gotten this far without your help. We're going to find Jeanine."

"I know. And then I'm getting the hell out of this town. You showing up has proven to me there are better things away from East Charlottesville. Much better."

Liam held her gaze for a long moment, then nodded.

Maybe if she was lucky, someone like him would be out there for her.

16

SLEEP WAS HARD TO COME BY FOR CAITLYN. SHE TOSSED AND turned most of the night. Liam laid next to her, but even his sure presence didn't calm her enough to let her fall fully to sleep. Every creak in the building had her eyes flying open and her heart pounding.

Her alarm went off early, forcing her out of bed to get ready for work. Liam got up with her and made coffee while she showered. He offered to drive her to the diner, but Caitlyn refused. She needed to be able to leave her apartment without him. She had to live her life. Even if it wasn't much of a life.

It was still dark outside when the first customers rolled into the diner. As usual, the earliest of the early risers took seats at the counter. They drank coffee and ate breakfast and said little. They never appeared happier to be there than Caitlyn was, so she served them and left them alone.

Almost two hours into her shift, Heather showed up. She had a sneer that was supposed to be a smile for Caitlyn before she took over at the counter.

Caitlyn double checked the tables in her section for napkins, salt and pepper, and cream and sugar, then wiped all the tables down once more, just in case. The menus in the center of each table got another wipe down before she slid them back into the holder. She was just finishing her last table when her least favorite customers sat down.

Liam's mother and her gaggle of friends. They came in every Tuesday on their way to work for what they called a staff meeting. Caitlyn served them about half the time and never once heard them talk about anything having to do with the school, unless trashing the other staff members and half the teachers counted. Caitlyn was fairly sure it didn't, but Mrs. Johnson always insisted she got an itemized receipt so she could submit it to the school for reimbursement.

Caitlyn pasted on a smile and approached the table. "Good morning, ladies. Coffee?"

Patty Johnson rolled her eyes toward her friends and lifted her mug toward Caitlyn. Caitlyn took the mug, not trusting the other woman to keep it still, and filled it three-quarters of the way to the top. She set the mug back in front of Patty and filled the rest of the mugs the same way, with plenty of room for cream and sugar.

"Would you ladies like a few minutes or are you ready to order now?"

"We need a minute," Patty said with a sneer.

Caitlyn forced back the snappy retort burning inside her mouth and nodded. She walked away, keeping her plastic smile firmly in place. There was nowhere to hide or run. She didn't even have a friend she could commiserate with. She was alone.

A wave of sadness washed over Caitlyn, surprising her.

The entire time Jeanine had been missing, she'd been determined and angry. At first, she believed her friend was hurt, but she never answered her door. After the police searched her apartment, Caitlyn thought maybe Jeanine went out of town for a few days and forgot to tell her. But the longer it went on, the more Caitlyn knew something had happened.

But until her files and the computers were stolen, Caitlyn was able to keep the anger in front of her. Lying in her bed all night, not sleeping, knocked down more than a few of her walls. The mad was failing and the sorrow was taking over.

"Excuse me!" Patty said loudly, drawing Caitlyn's attention back to the table. "We'd like to order. We're going to be late if you don't hurry up."

Caitlyn pasted her smile back on. She only walked away from the table because they said they weren't ready. Now, five seconds later, it was Caitlyn's fault. What a bitch.

"What can I get you?"

The five women ordered the same thing they did every week. Caitlyn wrote down every last bit of instruction they gave her, then read it all back to them. At Patty's insistence. And of course, she corrected something. Something she never said the first time. Caitlyn went with it and put in the order.

Two more of Caitlyn's tables filled up before Patty's order was ready. Caitlyn busied herself filling coffee cups and taking orders, then delivered the food to Patty and her friends. She hurried around the diner, trying to stay busy and out of their way.

"We need more coffee," Patty squawked.

Caitlyn held up one finger, not the one she wanted to use, and finished taking an order for another customer.

When she finished, she submitted the order and grabbed the coffeepot.

Their mugs were all full when Caitlyn got to Patty's table.

"Heather took care of us since you're not capable," Patty said.

Caitlyn nodded and walked away. She never liked Patty Johnson, but this was worse than usual. Caitlyn knew it was because of Liam. Not that she blamed Liam, but his mom was clearly not happy with the two of them spending time together. Even if it was innocent, which it wasn't, it hurt that Caitlyn was so strongly disliked that being tied to someone like Liam warranted the treatment she was getting.

Caitlyn mumbled her thanks to Heather when she put the coffee pot back.

The other woman gave her a sugary snarl and shrugged. "Some people just aren't cut out for working with the public. You have to pay attention to your customers, Caitlyn. And be friendly. You're not either of those. You're just a dumb, fat, former model."

Caitlyn drew in a breath. If she hit Heather, she'd get fired. If she got fired, she wouldn't be able to pay her rent. Caitlyn was planning to leave town anyway, but not until she found Jeanine. It wasn't worth it to hit Heather. Not yet. But one day soon, Caitlyn would enjoy it. Maybe Liam could show her how to throw a good, strong punch.

Caitlyn avoided Heather and Patty until Patty and her friends left. They barely gave Caitlyn a tip, but Patty walked up to the counter and slid a twenty across to Heather. She made sure Caitlyn saw her tuck it into her apron.

Maybe it was worth it to hit Heather and get fired. It would definitely improve her day.

Caitlyn cleared Patty's table and checked in with her other customers. It was a busy morning, which was good. Caitlyn preferred days where she wasn't standing around waiting for customers. Especially when Jeanine wasn't there to talk to.

Things were starting to quiet down at the end of Caitlyn's shift. She cleaned tables, making sure everything was ready for the next server, and counted out her meager tips. She put in a to-go order so she and Liam could have lunch and hoped no one else would sit in her section in the next twenty minutes.

Fifteen minutes later, Officer Nickolas Pattinson walked in. And made himself comfortable in Caitlyn's section.

With a heavy sigh and a long glance at her watch, Caitlyn made her way over. "Good morning, Officer. Can I start you off with a cup of coffee?"

She probably should have smiled or added some sweetness to her tone, but she didn't have any for him. Not when he could have been involved in Jeanine's disappearance. Even if it was only so far as to do a shitty job on the report.

"Um, I'm not sure yet. Let me think about it for a minute." He stared at the menu that hadn't changed in more than a decade and ignored Caitlyn.

She walked away, perching near the counter for when he was ready. He was her one and only customer, and until he left, she had to stay. If customers came in after her shift started, the next server would handle them, but until her time was up, she had to stick around. If the way Officer Pattinson was studying the menu was any indication, it was going to be a long end to her shift.

Another couple walked in and distracted Caitlyn. She silently prayed they didn't sit in her section and breathed a sigh of relief when they sat at the counter near Heather. Heather smiled politely and made small talk, laughing at something the woman said. When Heather turned to get the coffeepot, she caught Caitlyn staring and glared back.

Caitlyn huffed and approached Officer Pattinson again. "Have you decided what you'd like to order yet?"

"It would be nice if I could get a cup of coffee to start with," he snarled.

Her gut tightened. Heat flashed over her entire body. She squeezed the pencil in her hand. The snap of it breaking drew the attention of the officer.

The fucking asshole had the nerve to smirk at her.

Caitlyn wanted to stab the splintered pencil into his eye and walk out. But again, she did the adult thing and kept her mouth shut. She stuffed the two halves into her apron and tucked away her order pad. If she was lucky, the coffee would spill on the officer's pants and burn the pencil-dick she was sure he tucked inside his briefs every morning.

Her hand shook as she reached to pour the coffee. It splashed every so slightly out of the mug and onto the table. She finished pouring, then tossed a few napkins on the spill to absorb it.

"You almost poured that on me," he growled.

"You're right," she answered honestly, adding a smile of her own.

His eyes widened as her message sank into his thick skull. "Do you think you're funny?"

"No, I don't. I also don't think you're good at your job."

"Says the waitress who can't pour a fucking cup of coffee."

Caitlyn drew in a breath. It wouldn't do her any good to stoop to his level. She wanted to, a lot, but she wouldn't.

"Would you like to order something to eat?" Caitlyn asked, attempting to move things along so he would get the hell out of there and she could leave.

"That's why I'm here. Eggs, over easy. Bacon. Crispy bacon. Sourdough toast with butter on the side, not on top. Strawberry jam. And hash browns."

Caitlyn nodded. "It'll be out shortly."

She didn't give him a chance to say anything else before she walked away. The order was in and she was officially off the clock. Her replacement was there and would take any new customers, so she just needed to survive breakfast with the cop and she could go.

While his order was being prepared, Caitlyn hovered behind the counter. She didn't want to let his food sit once it was done. The faster she served it, the faster he got the hell out of there.

"Jeez, Caitlyn, can you take up more space?" Heather said. She bumped into Caitlyn, knocking her hip against the counter. The skinny bitch had three times more space than she needed to get past Caitlyn, but apparently it wasn't enough.

"I could, actually," Caitlyn said, turning on Heather. "I really wasn't blocking you, though. We both know that. You could have easily gotten around me. Unless you're having trouble walking straight. Did you start your day with a few too many glasses of wine again, Heather?"

Heather's mouth and eyes opened wide with a look of guilty anger. She carefully neutralized her features, then scowled at Caitlyn.

"Heather? Let's have a chat," the manager on duty said. Margaret didn't stand for any sort of crap.

"She's lying Margaret. She has no idea what she's talking about."

"Maybe so, but she's not wrong that there was more than enough room for you to walk by her. If you aren't able to do that, I have an obligation to find out why. For both of your sakes. I've already lost one employee. I'd rather not lose another." Margaret smiled kindly at Caitlyn before leading Heather away from the counter.

Caitlyn wasn't one to gloat, but it was nice to have someone believe her instead of Heather for once. The other managers fell at Heather's feet and listened to everything she said. Caitlyn was sure Heather wasn't actually drinking that morning, but the fact that Margaret didn't blindly follow Heather had Caitlyn feel a whole lot better.

"Order up!"

Caitlyn checked and found Officer Pattinson's order on the counter. She grabbed the plates and carried them to him. "Do you need anything else?"

"I asked for strawberry jam." He scowled up at her.

"I'll be right back." Caitlyn grabbed a bowl of jellies and jams, double checking that strawberry was there, and set it on his table.

"Finally."

"You're welcome," Caitlyn said brightly. *Eat and get the hell out.*

She retreated to the counter once more, glaring at Heather as she returned. Heather brushed past Caitlyn, bumping into her again. Caitlyn was ready for it and bumped back, sending Heather stumbling backward. Caitlyn raised a brow, daring Heather to complain. She snapped her trap shut and stomped to her doting customers, smiling and flirting and ignoring Caitlyn.

As soon as Officer Pattinson was finished with his food, Caitlyn took his plates. She asked if he needed anything else and dropped off his check. She was about to get away when he opened his mouth.

"I don't know how you managed to get released from

custody Friday night, but you never should have set fire to that apartment building."

Caitlyn spun toward him. "I didn't set fire to it. We were inside when the fire started. Someone was trying to kill us."

"You really think I'm going to believe that?"

Caitlyn straightened her spine and shook her head. "No, I don't. Because I know you suck at your job. You wouldn't know good police work if it climbed up your ass and crawled out of your mouth. You're the reason Jeanine is missing. You didn't even bother to look for her. She's been gone for two weeks, and because of you, and your shitty report that says she left town, no one's looking for her. You know it was all lies. You know she didn't run. And I'm guessing you also know where she is and are covering it up! So, no, I don't think you're going to believe anything I say because you don't care about the truth. You worthless—"

"Caitlyn!" Margaret shouted.

Caitlyn stopped and looked around the diner. Every single person in there was watching her. Conversation stopped. Forks paused in midair. Gazes flipped between Caitlyn and the smirking son-of-a-bitch Officer Pattinson.

"I think that's enough. I want to find Jeanine, too, but accusing our police officers is not going to do any good. Especially when you don't have proof. Now, let the man go back to work so he can find Jeanine, and solve any other crimes."

Caitlyn opened and closed her mouth. Ripping into him again would have been nice, but Margaret was right. It wouldn't change anything. It didn't matter what Caitlyn said, he wasn't going to find Jeanine.

Caitlyn turned and carried the plates she still held to the kitchen. She scraped off the food he didn't eat and rinsed them before setting everything in the dishwasher.

She stood at the sink and squeezed the cool stainless steel edge. She took a deep breath, her chest expanding to the point of pain before she let it out slowly. She did it twice more, finally loosening her white-knuckled grip on the sink.

Caitlyn straightened her shoulders and left the safety of the kitchen. Officer Pattinson was already gone, a stack of bills on the table the only sign he'd been there. Caitlyn grabbed the cash and his ticket and closed it out, pocketing the change he left her for her tip. *Asshole.*

No one was in the back when Caitlyn went to the break room. She put her tip money, broken pencil, and pens into her purse. The order pad got stacked with the others, ready for the next person. Caitlyn untied her apron and tossed it into the dirty bin. She grabbed her purse and dug out her keys, then turned to go.

She was almost out of the break room when Margaret came in. "Are you doing okay?"

Caitlyn shook her head. "I'm sorry for today."

"You know I have to give you a warning, right? You mouthed off to a police officer."

"He's barely a police officer."

"He wears the badge, Caitlyn. My late husband did the same, and I respect it."

All the anger inside Caitlyn deflated like a balloon. "I'm sorry, Margaret."

"Not all cops are great cops. Just like not all servers are great servers."

Caitlyn's cheeks heated. "I'll try to do better tomorrow. I'm just—"

"You're trying to find your friend. And you're keeping company with Liam Johnson. And you ran into some trouble the other night. I know. I like you, Caitlyn. I liked

Jeanine, too. But I can't let everything go. Today was a bad day. Let's make tomorrow a better one."

Caitlyn nodded, feeling rightfully shamed by a woman she respected. Most people's opinion didn't matter, but Margaret was one of the few Caitlyn liked.

She would do better. She had to.

17

———

ENGLISH CHECKED IN WITH DEX AND DUNN WHILE CAITLYN was at work. They were getting home from another all-night op, so he didn't talk to them long. Both assured him they hadn't seen anything on their end to indicate there was a breach in their system.

It was good news, but it didn't mean they were in the clear. English was itching to get his hands on a new computer. He hadn't been that long without one since he found out what computers were. And with his own missing, he knew the threat that was out there. If whoever took it knew what they were doing.

He hoped they didn't.

English went for a run, then did body weight exercises in Caitlyn's apartment. He hadn't kept up with his normal workouts since he came to town and was starting to feel it. His back was tight and his neck was sore from the lack of stretching.

After moving his body, he got in the shower and let the hot water soothe his muscles. He was grateful for the hot water for about twenty seconds, then it turned lukewarm. It wasn't long before even that was a generous descriptor.

English got out and changed into clean clothes. He hadn't brought a ton of stuff, assuming he'd be able to do laundry at his parents' house, and he was running low on clean tees. He hadn't noticed a washing machine at Caitlyn's. He needed to remember to ask her about it.

He sat on the couch and stared at the wall. It was getting close to midday. He didn't want to leave Caitlyn alone all day, but he wanted to get to the hospital during visiting hours to talk to John and Mickey. And if not them, their families and doctors. English needed answers. Answers only the two men who attacked them could provide.

English was about to give up on waiting for Caitlyn when a key slid into the lock. His body tensed, readying for anyone to open the door. The person wasn't being quiet, which meant it was either Caitlyn or someone who didn't care about being caught.

The door swung open and revealed Caitlyn. She yanked her key out and pushed the door closed behind her.

"Hey," English said when she didn't speak.

"Hi."

"Are you okay?"

She nodded and walked past him toward her bedroom. She smelled like greasy breakfast food and coffee. Her hair was tied up in a messy bun. Her clothes were streaked with stains that hadn't been there when she left. But it was the way she avoided his gaze and the downturn of her mouth that told him her morning was definitely not okay.

"Did something happen? Did someone threaten you?"

She shook her head, continuing her walk.

"Caitlyn, talk to me."

"I need a minute, Liam. Nothing happened, at least

nothing that's unusual. No one threatened me or said anything to me that would help with the case. It was just a bad morning, and I need a few minutes to myself. I'm going to take a shower. I know you have stuff to do today. If you need to leave, I understand. But I...I just can't right this minute. Okay?"

She glanced up at him, and English nodded. She turned and walked away, closing her bedroom door. He stared at the door, the first separation between them since she asked him for sex.

He wanted to beat down the door and demand she tell him what happened, but she deserved her moment. He'd had his fair share of shitty days, and he understood the need for solitude when that happened.

English waited for the water to turn off. When it did, he started lunch for the two of them. Caitlyn picked up bread, tomatoes, and cheese the day before, so English made them sandwiches. He'd just flipped one toasted sandwich out of the pan when Caitlyn opened the bedroom door.

"Did you cook?"

He nodded. "I figured we could both use some lunch before we went to the hospital."

"Thank you," she said quietly. She accepted the plate he held out but didn't move away. "I ordered lunch to go from work, but I forgot all about it until now."

"Sorry your day was..." He didn't know what to say. He watched her, waiting for her to say or do something else. He didn't want to scare her off, so he just waited.

She set her plate on the counter and stepped into him, wrapping her arms around his middle. She rested her head on his chest. Then she sighed.

English kissed the top of her head and held her tight. He got the feeling Caitlyn didn't let her guard down often, maybe ever. She didn't have people she counted on. She said Jeanine was her best friend, but Jeanine never told Caitlyn details about the men she was involved with. In a town as small as East Charlottesville, the fact that Jeanine kept secrets was nearly impossible. The fact that she kept them from her friend was most likely painful for Caitlyn.

Caitlyn let go a minute later. She picked up her plate and walked to the couch. She sat and ate while English finished cooking his sandwich and joined her.

Neither spoke as they ate lunch. Her knee brushed against his. The air was charged. It was nothing like English had ever felt before. Not just sexual tension, but more. Heavier, deeper. Something right there in front of him but just barely out of reach.

Caitlyn stood and whatever it was disappeared. She set her plate in the dishwasher and came back for English's. She put her shoes on and waited for him at the door. Then they were on their way.

English drove, letting Caitlyn relax for the forty-five minute trip to the closest hospital. She leaned back in her seat and closed her eyes for the first twenty minutes.

"I'm sorry I'm acting moody," she said when they were halfway there.

"You're not acting moody. You're acting like you had a crappy day and need time to shake it off. I get that."

"Really?"

"Yeah, of course. Happens to everyone. If you want to tell me about it, I'm happy to listen."

"I don't think you want to know," she said wryly.

He tilted his head to the side and tried to make sense of that statement. He glanced at her. "What does that mean?"

She sighed. "Nothing. Don't worry about it."

"Now I'm definitely worried about it. What happened?" The hair on the back of his neck stood up.

"It wasn't anything I haven't dealt with before. It just bothered me more after spending time with you. How did you turn out to be such a decent person?"

"Ah, my dad came into the diner this morning." English rolled his eyes and felt bad for Caitlyn.

"Actually, no. It was your mom."

"My mom? She's the one who made you feel like shit?"

Caitlyn shrugged and slunk back in her seat.

English fought the urge to argue with her. His mom was usually the quiet one. She let his father take the lead, and she followed along. But she wasn't always silent. When they went to get English's things from their house, his mom was the one who laid into him about spending time with Caitlyn.

"I'm sorry. I'll talk to her."

"Don't," Caitlyn said immediately. "It's fine."

English wasn't ready to let it go. Caitlyn might try to pretend it wasn't a big deal, but it clearly was. And it bothered English. He didn't like Caitlyn having to deal with anyone who treated her like she wasn't good enough, but especially his own family.

English reached over and grabbed Caitlyn's hand. It wasn't much, but he hoped it would show her he was there for her and with her. She turned her hand over and tangled her fingers with his. He squeezed her hand.

There was that feeling again.

English held Caitlyn's hand until they got to the hospital. They checked in at the visitors desk and got directions to the ICU where both John Valentine and Mickey Donnelly were.

They came to John Donnelly's room first. No one was in

there. English didn't know much about medicine, but he opened the man's chart and snapped a few pictures. He put the chart back on the edge of the bed just before someone in a white coat walked in.

"Who are you? What are you doing in here?"

"We're friends of John's. We heard about the accident and wanted to see how he's doing," English said without hesitation.

Caitlyn tensed beside him but didn't contradict what he said. She nodded when the doctor looked at her, and he appeared convinced.

"He's not doing well. He's in a coma still, and we don't know when he'll come out."

"Any idea what happened? He was in a car accident, right? With Mickey?"

The doctor nodded. "Yeah, that's what the police said. I don't know anything about the investigation. Do you know Mickey, too?"

English nodded. "We were going to see him next. Who was driving?"

"Mickey was. Neither of them were wearing seatbelts. John hit the windshield so his brain trauma is worse, but Mickey hit the steering wheel so his internal injuries were more critical."

"Are they going to survive?" Caitlyn asked.

The doctor shook his head. "I can't answer that. I'm sorry. They are both in critical condition. We've kept them sedated, but I don't think they'd wake up right now if we didn't have them on meds to let them sleep. If they had been found earlier, it would have been much better for them, but their injuries are severe."

Caitlyn rubbed her neck and stared at John. English grabbed her hand, hoping to not draw attention to the fading bruises around her throat from the last time she was in the same room as the man in the bed.

"Are you all right, miss?" the doctor asked. His gaze lingered on Caitlyn's neck before drifting to English's hands. He raised it to glare at English.

"Yeah, I'm fine."

"The bruises on your neck—"

"I said the wrong thing to the wrong man the other night."

"Do you need me to call the police? You don't need to leave with him." The doctor moved to block the door.

English wanted to defend himself, but the doctor already decided English was the one who put those marks on Caitlyn's neck. Nothing he said would change that.

"No," Caitlyn said firmly. "Liam had nothing to do with this. He's the reason I'm still alive. The man who choked me... Liam saved me."

"Are you sure?"

Caitlyn nodded. "Yes. He's a good man. A former SEAL and a friend. He'd never hurt me."

The doctor side-eyed English as he tried to look innocent and unthreatening. Apparently, he succeeded because the doctor moved to the side and let them pass.

"Be careful. If you want to look in on Mr. Donnelly, his room is right next door. Karen is in there with him."

English and Caitlyn nodded. The doctor moved toward John's bed, and they left the room. They exchanged a glance and nodded toward the other room, deciding silently to see what information they could get out of Karen. English hoped Karen was Mickey's wife.

English knocked on the door, drawing the woman's attention. She pasted on a smile as she lifted her head. Her brows drew together when she saw English at the door, then narrowed harshly when she saw Caitlyn.

"What the hell are you doing here?" Karen snapped.

"Mrs. Donnelly?" English asked.

"She's not welcome in here. She's been harassing my husband for weeks." Karen approached them, arms crossed, blocking their entry into the room.

"Your husband was sleeping with my friend, and she disappeared," Caitlyn argued.

"How dare you accuse him of that! My husband is many things, but a cheater is not one of them." Tears formed in Karen's eyes. Her shoulders slumped forward.

"Mrs. Donnelly, would you be willing to tell us what happened?" English asked.

"Why? So she can accuse him of something else? No. She needs to leave. She's not welcome here."

English looked at Caitlyn and nodded. Caitlyn sighed and walked out of the room, turning back the way they'd come in.

"Who are you?" Karen asked.

"My name is Liam Johnson. I'm—"

"Patty and William's son. I didn't recognize you. I work with your mom at the school."

"I'm sorry for what happened to your husband. Do you know anyone who would want to hurt him?"

"Aside from the woman you showed up here with?"

"Caitlyn was with me Friday night after we saw your husband at Sparky's. She had nothing to do with this."

"You saw him? Before the accident?" Karen moved toward English. She dropped her arms to her sides. "What happened? When did you see him?"

"We met at Sparky's around midnight. Your husband,

Mr. Valentine, and four other men attacked us. Mr. Valentine is the one who put the bruises on Caitlyn's neck."

Karen's shoulders hunched over again. "I didn't know. Mickey isn't a bad guy. He likes to drink and he can be an ass, but she's been harassing him. She accused him of sleeping with her friend, and—"

"Mrs. Donnelly, I think she's right about that. We don't have proof, but Ms. Waterford had a phone she only used to contact men she was involved with. She had your husband's phone number in it. They exchanged texts."

"What did the texts say?" she whispered.

English shook his head. "We don't know. They were all deleted by Ms. Waterford. But her phone records show they existed."

Karen drew a heavy breath and let it out slowly. Her eyes overflowed with tears. She moved away from English into the room. She went to the closet against the wall and opened it. She picked something up and stared at it, then turned and offered it to English.

"His phone. I don't know his password."

"Can I try his thumb print?"

She nodded, wrapping her arms around herself.

English walked over to the man. The cuts on his cheek and the bruise around his eyes were compliments of English. Mickey almost got the upper hand, but English was trained.

The phone unlocked with Mickey's thumb. English quickly scrolled through to the text messages and found deleted texts between Mickey and Jeanine. Not completely innocent ones.

"I'm sorry, but it looks as though Caitlyn was right about your husband and her friend." English showed Karen the text messages.

She read them, scrolling through all of them as tears fell from her eyes. Her tears rolled down her hands and disappeared into her sleeves as her husband's apparent affair played out in front of her.

After a few minutes, Karen handed the phone back to English. "This wasn't an accident, was it?"

English shook his head. "I don't know. I hope it was, but I have no way of knowing that. What I do know is Jeanine Waterford disappeared two weeks ago. These texts tell me she was supposed to meet with your husband and John that night. She canceled on both men."

"You think they had something to do with her disappearing?" Karen's voice shook with the question.

"Honestly? No."

"What?"

"Mrs. Donnelly, your husband and Mr. Valentine were angry we showed up. They wanted us to leave. They were being harassed, like you said, and they were upset about it. Did they mess up by getting involved with Jeanine? Yes, in my opinion, but her canceling is not enough for me to think either of them did something to her. Did you know Ms. Waterford?"

Karen shook her head. "She served me at the diner a few times, and I saw her in the gift shop at the church once or twice, but we weren't friends. I wouldn't even call her an acquaintance."

English nodded. "Do you mind if I keep your husband's phone for a little while? Try to find some more information."

Karen chewed on her lip.

"I'm hoping I can find something that proves he had nothing to do with Ms. Waterford's disappearance. And maybe something that will help us understand what happened in their accident."

Karen nodded before English finished talking. "He's a good man, Liam."

English squeezed her arm. "I know." He smiled at her and pocketed the phone, then left.

Caitlyn was outside the room, pushing off the wall as English walked out. They fell into step and left the hospital without another word.

"I need a new computer," English said when they got into his SUV. "Are you okay with stopping somewhere while we're here?"

"Of course." She paused while English pulled out of the parking garage and onto the street. "Do you believe her? That he was a good man?"

English shrugged. "Maybe to her, he was. Somewhat. I don't know many women who would defend their husband right after finding out he was cheating on them."

"I definitely wouldn't," Caitlyn said. "I'd probably pull out one of those tubes that was keeping him alive."

English chuckled. "I think I'd be the same. But Karen... she looked at him with love. She's already forgiven him."

"I'm not built that way. Not at all."

English nodded. He didn't know anyone who was. He just hoped he was right about Mrs. Donnelly and nothing happened to her husband.

18

CAITLYN NEVER THOUGHT OF JEANINE AS A CHEATER. As someone who wasn't honest. But it was getting harder and harder to be on her best friend's side when she read some of the texts Jeanine sent to Mickey. Jeanine was aware Mickey was married, and she encouraged him to lie to his wife to keep getting together.

Caitlyn wasn't sure she knew her friend at all. She felt dirty reading the texts the two of them exchanged. It was a violation of Jeanine's privacy. The texts were mostly about getting together and not sexual or explicit, but Caitlyn felt icky looking at her friend's life. She would never look at Jeanine the same way again.

Liam sat on the couch again, recreating the timeline they had on the table. He asked Caitlyn a question every now and then, but mostly, he worked quietly by himself. Watching him work was sexy. She admired a man who didn't let the outside world get in when he needed to focus on his task.

Caitlyn picked up her apartment and did a load of laundry in the basement laundry room. She was coming back up with her load when one of her neighbors opened the front door and scared Caitlyn. She dropped the basket at the poor guy's feet, a pair of her panties falling off the top and landing an inch from his shoe.

The guy raised an eyebrow at her, then moved past her to get his mail. He didn't say a word as Caitlyn picked up her stuff and hurried up the stairs. She was panting when she made it inside the apartment.

"Everything okay?" Liam asked.

"Yeah." Caitlyn heaved for breath. "I just scared myself. One of my neighbors walked in while I was coming up. It just freaked me out."

"Did they do anything?" Liam was up off the couch and approaching her before she could shake her head.

"No. I'm just paranoid."

"Are you sure?"

Caitlyn nodded. She carried her laundry past Liam and the couch and into her room. She needed to do something productive. Something that made her feel like she wasn't just sitting around and waiting. Her best friend was out there, and she was not going to let whoever took her win. Caitlyn was going to find him.

She folded her laundry and put everything away. Liam was back on the couch when she walked out of her room, so Caitlyn went to the kitchen to make dinner. She wanted comfort food. Something warm and cozy. Her pantry was not incredibly inspiring, but she did have a few cans of soup and a loaf of bread.

Caitlyn focused on cooking, pushing Liam and Jeanine and everything else out of her mind. She stared at the soup, mesmerized by the spoon as it moved through the liquid.

"Is that done?" Liam asked.

Caitlyn jumped, dropping the spoon into the pan. She swore and reached for the spoon.

"Don't," Liam warned. "It's hot."

She blinked, then nodded. She was more tired than she realized. "Thanks."

Liam moved in front of her and used another spoon the retrieve the one she dropped. He put it in the sink and turned off the burner. Caitlyn stepped back while he put the soup in bowls and added thick slices of Italian bread to the side. "Should we eat at the table or the couch?"

"Couch. I need cozy right now."

Liam nodded and carried the bowls over, setting both on the coffee table. He'd moved his computer and everything else he had to the floor and sat on the couch. He picked up the remote while Caitlyn joined him and queued up the next episode of the show they started the day before.

Caitlyn ate and tried to pay attention to the show. When she finished her soup, she curled up on the couch and let her eyes drift close.

"Let's go to bed," Liam whispered.

Caitlyn heard his voice, but she was not ready to move. She groaned and moved, tugging at her healing stitches. She winced and put her hand there. When she wasn't thinking about it, she was able to forget it had only been four days since she sliced her side open on a broken window escaping the fire in Jeanine's apartment.

"Did you hurt yourself? Let me see." Liam brushed her hand away gently and lifted her shirt. "I should be letting you rest. You lost a lot of blood that night. I keep forgetting."

"I'm okay," Caitlyn said. The pain woke her up enough to force her to go to bed. She trudged into her room and straight to the bathroom. She brushed her teeth and used the bathroom, then dragged herself to bed.

Liam did the same, then fitted himself behind her. "Are you sure you're okay?"

Caitlyn nodded.

"Good," he whispered. He kissed the back of her neck. "Get some sleep, beautiful."

She nodded again, already halfway there.

THE BED WAS cold when Caitlyn woke up the next morning. She rolled over and stretched. Her stitches pulled, but not as much as the night before. She lifted her shirt and looked at the healing cut. It was less red. The skin was definitely closed and holding together. A few more days until the stitches could come out.

Caitlyn used the bathroom and brushed her teeth before going to find Liam.

Holy shit.

Liam was in the middle of her living room in a plank position. He wore boxer briefs and sneakers only. His back glistened. His muscles were all tense. He moved, pushing himself up into a downward dog pose. His legs flexed, those muscles testing the edge of his boxer briefs.

Caitlyn's mouth was dry. Liam was strong and sexy, but seeing how dedicated he was to ensuring he stayed that way was beautiful. Wherever she moved after East Charlottesville, Caitlyn needed to join a gym. Just for the scenery.

"Good morning," Liam said when he finally rose to stand. He wiped his face and chest with a towel he must have brought with him.

"Morning," Caitlyn said.

"I made coffee. I haven't had breakfast yet."

Caitlyn nodded, her gaze unable to find his.

Liam chuckled. "My eyes are up here, Caitlyn."

Caitlyn shook her head. "I'll get there eventually."

He laughed but didn't hide his body from her appraisal.

Caitlyn finally looked him in the eye. She shrugged, unable to be embarrassed for staring at a gorgeous man. "Men get to look at hot women without any repercussions. Why can't I?"

"Are you saying I'm hot?"

"Do you honestly think I'm not going to say that? Have you looked in the mirror lately?"

Liam snorted. "If I didn't know any better, I'd think I was just eye candy for you."

Caitlyn shook her head and moved across the room to where Liam stood. "Definitely not. You're also brain candy and sex candy and mouth candy." She lifted up on her tiptoes and kissed him. She parted her lips and licked along the seam of his mouth, smiling when he groaned and took over.

Liam wrapped an arm around her back and yanked her body against his. He pressed his tongue deep into her mouth and rolled it around inside, tangling with hers as he tasted every inch of her mouth.

"That's a hell of a way to wake up," Caitlyn said when Liam pulled back. "I could get used to that."

Liam's brows pinched together, and his fingers tightened on her back.

Caitlyn realized what she said. Her cheeks heated. "I just meant—"

"Me, too," Liam said before she could explain herself. He waited until she looked up at him again, then kissed her nose. "I need a shower before I cover you in sweat. Want to join me or do you need a minute after that confession?"

Caitlyn breathed a laugh. "I need a minute."

"Okay," Liam said. He kissed her again, taking his time devouring her mouth.

Caitlyn held on to him, letting herself enjoy the fantasy. Kissing Liam Johnson every morning? Watching him exercise? Going to sleep in his arms at night?

Liam pulled back from their kiss. His erection was hard against her soft belly, but he didn't grind it into her. He smiled at her and smoothed her hair back from her face, then kissed her forehead and walked away. Whistling.

Caitlyn laughed as he closed the bathroom door. She noticed he did not lock the bathroom door.

She pressed her hands to her warm cheeks and sighed. Never in a million years did she think she'd date a guy like Liam Johnson. She wasn't good enough for him. She wasn't smart or strong or clever. She was lucky enough to have been pretty when she was young, but she didn't even have that anymore. She was just Caitlyn Marie Powers.

But Liam made her feel like she was something special. Someone special. And for the first time in years, Caitlyn wanted to trust someone other than herself.

Caitlyn went to the kitchen and started breakfast. Even with the groceries she bought the other day, she was already running low on things. She wasn't used to having someone else staying with her. But the idea of Liam leaving wasn't something she wanted to think about. It wasn't because she wouldn't feel safe without him there, even though that was part of it. It was more than that. It was Liam. She wanted him around. She wanted to spend time with him.

And she wanted to get to know more about him. Maybe even live close to where he was. If that didn't feel super sketchy.

The shower turned off, and Caitlyn shook her head. She

had to pay attention to what she was doing. Finish breakfast and feed Liam. It was the least she could do.

Caitlyn slid the breakfast pizza onto a plate just as Liam slid his hands around her stomach. He kissed her neck and inhaled deeply. "Still need some time?"

She shook her head.

"Good." He let go of her and grabbed the plate she put the pizza on. "Table?"

"Sure," Caitlyn said, following him with two smaller plates.

They sat and ate and talked about their plans for the day. Caitlyn realized just how boring her life was without Liam around. Normally, she'd sit around and do very little. It never bothered her, but it meant she wasn't living her life. She was simply existing. And she wanted more than that.

Like Liam.

Liam offered to clean up from breakfast while Caitlyn took a shower. She couldn't help but wonder why he didn't ask her anything else about what she said. Did he have a lot of women wanting more with him? Or was he just the kind of guy who brushed off comments like that?

Caitlyn didn't know much about him. He was doing his job finding Jeanine, but what else was there about him? What did he do in his free time? Who were his friends? When was his last serious relationship?

Caitlyn needed to know. She had to ask him. She was going to. Eventually.

ENGLISH TRIED NOT to think about what Caitlyn said. He was already marrying her in his mind, and she'd run screaming if she had any idea he was thinking about more than a few more days with her. He was surprised she hadn't kicked him out already.

After her shower, Caitlyn said she had errands to run. English volunteered to go with her, but she insisted he stay and work on the case. He didn't like her going out alone, but she promised to be careful. She would park where there were lots of people, and she wouldn't go wandering on her own.

English checked in with Dex and the rest of the team while Caitlyn was gone. They were getting close to closing their case. Dex offered to come out to Vermont to help English. They all agreed there was a lot more going on than any of them suspected, and they were going to pull all their resources toward the case as soon as they were able.

His next call was to the hospital. There hadn't been a change in either John Valentine or Mickey Donnelly. English asked to be informed if either of them woke up, and he was assured he would be.

English had just hung up with the hospital when his phone rang again. He didn't recognize the number, but the area code was local.

"Johnson."

"Liam, how are you? This is Daniel West."

"Hey, Daniel. I'm well. How are you?" English wasn't sure how Daniel got his number, but he wasn't going to come out and ask. Not when no one in East Charlottesville would have thought twice about giving it to him.

"Good, good. I was wondering if you wanted to grab that drink we were talking about the other day. I saw your dad today at work and thought about it. He gave me your number. I hope you don't mind."

"No, of course not. Yeah, a drink would be great. I was thinking of going to Sparky's tonight. Are you up for that?"

"Sparky's?" Daniel sounded less than sure.

"Yeah. Honestly, I'm working this Jeanine Waterford case. Do you know her?" English knew Daniel could be a valuable resource and wanted to tread carefully, but he was anxious to talk to the bartender.

"The name, sure. She wasn't an employee, though. I thought she left town."

English sighed heavily. Telling a civilian what happened wasn't a great idea, but Daniel was very well connected. Having someone like him on English's side could only help the case. "That's what everyone says, but I don't think that's true."

"Really? Why not?"

"I was at Sparky's after my parents' party and John Valentine and Mickey Donnelly attacked us. Because Caitlyn was asking questions about Jeanine."

"You two really did connect? Liam, I know it's been a while since you lived here, but you should know she's not great company. She's worked a lot of jobs because she keeps getting fired. I've never hired her because of the things I've been told. I know I shouldn't be repeating things, but she's a thief."

"Caitlyn? Really?"

"Yeah. She steals and lies. She never works the counter at the diner because the register is always off when she works there. They haven't been able to prove it, but Caitlyn's not the kind of woman you need to waste your time on."

English cleared his throat. He had a hard time matching the woman he'd been spending time with to the one Daniel described. But why would Daniel lie?

"Thanks for telling me. I appreciate it. But, um, anyway, this isn't really about Caitlyn. I'm trying to find Jeanine Waterford. And it's suspicious that the two men we talked to ended up in a coma just a few hours later. I want to talk to the bartender. See if he has any information he can share with me. Are you up for it?"

Daniel inhaled deeply and blew his breath out slowly. "Wow. Yeah, of course. John and Mickey are my employees. They're my family. If the bartender knows something, I want to hear it. They deserve answers. Their families deserve answers."

"I agree. I'll see you at eight?"

"That sounds good. Glad we could do this. Even though the circumstances aren't the best."

"We'll make the most of it," English assured him.

"We will. See you in a few hours."

CAITLYN WAS NOT happy when English told her he was meeting Daniel at Sparky's.

"I want to go with you."

"No. Last time was bad. And you have to work."

"But—"

"Caitlyn, this is not me sidelining you. Not at all. This is me wanting to solve this case. Daniel called me, and I took the opportunity. You have to go to work. If you didn't, I'd bring you with us."

Caitlyn pouted, and English chuckled. "It's not funny."

"It kind of is. You're not getting your way, and you're mad about it."

"I am mad. I've been helping, and now you're just running off with Daniel West."

"He's well connected. I think he could be an asset. And his house is next to the church. He might have seen something the night Jeanine disappeared."

"Do you think he had something to do with it?"

English shook his head. "No. He doesn't fit the profile."

"What profile?"

"If something happened to her, which is what I'm assuming, I've created a profile for the suspects. Married, late forties or early fifties, possibly serial cheater, regular at Sparky's, blue collar, likely drives a vehicle no one would notice blood in like a truck, and, most importantly, someone with a temper. Someone who will snap and lash out."

"An abusive husband who screws around on his wife, drives a truck so he can wash out the blood. Are you kidding me?" Caitlyn's voice was high and shaky.

"I know it's not easy to hear, but that's the person I'm looking for. It's part of why I wanted to go to the hospital. Their records will tell me if anyone local has ended up there recently. There's only been one name that's come up so far."

"What name?"

"Karen Donnelly."

"What?"

English nodded. "Caitlyn, I need to find out if she could be responsible for all of this."

"But we thought she was telling the truth when we met her at the hospital."

"I know, but some people are better liars than others." English didn't mean for his voice to be so harsh, but Daniel's words had been playing in his head. What if Caitlyn was a liar and a thief? What if she was just playing him?

"Are you accusing me of something? Because it sounds like you might be."

English hesitated. "I just heard—"

"Oh, you heard some gossip. Let me guess. You heard that I don't work the counter because I might steal money from the register. Or that I was fired for stealing. Or that I lie all the time. Any more I should mention?"

English shook his head.

Caitlyn crossed her arms over her stomach and nodded her head. "Well, I guess it's good you know who I am now. So you can stop worrying about me."

"Caitlyn..."

"No. I...I'm not perfect, Liam. I never have been. Those rumors...I worked the counter yesterday morning. And the job I was fired from for stealing? The manager was the one embezzling money and got caught a month after I was fired, but the damage was done. As for lying, no one believes me that Jeanine is missing, so that one's recent. But a lot of wives think I've slept with their husbands for some reason. And I'm not part of the inner circle, so people say whatever they want about me and there's no one to defend me. Except Jeanine. She always shut down the bullshit. A part of me was thinking maybe I could count on you for the same, but I guess not."

"Caitlyn..."

"I need to go to work. I—"

English spun her around and kissed the hell out of her. He wasn't willing to let her walk out the door without a word. He knew she was telling him the truth, and he hated that he even considered believing anyone else. He knew Caitlyn Powers. He knew every inch of her body. And he knew her heart. No one was going to ever tell him again that he didn't.

Caitlyn panted when he finally released her. She looked up at him with glassy eyes. "I can't take another person thinking the worst of me."

"I know you're not who anyone else thinks you are. You're smart and strong and beautiful. You're clever and talented and you can do anything. I don't know what you're going to do next, Caitlyn, but I hope I get to watch it because you are amazing."

Caitlyn sucked in a shaky breath and nodded. "I hope so, too."

English kissed her again, pulling back long before he was ready. "I'm driving you to work."

"Liam, I—"

"I know. But I need to make a stop before I meet Daniel. Karen Donnelly needs to answer a few more questions."

Caitlyn growled. "It is so not fair that you get to have all the fun."

English pulled her in tight. "I promise to save some fun for you. Starting in your bed later."

Caitlyn rubbed herself against him. "I like the sound of that."

English smiled and followed her out of the apartment, wondering if there was anywhere he wouldn't follow Caitlyn.

19

ENGLISH KNOCKED ON THE DOOR OF THE COTTAGE ON THE other side of town from where he grew up. There were never good and bad sides of East Charlottesville, but where the Donnelly's lived wouldn't have been good if there was one. An old truck was up on blocks, the grass was a few inches too long, and the sidewalk to the front door had more cracks than concrete left.

English knocked again when no one came to the door. Karen's hatchback was in the driveway, but Mickey's truck was at the local repair shop waiting for an estimate from the insurance company. English knew Karen was home.

He knocked a third time, pounding a little harder and trying to give her the benefit of the doubt. He didn't let up for a long minute. When he finally did, the door swung open and an angry Karen Donnelly glared at him.

"What?" she asked. Her eyes were red, and her brown hair was tangled and in her face. The shirt she wore had an orange stain near the collar. Her feet were bare, but she had sweatpants on that looked three or four sizes too big.

"Mrs. Donnelly, I wanted to ask you a few more questions," English said.

"Right now?"

English nodded. "It's important."

She huffed a sigh and pushed the screen door open. English followed her inside and to the kitchen. Dirty dishes covered the counters. The scent of burnt coffee hung in the air along with a faint hint of cigarette smoke.

"Did you hear anything new about my husband?" she asked after a minute.

"No, I haven't. Did you see him today?"

She nodded. "I spent the day there. I wanted to stay the night, but the nurses told me to come home and clean up and come back later. They said it would be good for me to change my clothes and take a shower and eat something."

"Especially since seeing your husband injured has to be bringing up some tough emotions."

She narrowed her eyes at English. "Of course it does. Why wouldn't it?"

"For you in particular. Since the last time you were there, you were the patient."

English let his words hang in the air. Karen stared at him, a mix of disbelief and anger in her gaze. She drew a shaky breath and ripped her gaze away.

"You don't know what you're talking about."

"Then why don't you tell me about it, Mrs. Donnelly."

"My husband is not a bad man."

"You keep saying..."

She tugged her lip between her teeth. Her eyes filled with unshed tears. She wrung her hands together, then squeezed them into fists. She released them and crossed her arms over her chest.

"I met Mickey in college. We had some of the same

friends. We were both going to community college, but we commuted from home. I didn't grow up here. We connected because we didn't live in town near school like a lot of our friends. We started talking and ended up dating a little off and on."

She took a breath and relaxed her arms, leaning back against the counter.

"Mickey wanted to move back here. John was another friend from school, but they were in high school together. Played football and wanted to be back in East Charlottesville. When we finished school, he asked me to marry him and move back. I said yes. I loved him, and I knew he would take care of me. I got a job at the school in the attendance office, and he started working at the factory. I met more of his friends and family and started to feel at home here."

English didn't move or speak. He could tell she needed to talk to someone, and he needed a confession. If she killed Jeanine, he wanted to know.

"About a year after we moved here, Mickey started spending time with his high school sweetheart. Sally was best friends with John's wife, Jenny. I heard rumors that Mickey and Sally were sleeping together, but he told me it was all lies. I believed him. At least, I tried to believe him. I followed him one night. He went to Sparky's with John. I saw him leave with Sally. They got in his truck and went to her place. She was all over him when they walked inside. I don't know what happened, but I have a pretty good guess."

She wiped a stray tear and straightened her spine.

"Anyway, when Mickey got home, I confronted him. I'd just found out I was pregnant and told him I wasn't going to stick around and have a baby with a man who couldn't be faithful to me. I had a bag packed, and I was going to leave him."

There was no indication there was a child in the house. Before she said it, English knew what was coming.

"Mickey was drunk. And angry. And he has a temper. I grabbed my bag and headed for the door. He tried to yank it out of my hand. I wasn't prepared for it, and the force of it threw me off balance. I fell, landing on the coffee table. Mickey just yelled. He didn't know I was hurt. I couldn't breathe, and I couldn't really move. By the time I got to the hospital, I'd lost the baby. I had two broken ribs."

English closed his eyes. He felt for her, but nothing in her story gave her the right to go after anyone else.

"Mickey promised me he'd never cheat on me again. He was sorry. Sally left town before I got out of the hospital, and Mickey was a doting husband. He still goes out with John sometimes, but not as much. And he promised me...he promised he'd never cheat on me again if I didn't leave him."

"But he did," English said, the first words since she started her story.

Karen nodded slowly. "I know that's what it looks like. I can't explain the texts. But I have a hard time believing them. He made a mistake, and I forgave him. We lost our child because of it. He's not going to do it again."

"Did you know Jeanine Waterford?" English asked.

Karen shook her head. "Not more than from the diner and the church. I didn't know she knew Mickey. I know you think I had something to do with her disappearance, but I didn't. I wish I could help you find her."

English nodded. Either Karen Donnelly was an excellent liar, or she was telling him the truth. Her story would be easy enough to verify. He saw her name as a patient, but he didn't have access to her medical file. Situations like that could also have a police report, but English was fairly certain she wouldn't have pressed charges against her husband.

He needed to do a little more digging into her, but if she was telling the truth, she wasn't a suspect. And if she was right about Mickey, he wasn't a suspect either. Which meant Mickey could have gotten upset with Caitlyn's questioning because he knew it would ruin his marriage for good.

English thanked Karen for her time and asked her to let him know if she could think of anything else or if her husband woke up. He didn't think he needed to talk to them again, but he wanted to be sure before he closed that part of the case.

Sparky's was busier than English expected for a Wednesday night. He found a seat at the bar and flagged down the bartender from Friday, not surprised at all when the man did not look happy to see him.

"You shouldn't be here," the bartender said as a greeting.

"I'm meeting a friend."

"The same friend? Definitely not a good idea."

English shook his head. "A different friend."

Daniel joined him as he finished speaking, and the bartender's entire demeanor changed.

"Hello, Mr. West. So happy you could join us today. How are you? What can I get you?"

"Whatever my friend is having. Did you order yet?"

"I was just asking what he wanted, sir. I can get you two anything."

"A beer for me," English said. "And some answers."

The bartender slid him a glare but kept his smile firmly in place for Daniel's sake. "Of course."

"Same for me," Daniel said.

"Yes, sirs. Coming right up."

The bartender scurried away. He grabbed glasses and watched English and Daniel while he filled both to the very top.

"Thanks for meeting me," Daniel said.

"I should be thanking you. I wouldn't have gotten anything out of him without you sitting here. I think he was about to kick me out."

"Sparky's fairly harmless."

"He's Sparky?"

Daniel chuckled. "Probably not, but that's what everyone calls him. I have no idea what his name actually is."

"That's interesting."

"Why is that?"

English watched the bartender. His first guess was the guy was just protecting his bar, but if no one knew his name, he could be protecting a lot more than that. Like his identity. Especially in a town so small everyone knows if someone gets a cold.

"How is it possible not to know the name of someone in a place like this?"

Daniel shrugged. "Never really thought about it. He serves my drinks and keeps people's secrets. Isn't that what bartenders do?"

English nodded. "It sure is."

Sparky set the beers in front of them and asked if they needed anything else. Before he got slippery, English stopped him.

"I heard Mickey put his wife in the hospital a year ago."

Sparky froze. So did Daniel.

"Who told you that?" Sparky asked.

"Karen Donnelly told me all about it. Mickey ever tell

you?" If English couldn't ask Mickey, he figured the bartender who saw him with Sally might know something.

"It was an accident. And Mickey felt bad about it. Didn't touch a drop for months afterward."

"What happened to Sally? She left town?"

"Yeah. Her sister's down in Rhode Island. She went there. Got away from here and all the rumors. Course the rumors were all true. Sally's mama and daddy were about run out of town, too."

"Doesn't seem fair. Sally wasn't the married one. Why didn't anyone blame Mickey?"

"He had enough of that on his own head. It's why he was so mad when that friend of yours started asking questions. If it got back to Karen, he could have been in some big trouble."

"So everyone lied for him? Told Karen he wasn't sleeping with Jeanine?"

Daniel stiffened. He took a drink of his beer and shifted his weight.

English glanced at him. Someone sat on the other side of Daniel, and even from where English was, he could smell the booze on the man.

"No one lied for Mickey. He wasn't sleeping with her. John was, but John and Jenny have one of those open things where they both sleep with whoever they want. Jenny was the one who introduced John and Jeanine. Mickey, he was never involved with her."

"I saw text messages between them. I know there was something going on," English pressed.

Sparky shook his head. "Not sure about the texts, but I never saw them leave together. Not unless the three of them walked out at once. Mickey wasn't looking to mess up his marriage again."

A glass broke at the other end of the bar, and Sparky left to clean it up. English tried to piece together everything in his mind. None of it worked. There were too many pieces missing.

"You think something happened to Jeanine Waterford?" Daniel asked, his voice tight.

English nodded. "You want to grab a table?"

Daniel nodded and stood. He led the way to a table in the back, away from most of the noise. "Why do you think something happened to Jeanine?"

"I came here to find out if something did, and since I've been here, I was in a bar fight, in a fire, arrested, the men from the fight are in the hospital, and my computer and all my research was stolen. And all of it has been around Jeanine."

"Wow. That's a lot of activity. The fire at Jeanine's? You were there?"

English nodded. "Yeah. Caitlyn and I went there after Mickey and John attacked us. I wanted to get a look at her place."

"What did you find?"

"Caitlyn said her favorite sweatshirt was there. All her clothes were still there. Her phone charger, mail, even her toothbrush. It looked like she was just gone for the night. Hard to believe someone packed a bag and skipped town by the looks of the place."

"Huh. That's interesting. What did the police say?"

"Nothing. They're pretty useless. They barely investigated the case. And the FBI did even less. That's why I'm here. I'm doing their due diligence."

"Wow. And you figured out that she is actually missing. That's hard to hear."

"Did you know her?"

Daniel shook his head and took a sip of his beer. "She was my server a handful of times, but we didn't know each other well at all."

"That seems to be the case with everyone."

"She never worked for me. I try to get to know all of my employees, and their families, but outside that, it's hard to know everyone in town well."

English nodded. He knew the other ninety-seven students he graduated with, but he didn't know everyone in the classes ahead or behind him. It still surprised him no one seemed to know Jeanine except Caitlyn.

"She was dating someone. I'm surprised whoever she was dating hasn't come forward. This whole case is just strange to me. I can't figure it out."

"Maybe whoever she was dating had something to do with her disappearing."

"That's what I've been thinking, but Caitlyn has no clue who Jeanine was dating. I haven't found anything that tells me. Her phone records don't show any numbers I can't identify. It's all a big mystery. What kind of woman doesn't tell her best friend who she's dating?" English huffed a laugh.

Daniel chuckled a few seconds after English. He shook his head. "Sounds like a strange one."

English nodded. "Yeah. My only leads have been Mickey and John. I'm hoping one of them knows something about who else Jeanine knew. Or maybe even one of them was the one who did something to her. I don't know. She canceled on them the night she disappeared, but I don't know who she met instead. I definitely feel like I'm not making any progress."

"I'm sure that's not true." Daniel drained the last of his beer and set it on the table with a thunk. "I need to head out. Early morning and all. But thanks for getting together."

English finished his beer and stood with Daniel. "Definitely. I hope we can do this again before I leave town. Hopefully with a lot less of a mystery to solve hanging over my head. I'm sure I wasn't great company."

"Not at all," Daniel said.

They walked outside together. English headed to his SUV while Daniel pulled out in a fancy SUV of his own. English couldn't remember seeing the vehicle on the roads since he got to town. Not even in the parking lot at West Textiles the few times he was there.

English's phone buzzed with a text from Caitlyn.

```
So bored. Dead quiet tonight. Hate that I
have to stay here for another hour.
```

```
    Mind some company? I was going to kill an
      hour, but I can do that while looking at
                    you if you're up for it.
```

```
Yes! Please! Save me from these annoying
people.
```

```
                                    On my way.
```

English parked half a block from the diner and walked back toward it. The street was quiet. The whole town was quiet. He wondered why they stayed open until ten on a weeknight, but his guess was because they always had.

Caitlyn was leaning against the counter when he walked in. Her lips curled up in a smile, and her eyes brightened. She pushed off the counter and walked over to him, stopping just before she reached him.

"Am I not allowed to touch you? No PDA?"

Caitlyn shook her head. "No one cares."

"Good," English said, already closing the distance between them. He wrapped his arm around her waist and pulled her close, pressing his lips to hers as soon as she was close enough for a taste.

Caitlyn sighed happily and eased her hands up his chest and around the back of his neck. She tilted her head to the side and parted her lips, inviting him in.

English didn't hesitate to accept her invitation, pulsing his tongue in and out of her mouth. It had been entirely too long since he'd had her in his arms. A thought that should have scared him but only made it that much harder to pull back from her.

"I missed you," she whispered. Her cheeks flared red immediately at her unintended confession.

"I missed you, too," he told her. He meant it, too. Being away from her for a few hours was not easy. Or fun.

"Well, you're here now."

"I'm here now. And I'll be in your bed later."

Caitlyn's grin turned sinful. Her eyes dipped to half-mast. His cock soared right past that to fully hard. Ready for her. Waiting for her. She rolled her hips ever so slightly, enough to make him groan. "I can't wait," she whispered.

"Tease," he said as she pulled away.

Caitlyn shook her sexy ass as she walked away from him. English followed her, claiming a booth in the section she indicated was hers. She brought him a slice of pie with two forks and sat across from him at the table.

Did life get better than that?

English almost snorted. It was going to as soon as he had her in her bed. It was going to get a hell of a lot better.

20

CAITLYN FELT AWKWARD WITH LIAM AT THE DINER. SHE TRIED to play it off as no big deal, but having him there, watching her, was weird. She'd never been with anyone who was content to simply sit. The men she knew wanted sex without much of a connection.

That worked for Caitlyn before, but she wasn't sure it was something she wanted to go back to. She liked having Liam around. She liked that he paid attention to her, when he wasn't absorbed in work. And she liked that he wanted to just be in the same space as her.

She tried to stay busy for the last hour of her shift, but no one came in. She stocked salt and pepper shakers, wiped down tables and menus, and did what she could to set up the morning shift. But mostly, she stood near Liam's table and talked to him.

He filled her in on his visit to Karen Donnelly's house. Caitlyn wasn't sure she believed the entire story, but Liam was right. It would be easy enough to check it out and get records.

"How did things go with Daniel?" Caitlyn finally managed to ask.

Liam looked up at her and waited until she met his gaze. Caitlyn didn't want to ask the question, but she didn't like that Liam was so open with Daniel. She didn't trust anyone who looked down on her without even trying to get to know her, no matter how many times Jeanine and the rest of the town said he was a good guy.

"Daniel was fine. He was surprised to hear about John and Mickey and their extracurricular activities. He also didn't know about Mickey and Karen."

"Why would he? Just because they work for him doesn't mean he actually knows them," Caitlyn spat.

"I know you don't like him, but he really seems like a good guy. He's worked hard to make sure his employees feel like they can go to him. I think he was hurt that Mickey went through that with Karen and the baby and never talked to him."

"And what would he have done? Can Daniel bring unborn babies back to life?"

Liam tilted his head and chuckled at her. "I think you're being too hard on him."

"I just don't appreciate that he's never bothered to try to know me. And then he's warning you to stay away from me and spreading rumors about me. I don't know him. We've lived in this same town for most of our lives, and I don't know him. He's short and dismissive of me when I see him here, and if I see him out in public, he just pretends he didn't notice me. I know I'm worth less than the gum on his shoe, but it sucks to be treated that way."

Liam stood from the booth and grabbed her arms. He squeezed gently and ducked down to catch her eye. "You are not worth less than anyone else. And yeah, it does suck to be treated that way. I'm sorry anyone does, let alone so many people in this town. It's not right." He pulled her into his arms and breathed deeply. "I wish they could see the woman I see."

Caitlyn snorted. "Flat on my back and begging to come."

Liam groaned. "That's just for me."

She chuckled and leaned into him, taking strength from him. She didn't know how he did it, but he made her feel like everyone else was wrong about her. That he was the only one who knew who she really was.

Liam kissed the side of her neck, then pulled back. "How much longer?"

His rough voice skittered down her spine and settled between her thighs. Caitlyn looked at the clock above the kitchen door. "Six minutes."

"Good. I'm not sure I can wait seven."

Her entire body flashed with heat and desire. She wasn't sure she could wait six.

Caitlyn forced herself away from Liam and went through the motions of closing the diner with her fellow employees. When they all headed to the door, Liam reached for her hand and pulled her outside into the chilly night with him. The cold did nothing to calm the fire raging inside Caitlyn, but she didn't want it to. She wanted to let it burn.

Liam did not take his time getting back to her apartment. His fingers drew circles on her inner thigh as he drove the dark streets. His other hand gripped the steering wheel tight, barely stopping at stop signs or red lights. When he parked in front of her building, he slammed the vehicle into park and jumped out.

Caitlyn met him next to the vehicle. He grabbed her hand and dragged her toward the door as he locked the SUV with a loud beep in the otherwise silent night.

They hurried upstairs. Caitlyn fumbled with her keys when Liam pressed himself against her back. She paused long enough for him to bite her earlobe and whisper, "Let us in, Caitlyn."

She shook her head and jammed the key into the lock. It clicked open, then they were inside and all of his teasing was no longer promises. It was reality.

Liam kicked the door shut and flipped the locks back into place. Caitlyn tossed her keys on the table and reached for the hem of her shirt.

"Let me," Liam growled.

Caitlyn stopped, her breath tight in her chest as Liam took two steps and put his hands on her hips. He skimmed his palms up, letting the rough pads of his fingers brush her bare skin. She shivered against his gentle touch.

Her shirt got caught on her arms. She lifted, and he took the offending item off. Liam stepped forward, one hand going to her cheek and the other resting on her hip.

Caitlyn opened for him without a thought. She wanted him. She wanted this. Whatever it was for however long she could have it. Liam Johnson was quickly becoming her favorite part of the day. Maybe of her life. And she was going to savor every last minute of it before he returned to his life that didn't include her.

Her hands moved to his waist and tugged at his shirt. She wanted to feel his skin against hers. He pulled back from their kiss and yanked his shirt off. They reached for each other at the same time, colliding in the middle with tongues and bodies.

Caitlyn explored Liam's chest with her fingertips. She traced his muscles and scraped her nails down his abs. He growled and backed them up toward her bedroom. She undid the button on his jeans and pushed the zipper down, loving that he didn't stop kissing her to do it himself. She shoved his jeans over his hips, and he stepped out of them before they made it past the couch.

Liam slid his hands down her sides and cupped her ass. He dug his fingers in, like he wanted her to straddle him. In the middle of the living room.

"What?" she asked, reluctantly pulling back.

"Need you. Come here." He lifted one leg and tried to pick up the other.

"I'm too heavy."

"I already carried you. I need to feel you, Caitlyn."

She was sure they were both going to end up on their asses, but she jumped anyway, trusting him to catch her. His erection nestled between her thighs. Her leggings did nothing to hide it from her. She sank down, rubbing herself against him.

Liam's fingers dug in deeper, urging her to ride him. He stalked to the bed, not slowing down until she was on top of him on the mattress. "Ride me, beautiful. Take what you need."

"I need a lot less clothes on," she said. She was frantic, desperate for an orgasm. She wanted to let go, to forget about everything except Liam.

He urged her hips to move anyway, pushing her back and forth over his cock. Caitlyn couldn't stop herself from enjoying the feel of him beneath her. She put her hands on his chest and gave in to the pleasure. He surged up at just the right time, giving her the added push she needed to carry her up and over the edge.

"Oh, God," she whimpered, the pulsing need inside her strong and sudden and very welcome. She couldn't remember the last time she came without getting naked, but she wasn't going to complain about it.

"Now we can get the rest of these clothes off," Liam said.

He was already undoing the clasps on her bra. He slid it just far enough to grab two overflowing handfuls of her breasts. He rasped the pads of his fingers over her nipples, and her entire body responded.

"More," she whispered.

"Less clothes first," Liam argued.

Caitlyn didn't like that answer, but she climbed off him anyway. She pushed her leggings down ruthlessly, stepping on them when they got stuck on her ankles. She flailed like a baby deer when they still didn't come off.

Liam pressed his naked body to her back and wrapped his hands around her, cupping her breasts. He rolled her nipples between his fingers.

"Oh, God. I thought you said less clothes."

"I already got rid of mine. You need some encouragement."

"I need some help," Caitlyn confessed. "I should have worn a dress to work."

"Next time. Skip the panties, too."

"Yeah, I'll definitely have everyone in town talking about me if I do that."

"Fuck them. The only opinion that matters is your own. And you know you're better than this place and their shitty rumors about you."

Caitlyn took a breath and nodded. He was right. She knew in that moment nothing was going to stop her from leaving as soon as she found Jeanine. She was done hoping her mom would come back or hoping the town would approve of her. She was done looking outside for acceptance.

"There's my woman," Liam said, licking the shell of her ear. "I can feel it. This is the Caitlyn Powers I remember. The one who knows exactly who she is and says fuck you to anyone who thinks differently. I just hope this woman still wants me."

Caitlyn turned in his arms and looked up at him. She wrapped her arms around his neck and appraised the man in front of her. The only man she'd ever known who saw her for more than a pretty face or a pussy to sink into. The only man who thought she was smart and capable and worth something. How could he ever think she wouldn't want him?

"I've never wanted someone more than I want you right now," she told him honestly.

His gaze narrowed for half a second before a satisfied smile tilted the edges of his lips up. "I'll take that."

She grinned back at him and pulled him in for another kiss that made her leggings and panties finally melt away.

Together, they moved to the bed. He laid on his back and urged her on top of him. They kissed and touched and explored each other in a way that would have been chaste if they weren't naked. They learned each other's bodies and minds, but also their hearts. Making out like they had all the time in the world to get to the rest of their night.

Caitlyn finally pulled back from their kiss and licked her way down his neck. She flicked the peak of his nipple, then kissed farther down his body. When she reached his erection, she looked up at him.

His eyes were locked on hers, watching her every move. He gave her a nod, either of approval or request. Whichever he intended, Caitlyn was desperate to taste him.

She licked the underside of him, letting the musky scent of him fill her lungs. Her thighs slicked together.

He jerked at the tip of her tongue on his sensitive cock. His hands went to her hair and pushed it out of her face.

Caitlyn looked up at him and held his gaze as she parted her lips and brought him inside her mouth. He swelled instantly and surged up. She retreated, then swallowed more of him into her mouth. Her breasts felt heavy, needy, and her thighs tingled in anticipation.

Liam grunted and held her face tighter in his hands. His muscles were tight, holding himself back from fucking her mouth. She loved that he was letting her explore. Letting her take her time with him.

Caitlyn relaxed her throat and took him in deeper. He grunted again, his muscles tightening more. She loved the feeling of power, being in control. Knowing she was the woman who made the strong man beneath her shiver with the same desire that was making it hard for her to breathe.

"Fucking hell, Caitlyn. You have about two more seconds, then I'm dragging you back up here," Liam growled.

Caitlyn was going to make those seconds count. She closed her eyes and sucked him as far down her throat as she could. The urge to pull back made her eyes well up, but she trusted Liam. She slowly backed off him, releasing him with a soft pop. Then she looked up.

He didn't give her a chance to react to the fiery look in his eyes. He yanked her up his body and flipped them. He held himself off her long enough to roll a condom down his length with a shaky hand, then he thrust into her deep and hard.

Caitlyn came instantly.

"Oh, God," she moaned. Liam held still, letting her come. She twitched and struggled, not wanting to push him out at the same time her body needed to squeeze him hard.

"Don't stop, Caitlyn," Liam said as he finally moved. He slammed into her again, not letting the orgasm end before he was fucking her hard and sending her toward another orgasm.

"Liam."

"I'm right here, baby. I'm with you. Fucking hell, you feel so good. It's just you and me, Caitlyn. You and me. Look at me, beautiful."

She pried her eyes open and blinked up at him. He smiled at her, the edges tight. His eyes shined like the brightest stars in the sky. It was the most beautiful thing she'd ever seen. A man looking at her like that. Like it wasn't just sex for him. Like he wasn't going to disappear as soon as he was finished.

"Caitlyn," he whispered. His voice was reverent, tender, intoxicating.

Caitlyn wanted more of him. More than a few nights. More than a week or so. More than a lifetime. She wanted forever with Liam Johnson.

And she wasn't sure it could ever happen.

But she wasn't going to let that kill her mood. She was going to enjoy it. She was going to love him in that moment and show him how good it felt to be truly loved by another person. Because she knew without a doubt, for the first time in her life, Caitlyn loved someone.

And Liam Johnson was it.

"Caitlyn," he groaned. His hips pounded hard into her, his control slipping. Sweat beaded on his forehead and upper lip. But all she saw was the look in his eyes. The look that said maybe, just maybe, a part of him was feeling the same thing she was.

"Liam," she whispered back. She reached up and cupped his jaw. He turned his face to kiss her palm and tilted his head to trap her hand between his cheek and shoulder. The whole time, he pumped into her, chasing the orgasm that was barreling down on them both.

Caitlyn broke first, her orgasm jumping ahead and grabbing her around the throat. She screamed at the shock of it, locking her thighs around his hips.

Liam grunted and threw his head back as he surged into her one more time, as if he was waiting for her. He throbbed and pulsed deep inside her as he spilled himself into the condom.

Her hand was still against his cheek. She moved it to the back of his neck and pulled him down. He settled gently on top of her, his sweaty body warm against hers.

They laid like that for a while. Neither moved nor spoke. Caitlyn didn't want the moment to end. She wanted to put a bubble around them and never leave. Never let the real world back in.

Liam finally rolled off and went to the bathroom. When he came back, Caitlyn took her turn. He was on his back when she got to the bed. He pulled the covers back and tugged her close when she slid under them. It wasn't long before they were both snoring.

ENGLISH DID NOT WANT to get out of Caitlyn's bed and face the world again. He finally understood what his teammates were talking about when they said they couldn't bear to leave their wives and girlfriends some days. English couldn't imagine ever wanting to leave Caitlyn.

A noise put him on alert. He was somewhere between sleep and awake, but something woke him. He laid perfectly still so he didn't bother Caitlyn and listened for it again.

His phone. Three beeps and three buzzes. A text

message. An important one if that was the alert. Usually that meant it came from his team.

The phone was still in the pocket of his jeans on the floor of Caitlyn's room. English carefully eased out from beneath Caitlyn and climbed over her and off the bed. She rolled toward the wall and nuzzled her head against the pillow he just left.

English smiled. He could get used to that sight.

The phone buzzed again, and English turned his attention to it. Adam. English forgot he assigned the same tone to his cousin's texts.

On my way back to town. Caught a case. Think it might be connected to yours. Are you staying with Holly or Caitlyn?

English glanced at Caitlyn and grabbed his jeans and boxer briefs. He went out into the living room, closing the bedroom door so he didn't disturb her.

He called Adam instead of replying with a text.

"Morning," Adam said. "I wasn't sure you'd be up yet."

"I wasn't, but I heard the text. What case are you working on?"

"It's a suspected homicide."

"The FBI comes in for something like that?"

"We do when the two people who are dead were the two lead suspects in a kidnapping case the bureau botched."

"Whoa, what?"

Adam sighed. "You need to check your messages. Mickey Donnelly and John Valentine died last night."

21

———

ENGLISH GLANCED AT THE BEDROOM DOOR. HE WAS WRAPPED up in Caitlyn all night. He didn't bother with his phone. He didn't care. All he cared about was Caitlyn. And two men died.

"No. That's not possible. I was told they were improving. The doctor had hopes they would wake up in the next day or two."

"And that's why we're on our way. No one wants to fuck up two cases in the same small town. Are you at Holly's?"

"No," English said, still trying to piece together the whole thing. John and Mickey were dead. He'd already somewhat removed Mickey as a suspect, but not Karen. But if it was Karen, why would she kill John, too? And if it wasn't Karen—

"Liam!" Adam shouted.

"What?"

"Where the hell are you?"

"I'm staying with Caitlyn."

"Who's Caitlyn?" a woman asked.

"Who are you?" English barked. Adam didn't say

anything about someone else being able to hear their conversation.

"That's Lorelei. My partner. We'll be there in an hour. We need to get together. Breakfast at the diner? Bring Caitlyn."

English nodded to himself. He hated to wake Caitlyn up after their late night, but she needed to be there for whatever Adam wanted to talk about. "We'll see you then."

English hung up the phone and stared at it. He had twelve missed texts.

"See who?" Caitlyn asked from behind him.

English spun. She was wearing his tee from the night before. It fell to her hips, and she wore pink panties underneath. All he wanted to do was strip her naked again and go back to bed.

"John and Mickey are dead. Adam and his partner are on their way to town to look into it."

Caitlyn leaned against the doorframe, wobbling where she stood.

English rushed to her, catching her before her knees gave out and she sank to the floor. He helped her to the couch and sat next to her.

"They're dead?"

English nodded. "I was just going through messages from last night. Adam sent me a few texts when he heard. And I have a call from the doctor we met when we were there."

"What does it say?"

"I haven't listened to it yet."

"Play it."

English tapped the voicemail button and hit play.

"Mr. Johnson, this is Dr. Romero. Just before eleven tonight, Mr. Donnelly and Mr. Valentine were both pronounced dead at the hospital. Mrs. Donnelly was here with her husband, but Mrs. Valentine was not. Both men had cardiac events around the same time. We did everything we could, but we were not able to save either of them. Mrs. Donnelly asked me to call and let you know. I apologize for leaving a message, but I wanted to inform you as soon as possible."

English's mind turned over and over with the possibilities. It was highly unlikely both men died at the same time days after their accident. It was also highly unlikely they had cardiac events at the same time. Either someone did something, or... Nope, English couldn't come up with another answer.

"Do you think Karen did this?" Caitlyn whispered.

"I don't know."

"Do you still think this is connected to Jeanine?"

"I don't know that either. What I do know is someone killed those two men, and Jeanine is still gone. And I feel like we're running out of time before something else happens."

Caitlyn rubbed her hands up and down her arms. "Whoever did this isn't going to stop until I'm dead, are they?"

"Not necessarily. But we need to be careful. You need to be careful."

Caitlyn nodded. "Do I have time for a shower?"

"Yeah, go ahead. I'll jump in after you."

Caitlyn nodded absently and walked away.

English watched her, hating the way her rounded shoulders pulled her down. She didn't deserve all of this. Neither did John or Mickey or Jeanine. But someone out there thought they all did.

CAITLYN HAD NEVER BEEN SO tense in her life. She jumped at every noise when she was in the shower. She almost hit a neighbor when they walked out of their apartment as she walked past. At the diner, she practically ran to a booth in the back and dragged Liam in next to her to protect her in case bullets started flying.

She was a mess. And she did not like the feeling.

Her mind kept repeating the same thing over and over again. *They're all dead, and I'm next.* She couldn't stop the thought. Whoever killed Jeanine, she had little doubt that wasn't true anymore, had now killed two more people. Caitlyn wasn't smart enough to figure out who it was. She couldn't beat them.

The diner door opened, and Caitlyn jumped again. She watched as Adam and a beautiful Black woman with spiral curls and dark brown skin approached. The woman looked around the room as they moved, confidence pouring off of her. She was beautiful, smart, and strong, and Caitlyn wanted to be her. She wanted to have herself together as well as the woman who approached. She wanted to not be terrified.

Adam nodded at them both as he slid into the booth opposite them. The woman sat next to Adam and appraised them closely.

"This is Lorelei Sloane, my partner. Lorelei, my cousin Liam and Caitlyn Powers."

Lorelei nodded at them both but didn't say a word.

Caitlyn didn't like that about the other woman. Lorelei was assessing her, watching her. And Caitlyn was sure she would decide she wasn't good enough.

Liam's hand landed on Caitlyn's knee, and she jumped. He squeezed gently. Caitlyn looked at him.

"You okay?" he asked.

Caitlyn nodded, but it was an obvious lie. She was not okay. She wasn't sure if she would ever again be okay.

Heather came over and poured them all coffee and took their orders. She glared at Caitlyn and rolled her eyes when she ordered oatmeal. With the way her stomach felt, anything more would not sit well, but Heather hated when people didn't order big breakfasts. She wanted big tips.

"Caitlyn, I'm sorry about your friend," Lorelei said when Heather went to put in their order.

Caitlyn met her gaze and nodded.

"I promise you, we are going to do everything we can to find her while we figure out what happened to the two suspects. I would tear the world apart if something happened to my sister. She's my best friend. Having that one person you turn to for everything disappear has to be gut-wrenching."

Caitlyn nodded, her emotions welling up. She appreciated Lorelei's words. It showed her more about the woman than anything else could. She was everything Caitlyn wanted to be on the outside, but she was also kind and compassionate on the inside. And fierce if the look on her face when she mentioned John and Mickey was any indication.

"What do you know about John and Mickey?" Adam asked Liam.

Liam handed over his phone. "Both spent a lot of time at Sparky's. We think both were involved with Jeanine, but Mickey's wife insists that wasn't the case for him. Karen said he cheated before and she threatened to leave him. He grabbed the bag she was trying to walk out with and she fell and hit a coffee table. She just found out she was pregnant and lost the baby. She said Mickey would never cheat again."

Lorelei whistled. "Sounds like a woman with motive if I ever heard of one."

Liam nodded. "I agree. I was looking into her. Them, too. Their accident is suspicious, but that makes me wonder if either of them was actually involved."

"These are the two ringleaders who jumped you last weekend. Why change your story about them now?" Adam asked.

"Caitlyn was asking questions. If Mickey really didn't cheat on Karen, we think he might have been worried Caitlyn's questions and accusations would get back to Karen and she'd leave him."

"But you said you thought he was cheating," Lorelei said.

Liam nodded. "Karen gave us his phone. There were texts between Mickey and Jeanine that didn't seem innocent. Because we knew they were in contact, we went into them looking for a connection between the two of them. Looking at them again, we could say they were friendly, not flirty, but it's a bit more of a stretch than I would normally make."

"So, the wife might be behind all of this. But the husband and his buddy could be the ones who made the woman disappear. And now the men are dead and we still don't have the woman's body," Lorelei said succinctly. No emotion, just facts.

Caitlyn struggled to breathe. It didn't matter how much she believed Jeanine was dead, she still had a tiny bit of hope. She didn't want to imagine what her friend was going through, but she had hope. Alive was always better than dead.

"I'm sorry," Lorelei said a minute later. "I can't get

emotional about cases or it'll destroy me, but I shouldn't be so callous. I apologize. Shit, hit me or something." She elbowed Adam.

Adam grunted. "I tried to give you a signal, but you just wouldn't stop. Sorry, Caitlyn."

Caitlyn forced her lips to lift in a smile.

Heather delivered their food and left again, promising to check on them soon. Caitlyn took tiny bites of her oatmeal, hating the bland flavor. She wanted to ask for some brown sugar or cinnamon or something that would make it tolerable, but she wasn't sure she could eat it anyway.

The others didn't have the same issue. They ate and talked and made a plan. Adam and Lorelei were going to talk to Karen and find Mrs. Valentine and talk to her. Liam was going to go to the hospital and talk to Dr. Romero. They decided to meet back up for dinner to discuss what they found and go from there.

Caitlyn followed Liam to the car. She stared straight ahead as he pulled away from the curb and headed south toward the hospital. She could see him glancing at her every few miles, but she didn't say anything. She felt like they missed an opportunity. They spent the night wrapped up in each other and two men were dead. Two men who might have had information about where her best friend was.

Liam parked in the lot and turned off his SUV. He didn't make a move to get out, and Caitlyn turned to look at him. "Talk to me."

She shook her head. Not saying no, but she didn't know what to say. Her thoughts were jumbled. Guilt and anger, frustration, acceptance, fear, sadness. It was a lot. And if she opened her mouth and let it out, she wasn't sure she'd be able to bottle it up again. She had to keep it together. For Jeanine.

"Caitlyn," Liam said softly. He reached for her, tucking her hair behind her ear. His fingers lingered on her jaw.

The touch sent shivers through her body. Shivers that brought the guilt to the forefront. "What if we'd been here instead of in my bed?"

"Caite, you can't think about that. You can't blame yourself."

"But if you were here protecting them instead of protecting me with multiple orgasms, John and Mickey might be alive and we might be able to find out where Jeanine is."

"We're going to find her," Liam said. The steel in his voice was a promise. He was not giving up.

Caitlyn drew a breath and let it out slowly. She closed her eyes and pushed all the emotions back down where they belonged. When this was over and she was alone again, she could let them out. She could feel all her feelings and have a massive pity party for herself. Until then, she had to act like she did when she modeled and bottle all that shit up. She wasn't Caitlyn Powers, she was whoever they needed her to be. And right now, she needed to be like Lorelei. Unfeeling and unemotional.

They walked to the hospital and asked at the visitors desk to see Dr. Romero. They were given passes and directions up to the ICU floor again.

The nurse at the desk upstairs paged Dr. Romero. Caitlyn watched the doctors and nurses as they rushed around and tried to save all the patients. An overhead alarm called out a code blue at one point and a dozen people rushed into the room.

Caitlyn told herself not to care even as she sent up good vibes for the person dying a few feet away.

"Mr. Johnson, you didn't have to come down. Did you get my message about Mr. Donnelly and Mr. Johnson?"

Liam nodded. "I wanted to ask you a few more questions, though."

"Sure. There's an empty room right there." Dr. Romero pointed to the room next to the code blue and led the way. He stepped aside for Liam and Caitlyn to go in ahead of him, then closed the door behind them. "I get the feeling this requires privacy."

"Yes, it does. Thank you. We have been looking into the disappearance of a woman, and we have reason to believe one or both men might have been involved with her. And because of that, we also have reason to believe their wives could have had something to do with all of this."

Dr. Romero rocked back on his heels and ran a hand over his salt and pepper beard. He shook his head slowly. "I don't deal with this side of things, but my guess would not be that Mrs. Donnelly had anything to do with it. She barely left her husband's side. She seemed like a doting wife to me."

"She was a patient here. About a year ago. He was cheating on her and when she tried to leave him, they got into a scuffle. She fell, broke a few ribs, and lost a baby."

"I'm sorry to hear that," Dr. Romero said. "How do you know that?"

"She told me. One thing I want to do is confirm her story. Is there a way you can get me access to her medical records?"

Dr. Romero sighed. "That's a violation of patient privacy. It's not something I can authorize. Not without her permission."

"But if I get her permission?"

"Then of course."

"Good. What about Mrs. Valentine? You said Mrs. Donnelly wasn't someone you'd think had anything to do with this. Not Mrs. Valentine?"

Dr. Romero shrugged. "She struck me as more annoyed than anything else. Like she didn't want to be here. We see that sometimes, but usually it's people who don't like hospitals. She only came once. She asked a few questions, wanted to know if he'd survive, sat for about five minutes, then left. When I informed her he'd died, she asked to have his things ready for her to pick up. She doesn't want to see him."

"That seems strange," Liam said.

Dr. Romero nodded. "I thought so, too."

"Can we see his stuff?" Caitlyn asked.

Dr. Romero shook his head. "Unless there is an investigation, I can only release his personal effects to family."

"We're working with the FBI." Liam pulled out cards from Lorelei and Adam and handed them over. "These two agents are in charge. We volunteered to speak to you while they go talk to Mrs. Donnelly and Mrs. Valentine."

"And you don't mind me confirming this?"

"Of course not."

Dr. Romero took the cards and dialed Adam's number first. When he got confirmation from Adam, he repeated the process with Lorelei. With assurance from both of them, Dr. Romero led Caitlyn and Liam to another room where John and Mickey's things were stored.

"We cut them out of their clothes, but we keep them in situations like this just in case the police come back and need the clothes for some reason. Mr. Valentine had a phone and a wedding ring, his wallet and keys, and a few other things, but not much. Mr. Donnelly had about the same."

"Thank you," Liam said. "The agents you spoke to will

let their wives know we've taken these items into our custody."

Dr. Romero nodded. "If there's anything else…"

"Actually, I had one question," Liam said. "What is the likelihood these men both died minutes apart from cardiac events five days after their accident?"

"Best guess? A million to one."

Liam nodded. "That's about the same odds I thought. Thanks, Dr. Romero."

Liam grabbed the boxes and led the way back to his SUV. He stashed both in the trunk and headed back toward East Charlottesville.

Again, the ride was quiet. He reached over and put his hand on Caitlyn's knee. She wrapped her fingers through his and held on tight with both hands.

Liam carried the boxes up to Caitlyn's apartment. He checked to make sure no one had gotten in while they were gone, then laid all the items out on her table.

Clothes, phones, rings, wallets, keys, and one lighter.

"A lighter?" Caitlyn asked. "Could they…?"

"Have been the ones who tried to burn Jeanine's apartment with us in it? Yep. Or John could be a smoker."

"What do you think about what Dr. Romero said about John's wife?" Caitlyn asked.

"I think she could be a suspect or she could be sad or she could hate her husband so much that she didn't want to be in the same room as him. Hopefully Adam and Lorelei get some answers out of her."

"Can you get into his phone? See what kind of texts he sent to Jeanine?"

Liam nodded. He put on a pair of rubber gloves and reached into the bag holding the phone. He plugged it in and waited for it to power up. After a minute, Liam had the phone unlocked and was reading all his texts.

"He was definitely involved with Jeanine. And he was pissed because she canceled on him the night she disappeared. He threatened her."

"So, he's the one who took her. Who...?"

"It's looking like he might be. But that still doesn't explain who killed him."

"Who cares? He killed my best friend! He deserved to die."

"Caitlyn, you can't say things like that. You'll get bumped to the top of the suspect list."

"I was with you all night. How can you say that?"

"I know, but all of this... Something isn't right with it. Something is missing."

"What? What's missing?"

Liam stared at the phone, then scanned the table. "I don't know. And that's what worries me. Because whatever it is, I know it's the truth. The truth about who Jeanine was, the truth about who she was dating, and the truth about what actually happened to her."

"You don't think it was John, do you?"

Liam shook his head. "I don't know, but I think it's suspicious she was dating someone and no one has come forward. I think he might be involved with this."

"We don't know who he was."

"I know. But I think if we can find out, we'll find out what really happened to her."

22

———

HE WALKED IN AND LOOKED AROUND. HE KNEW NO ONE recognized him, but he kept his gaze hidden behind glasses that were for show just in case. The clothes he had on were clothes he never wore out. They were special clothes. Clothes he had for meeting women. He couldn't risk being recognized.

He sat at the bar and ordered a beer. Men drank beer. His father always drank beer. He hated the shit, but it was what men drank, so he choked it down. It was only for show anyway.

It didn't take long for a woman to approach him. He knew it would happen. It always did. He made sure of it. His shoes were fancy, his clothes screamed money. He was the kind of man women were drawn to. Women who only cared about money.

"Buy me a drink?" the woman asked. The pout on her lips was supposed to be sexy.

He nodded and lifted a finger to catch the bartender's attention. "Whatever the lady wants."

The bartender nodded and fixed the fruity, sweet drink she ordered.

"You live around here?" she asked, her hand running up and down his arm.

"Not too far."

"Yeah? I don't recognize you. I figured you were visiting."

He shook his head. "I've never been here before." That part was the truth. He always picked a new bar when he went out looking for a woman. It wasn't often he had the urge to bring someone home, but when he did, he found a bar a few towns away where he could be somewhat anonymous.

She twirled the straw in her pink drink and looked up at him. She wrapped her lips around the straw and sucked her cheeks in.

The move didn't do much for him, but she was pretty enough. Her blonde hair came from a bottle. Her red lips were extra plump. Her tight dress left little to the imagination. His cock grew hard looking at her. She'd do for the night.

"Want to get out of here?" he asked.

She smiled and nodded eagerly. He tossed a hundred dollar bill on the counter for the bartender knowing the tip would be more than enough to ensure he kept his mouth shut about them leaving together. Not that it mattered. He wasn't doing anything wrong.

"Should I follow you?" she asked.

"Yep. I'm in the black SUV." He pointed to his vehicle. She nodded and went to hers. He definitely picked the right one if she was going to drive herself. He hated when he had to take a woman home afterward. Or when they tried to hang on longer than it took for both of them to orgasm.

He watched his mirror as he drove, making sure she was

behind him. He took back roads and pulled into his driveway seventeen minutes later. If things worked out, she'd be gone in ten.

She parked behind him and got out of her car. He didn't wait for her before he walked to the door and unlocked it.

"What the hell are you doing, boy?" his father shouted as soon as the door swung open.

He stopped dead in his tracks.

"What's wrong?" she asked, stopping right behind him.

"Nothing," he said quickly. "I just thought I heard something."

"Was it the sound of me taking off my panties? Because I did that in the car."

He smiled at her and walked inside. He pushed the door closed, then pushed her against it. He leaned his body against hers and claimed her mouth.

She met his with parted lips and an eager tongue. She cupped him through his pants, squeezing hard.

"Seriously? This slut?" Jeanine asked.

Again, he jumped. He spun and looked around the kitchen. No one was there.

"What happened?" the woman asked.

He shook his head. "Nothing. Bend over the counter."

She smirked at him and moved to where he indicated. She hoisted herself up on it and crossed her legs. She raised an eyebrow.

"What?"

"I like to see it before I fuck it."

He grunted, annoyed the woman wasn't doing what she was supposed to do. "So do I."

She smiled and uncrossed her legs. She spread them wide, letting him look his fill of her.

He didn't really care what she looked like as long as she

was going to let him come. He dug a condom out of his pocket, then dropped his pants and briefs.

"Nice. I like long, thick ones. Leans a little to the left, though. You must be left-handed." She smirked at him like she knew a secret.

Instead of answering, he grabbed himself with his left hand and stroked.

"Ooh, I like it a little dirty." She dipped her finger inside herself and trailed it up to her clit. "Let me watch you for a minute."

He stroked himself again. He wanted her gone, but it felt too good to kick her out right away. Her pussy dripped as she toyed with it. Precum leaked from the tip of his dick. She dipped her finger inside again, then leaned back and put her feet on the counter next to her hips.

"Seriously, on my counter? Your father is going to have a fit when he gets home," his mother shouted.

An icy chill skittered down his spine. He stopped stroking himself and looked around. She couldn't be there. None of them could be. But he heard them.

"What's wrong?" the woman on the counter asked. "Why did you stop? I like it better when you stroke it."

He shook off the feeling and focused on the woman again. He gripped his cock tighter, staring at her pussy. She pumped her hips, riding her fingers as she started to come.

"Come here. Fuck me. Now. Get that condom on." She reached out for him, beckoning him to her.

He rolled the condom down his length and walked over to her. He thrust inside her in one quick stroke. She screamed and fucked him back, leaning back on one hand while the other stayed busy on her clit.

"Fuck me. Yes, harder. Use that crooked dick to fuck me, dammit."

Laughter rang out all around him. "I told you it was bent weird. She can't even get off with it."

He stopped fucking the woman and looked for Jeanine. She was there. She couldn't be, but she was.

"Jeanine?"

"I'm Heather, you dumb fuck. Now fuck me harder."

He kept looking for Jeanine while he tried to fuck Heather. Jeanine's laughter echoed through the empty walls of the house.

"What is wrong with you?" Heather demanded.

"See? You're ruining my counter. I told you not to let her up there," his mother admonished him.

"Why the hell can't you ever listen, boy? You too stupid? What a waste of a fuck. If I'd have known how you'd turn out, I'd have made your mother suck me off instead," his father berated him.

"Stop it!" he shouted. "Stop it! Stop it! Stop it!"

He backed away from the counter and held on to his head. It hurt. Everything hurt. They were all there. Talking to him. Torturing him. Dead. They were all dead. He knew they were because he made sure of it.

"You're not really here," he whispered.

"Not for long, psycho. What the fuck is wrong with you?"

Heather. He'd forgotten about Heather. "Get the hell out," he growled.

"Don't worry, I'm going. Worst fuck ever." She climbed off the counter and pulled her dress down. She walked to the door and opened it. "Guess all you are is a pile of money and crazy."

He started to go after her, but Jeanine laughed at him.

"She has you pegged."

"Fuck you, you bitch! You're dead."

"Yeah, but you're the one who's fucked. Not physically, though!" She cackled loudly, the sound echoing in his head.

He squeezed his temples, willing the sound away. She just kept laughing. After a minute, his parents joined her. Laughing at him.

He went to the garage where Jeanine's body was rolled up in a tarp. He kicked it, and the laughter in the house stopped. He kicked it again, and again, his laughter starting. Then he put on a pair of gloves, picked up the tarp, and loaded it into the back of her car.

He put a hat on to hide his hair and got her keys from the drawer he stashed them in after he used them to get into Caitlyn's apartment. He opened the garage door, darkness and silence surrounding him.

He backed out of the garage and closed it again, putting the remote into his SUV so he didn't forget it. He drove to the church next door, the tires crunching on gravel as he pulled around the side of the church and crossed the border. He kept driving through the lot and into the remote area that laid just on the other side of the border from his house.

He found a good spot and pulled over. He left the vehicle running and turned the wheel hard to the right. He opened the door and jumped out, feeling the car start to fall into the ditch before he managed to get fully clear.

The car tipped, then went over, nose first into the ditch. It was shallow enough that someone would see it. Eventually. The road was not a well traveled one. He knew that well.

He nodded at the car and turned back toward where he came from. He walked across the road and through the field. The border was nothing more than an invisible line in his backyard, a line he never cared much about except when he needed to move undetected. In the shadows.

He made it to his back porch and took all his clothes off. He put them in the barrel and poured oil on them. He lit a match and tossed it in, the familiar smell of fire infiltrating every inch of him.

He waited, naked in the darkness, until the flames died down and the evidence was gone. Nothing would tie him to Jeanine again.

He walked into the house and turned on the light. Silence met him. His mother was gone, dead and burned alive years ago. His father went with her, a needle in his neck ensuring he wouldn't leave when the fire started. He told them both everyone would know the truth about the way they treated him if they tried to leave the house. His mother never left his father's side, laying in bed beside him as the fire ignited the entire house.

He walked into the room that was once theirs. The room he rebuilt in the same spot so he would never forget that he won. That he came out on top.

He closed the door and went back to the kitchen. Heather's ass print was still on the counter. Jeanine sat there once when they had sex, screaming his name like he was the only one who made her feel good.

Then she laughed at his proposal. Threw it in his face that she fucked someone else the night before.

John and Mickey got the same needle his dad got years ago. Potassium wasn't something most autopsies tested for. He enjoyed adding the serum to their IVs. He only wished he could have been there to see them die. To watch as their punishment took effect. They thought they had a right to fuck Jeanine. She belonged to him.

Well, he got the last laugh on all of them. Fuck them.

No progress. No news. No updates. Everywhere Caitlyn turned, the answer was no. She was sick of it. Someone had to know what happened to Jeanine. Another day had passed without finding her, and now the men Caitlyn was sure were behind her friend's disappearance were dead.

Caitlyn trudged through the first hour of work without her mind really there. She tried to pay attention to her customers, but it was more of a struggle than usual. John and Mickey were dead, which meant they were going to get away with whatever they did to Jeanine. Caitlyn might never find Jeanine. Might never know what happened.

Adam and Lorelei questioned both wives about Jeanine and about their husbands. Both wives said they knew nothing about Jeanine. Karen stuck to her story that Mickey would never cheat on her. And Jenny just didn't care. She said her husband slept with whoever he wanted, and she did the same. There was no reason for her to kill her husband, or any of the women he screwed, because she was only with him for the paycheck he brought home.

Adam looked into both of their alibis. Jenny was nowhere near the hospital for more than an hour before the men died. Karen was there, but more than one nurse said she left to get dinner and was back at her husband's side. She never went into John's room.

The hospital was running tests on both men to determine if they were given something, but so far, they hadn't found a thing. Or a suspect.

No, no, no. Caitlyn wasn't sure if she could take it anymore.

She refilled coffees and took orders and tried not to scream or cry or hit someone. Heather was working the counter again, a friend of hers sitting on the end. Heather leaned over, talking quietly to her friend and ignoring the other customers.

Caitlyn walked by to turn in an order and heard Heather say, "It was huge, but it had a big curve to it. Like it took a hard left somewhere."

"That's so weird. I've never seen one like that. How was it?" Heather's friend had her chin in her hand, staring up at Heather like she was a goddess.

"He couldn't even finish. It was fun until he started yelling. I don't think I'd go home with him again. I mean, he's definitely fucking nuts."

"Sometimes those are the good ones. I mean, do you want one who's going to ask where you're going and who you're fucking? I don't. We're too young for that shit. We might end up like Caitlyn," the friend said.

Caitlyn spun to them, no longer pretending not to listen to their conversation. "Who were you with last night, Heather?"

"Why the hell would I tell you?" she spat back.

Caitlyn's heart thumped hard. She'd never heard of a man with a sharp left turn on his cock either, but Jeanine did. "Just fucking tell me."

"No. Get the fuck away from me," Heather said. She took a step away like she was actually going to do her job.

Caitlyn grabbed her arm. Heather opened her mouth to say something, but Caitlyn squeezed tighter.

"What the hell, Caitlyn? Why do you care who I went home with? It's not like anyone would want to fuck your fat ass anyway."

The urge to slam her head into the counter was strong. Very strong. But Caitlyn needed Heather to talk. She needed her to tell the truth. She needed to know who she was with the night before. Because if it was the same guy Jeanine called Lengthy Lefty, Caitlyn might have a new lead on where Jeanine was.

Caitlyn twisted Heather's arm back, making the woman cry out. "Fucking hell. What is wrong with you?"

"Tell me who it was, Heather. Just fucking tell me."

"It was Daniel West, okay? Jesus Christ. Why do you care?"

"Daniel West," Caitlyn breathed.

"Yeah, and you're welcome to him. He's fucking nuts, and he couldn't even remember my name. He called me Jeanine."

Caitlyn's knees gave out, and she sank to the dirty floor of the diner. Heather stepped over her, muttering to her friend about not wanting to get old and fat like Caitlyn.

Caitlyn just sat there. Daniel West. Was he the man Jeanine was seeing? Was he the one who took her? He had the money and the power to do it, but would people actually go along with it? The police? The FBI? Could they be bought?

Caitlyn didn't know the answer, but she needed to get the hell out of there. She needed to go to Daniel's house. But first, she needed to go tell Liam what she found out. He wouldn't believe her, but when they found Jeanine, it wouldn't matter.

"I'm not feeling so well," Caitlyn said to absolutely no one. "I'm taking off early." She pushed herself to stand and headed for the break room. She might get fired, but she wasn't even sure she cared at that moment. She was going to find Jeanine.

Caitlyn got back to her apartment in record time. She was panting and excited. It was all going to be over soon. She could feel it.

She rushed up the stairs and hurried to unlock the door. She burst inside, grinning from ear to ear. Until she saw Liam's face.

"What's wrong?" she asked. Her stomach bottomed out. Her hands shook. Her heart pounded.

"We need to talk, Caite."

She shook her head. "Just say it, Liam. Tell me."

"They found Jeanine. She's dead."

23

<hr>

ENGLISH STARED AT CAITLYN AS THE NEWS SANK IN. HE couldn't remember how many times he'd delivered death notices to families in the past, but none of them, not even the first one he did, was as hard as telling Caitlyn her best friend was dead.

"No," Caitlyn breathed. "You're wrong."

"They found her car this morning. She was in the backseat."

"No. No. You're lying!"

English knew the news would be hard for Caitlyn to hear. It was hard for everyone. Hope was dangerous, and while he wanted Caitlyn to have it, when he blew that hope up, it was worse than not having it in the first place.

"Caitlyn—"

"No." She held up her hand to stop his approach. "It's not her. She always wore a silver necklace with a blue crystal pendant. Was it on her?"

"I don't know, but the Canadian Provincial Police have no reason to think it's not her."

"Canadian? What are you talking about?"

"Her car was in a ditch just across the border. Whoever had her drove her there and dumped the vehicle and her body. They didn't push it all the way off the road, leaving it sticking out, so the police said it was definitely done last night."

"Last night?" Caitlyn asked. She glared at English. "Last night. While we were having sex instead of looking for her, my best friend's body was dumped in Canada?"

"This isn't your fault, Caitlyn," English said. He took a step toward her again.

She laughed. A cruel, sick sound he'd never heard from her before. "My fault? No, it's not my fault. It's your fault, Liam! You were here to find her. You were supposed to be looking for her. And instead of doing your fucking job, you were here with me. Instead of finding my friend, you were fucking the teenage model. Do you feel better about yourself? About your life? You can add me to the notches on your bedpost."

"Caitlyn!"

"Just go, Liam. Just get out."

"Caite…"

"I said leave. I don't want you here. I can't even look at you. Get out! Get out! Get out!"

She beat him on the chest with each shout, pushing him toward the door. English kept his hands up, trying to show her he wasn't a threat. His back hit the door as a tear rolled down her face.

"Caitlyn." He reached for her, wiping the tear from her cheek.

"I hate you!" She pounded on his chest again, not letting up until he opened the door. She shoved at him, pushing him into the hallway and slamming the door in his face.

English stood in the hall. The locks clicked, and the

chain slid into place. Her body hit the other side of the door and slid to the floor. Then she cried, wailing and sobbing and crying out Jeanine's name.

English couldn't leave her. He wanted to be on the other side of the door with her, holding her and doing anything to make her feel better. There was no fixing this for her, but he could hold her through her grief.

Except she hated him.

He tried to tell himself she didn't mean it, but he wasn't sure. Her best friend was dead. And he was supposed to be there to find her. Instead, he was playing house and falling in love with Caitlyn.

English didn't know how long he stood there listening to her cry, but when she was finally quiet, he went out to his SUV. He called Dex, needing an update from his team, and some manpower to find out who was behind Jeanine's death.

"Morning," Dex said, sounding barely awake.

"My missing person case is now a homicide. I need help."

"Fuck," Dex breathed. Blankets rustled on his end of the phone, then a door closed.

"Are you guys done with the case you're on? Because I could really use a friendly face or two."

"Yeah, we're done. Had an all-night op, so everyone is off today to rest. Jack's got a few bruised ribs, and Slade has a concussion, but otherwise, scrapes and bruises. Nothing we don't have every day."

"Think you can get some help here tomorrow for me?"

"Yeah, I'll talk to Dunn later today and pull a team. Did you get an autopsy yet?"

"No. They found her this morning. Someone dumped her across the border."

"Is that where she was being held?"

"I don't know. Nothing about this case is adding up for me."

"You got a spot we can stay? Someplace we can talk things out without being overheard?"

English sighed and looked up at Caitlyn's apartment building. There was exactly one motel in town. It was rundown and shady, but it always had rooms available. "I'll take care of it."

"All right. See you tomorrow. Sorry about the missing person. Hey, how's Caitlyn?"

"She kicked me out. Blames me."

"She'll come around. Hang in there."

"Yeah," English said. They hung up, and he kept looking at the building. He didn't want to leave Caitlyn alone. He had no idea who killed Jeanine, and if they were done with her body, there was no telling if they would go after Caitlyn to make sure no one found out.

English was still debating what to do when his phone rang.

"Yeah?"

"It's Adam. I need you to come down to the hospital. Now."

"On my way."

English told himself nothing would happen to Caitlyn during the day and left. He drove south to the hospital, hoping whatever Adam wanted him there for would help catch whoever was behind Jeanine's death.

English parked and sent Adam a text that he was there. Adam gave him directions into the hospital and down to the morgue. He was waiting at the elevator when it opened.

"What's going on?"

"John and Mickey were definitely killed. We got a rush

on their autopsies and both men had potassium in their systems."

"Don't we all have potassium in our systems?"

"Yeah, but not at this level. Come on."

Adam led the way through the basement to a door marked Medical Examiner. A thin, pale man was talking to Lorelei. They stopped when Adam and English walked in.

"This is Liam Johnson. He's with F-BOMB, a special task force out of Niagara Falls. He's been looking into the disappearance of Jeanine Waterford. Her body was found this morning, and Mr. Valentine and Mr. Donnelly were two of his prime suspects. He needs to know what you told us, Dr. Reed."

The ME looked at English before nodding. "As I was telling the agents, both men were given high doses of potassium. Our bodies can process it, but the levels they were given were too high for a body to get rid of. Especially in the states they were in. The men's hearts slowed almost immediately, but they did not stop right away. The potassium was like a drug, and as their bodies pumped it through, it slowed all their muscles down until they wouldn't work. The most important muscle, of course, was their hearts."

"What does this tell us?" English asked.

"It tells me that neither of their deaths were accidents. They were poisoned. But whoever did it was smart. They could have been dressed as a medical professional so no one would notice them. The doses were low enough that I wouldn't have thought anything about it if I wasn't looking for them," Dr. Reed told them.

"Do you have Jeanine Waterford here?" English asked.

"Yes, she came in earlier. My friends in Canada were happy to pass on her since there was already an open case in the US. I've only just started her autopsy."

"Any guesses on her cause of death yet?"

Dr. Reed moved to another table that was covered with a white cloth. He picked up a clipboard from a stainless steel table next to the draped body. "Ms. Waterford appears to have been strangled. There is bruising to support the theory. There's also damage to her side, but no bruising there, which leads me to believe it happened after her death."

"Could that have been caused when her car was pushed into the ditch?" Adam asked.

Dr. Reed nodded. "It's possible, but until I'm able to see inside, I won't be able to give a plausible explanation."

"Did you find a necklace on her?" English asked. He wasn't sure if Caitlyn would want Jeanine's necklace or not, but it would definitely bring her closure.

Dr. Reed checked his clipboard again. "No. No necklace on the body, and none noted with her personal effects."

"No? Silver with a blue crystal pendant?" English asked.

"No necklace at all. Do you know she was wearing it?"

"What's up with the necklace?" Lorelei asked.

English shook his head. "Caitlyn was adamant about Jeanine's necklace. I don't think she'll believe it's her unless the necklace is here."

"Maybe it's in her car," Lorelei suggested

"Or wherever she was held," Adam said.

"Would you like to see her personal effects?" Dr. Reed asked.

English nodded and followed him to a small bank of lockers. He opened one and pulled out a clear plastic bag. He handed it to English.

English took the bag and lifted it to look at the contents. A purse, two phones, a ring, and a bracelet. No necklace. "She was supposed to have a necklace."

"You're positive?" Adam asked again.

English shook his head. "I don't know anything about this. But if Caitlyn said Jeanine never took the necklace off, I have to believe she would have been wearing it that night."

"Then where is it?" Lorelei asked.

English studied the bag again. He grabbed a pair of gloves and opened the bag. He pulled out the purse and searched through it. No necklace. "We need to find that necklace. Wherever it is, we'll find our killer."

CAITLYN DRAGGED herself off the floor and onto the couch. She couldn't wrap her head around Jeanine being dead. She knew it was possible, but it was hard to accept it. Especially when she finally figured out what happened to her.

Daniel West. Caitlyn never would have suspected him. She was fairly sure no one would. And now... The only way to get anyone to believe Daniel killed Jeanine was to prove it.

Caitlyn tried to come up with a plan all day. Walking up to Daniel's door and asking him nicely if he killed Jeanine wouldn't get her anywhere. If he'd gotten away with holding Jeanine for two weeks, he was smart. He'd hidden her car and—

Her car! If Daniel hid Jeanine's car, he had to have kept it in his garage. That was the only place it could have been without someone noticing it.

Caitlyn had to get into the garage. There had to be something that would prove Jeanine had been there. Hair or skin cells or something.

Caitlyn's phone rang off and on all day, but she ignored the calls. She was sure they were from Liam, but talking to him was too painful. He wouldn't believe her if she accused Daniel. And she couldn't take one more hit.

Caitlyn waited until it was starting to get dark. She dressed in all black clothes with her hair piled up high on her head. She grabbed her phone and glanced at the screen, needing a little strength from him before she faced the truth about her friend.

She had six missed calls from Liam. He left voicemails for all of them. She had no idea what he would say, so she didn't listen to them, but she saw one line from the last text.

```
I'm sorry.
```

Caitlyn's eyes watered. Her chest felt too tight. She didn't want to think about Jeanine, scared and fighting for her life or dying alone. She didn't want to think about anything happening to Jeanine. But it did.

Caitlyn opened the texts and read them all.

```
I need to talk to you. Please answer your
phone.
It's important. Jeanine's autopsy has
started.
Are you sure she was wearing a necklace?
It's not with her.
Caite, please call me back. I don't want
you to go through this alone.
I'm here for you if you decide to call. Any
time.
I'm sorry.
```

Jeanine was being carved apart, some stranger trying to determine why she died. Caitlyn hurt. Everywhere she hurt.

She pushed the pain down and drew a deep breath. She straightened her shoulders and closed her eyes. It had been a long time since she had competition. Someone who thought they could outwit and out-strut Caitlyn. Daniel West had no idea who he was dealing with. Caitlyn was a damn model. She grew up fighting for everything. There was no way in hell she was going to stop fighting for Jeanine.

Caitlyn snuck out the back door of her apartment building into the cool night air. The hairs on the back of her neck stood up. She held still against the old building, listening to the sounds of the night.

It was only about eight o'clock. She didn't know if Daniel would be home or not, but she wasn't going to wait another day to find Jeanine's killer and bring him to justice. If Jeanine's necklace was not with her, it had to be at Daniel's.

Caitlyn stayed away from streetlights and busier roads as she walked through town to where Daniel lived. Holy Trinity Christian Church came into view, and Caitlyn said a silent prayer that if there was a God, He would watch over her.

The house and garage were both dark. No vehicles were in the driveway. Caitlyn never thought much about Daniel West or the things he did, but she was fairly sure he didn't normally park in his garage.

Caitlyn walked up the driveway for the church and watched the house. Nothing moved except the trees in the backyard, a barrier between the United States and Canada. A barrier that had a road on the other side. A road where Jeanine's body was discovered.

The how didn't matter to Caitlyn, even as little pieces came together in her mind. Liam said Jeanine was at the church, but with how close the church was to the West house, Caitlyn thought it was reasonable Jeanine was actually with Daniel that night.

If that was the case, Caitlyn wanted to know why. Why did Daniel kill Jeanine? Why did he decide she wasn't worthy of another breath?

Caitlyn stepped off the gravel driveway of the church and onto the damp grass that separated the two properties. She scanned the area, straining to see or hear anything that didn't belong. All that met her was silence and stillness.

The garage had a vehicle door in the front, a window in the back, and a person door on the side near the house. Caitlyn didn't like moving around the garage toward the house, but she wanted to get into the garage. If that was where Jeanine's car spent the last two weeks, something had to be there.

The door was unlocked. Caitlyn didn't want to think about her fortune. How likely was it that Daniel hid a body and a car in a garage he didn't keep locked?

A trickle of doubt tingled in the back of her throat. If she was wrong, she'd just leave. But if she was right...

The garage was not much bigger than the size of one vehicle. It was old, old enough that Caitlyn wondered if it was a part of the original home that stood in the exact place. The house burned to the ground, but the garage wasn't touched. Faulty wiring had been the fire investigator's report, Caitlyn remembered.

The ground was paved, but the pavement was cracked and littered with dirt and oil and grease. Tire tracks were clearly visible, but there was no way for Caitlyn to prove where they came from. Caitlyn tiptoed around them, doing her best not to mess them up. She couldn't tamper with evidence if the police were going to convict Daniel.

Moonlight streamed through the window at the back of the garage. It was the only light in the space, and not nearly enough for Caitlyn to see anything. She looked around, the darkness swamping her vision not more than three feet away. She needed light.

Caitlyn pulled out her phone and turned on the flashlight. It was bright in the dark space. She immediately pointed it at the ground. If someone saw the light through the window or under the door, she'd be arrested for trespassing.

Her heart thumped hard in her chest, echoing in her ears. Caitlyn wasn't used to breaking and entering, even though technically she didn't break anything. She needed to search quickly and get out of there before Daniel got home.

She swung the flashlight around, not finding anything that made her suspicious. There were no flashing signs saying this was where Jeanine died, or Jeanine was here. Caitlyn sighed heavily. She was wrong. It wasn't Daniel.

She moved her phone to turn off the flashlight and stopped. Something caught the light. She didn't know what it was, but it sparkled when the light hit it. Caitlyn moved closer, toward the wall of the garage. She crouched down and dug.

She lifted it from the dirt and gasped. Jeanine's necklace swung in the light.

Tears fell from Caitlyn's eyes. She did it. She had proof. Everyone would know she was right and Daniel would go down for killing her friend.

Caitlyn unlocked her phone to call Liam. She could tell him to meet her there. He would bring the authorities. And Daniel would never hurt anyone again.

"What the hell do you think you're doing in here?"

Caitlyn turned toward the snarl and found Daniel blocking her exit.

He held a golf club like a baseball bat. His shirt was untucked, his eyes glazed and a little crazy.

Caitlyn lost what was left of her composure. This was the man who killed her best friend. The man who stole Jeanine away. And Caitlyn had the proof right in her hand. She lifted it up so it glinted in the light from her phone.

"I was looking for proof that you killed Jeanine. And I just found it."

Daniel's face twisted. He looked at the necklace, then back at Caitlyn. Then he closed the garage door and slid a board over the door.

"Thank you. I was looking for that. Last piece of that fucking whore I need to destroy. And the perfect piece of evidence for the police to find on your corpse."

24

ENGLISH PARKED OUTSIDE CAITLYN'S APARTMENT AND STARED up at her window. He hated that he wasn't in there with her, comforting her. Helping her to feel better.

He sighed. It wasn't a shock that she hated him, but he still felt like an asshole. An asshole who needed advice.

He scrolled through his contacts and found the only person who could actually help him. English glanced at the clock, but it didn't really matter what time it was. He needed the help.

"Yo," Jack said as a greeting.

"I need some help."

"What's wrong?" Jack asked, his tone on edge and ready to do whatever it took to help.

That was what English loved about his team. They were always there for each other. "I fucked up with Caitlyn. We found her friend's body. It was dumped. Do you think Pilar would be willing to talk to me?"

"Hold on."

The phone went silent. English pulled back to make sure

Jack hadn't hung up. The call was still live. Jack was on mute.

"English?" Pilar said, her voice soft.

"Hey, Pilar."

"I'm so sorry about Caitlyn's friend."

English nodded. "Me, too. I didn't expect much coming in here, but I didn't think it would really matter."

"It matters when you care. You care about Caitlyn?"

"Yeah, I do. I tried not to, but I do."

"Are you in love with her?"

Love. The word was a punch in the gut. He grew up thinking love meant keeping each other's secrets and tolerating each other enough to not ruin the picture you presented to the outside world. After watching his brothers all find a very different kind of love, English was learning love meant putting someone else's happiness above your own. It meant doing anything to see that person smile. It meant giving all of yourself to another person, whether they felt the same or not.

"Yeah, I am."

"Then be there for her."

"She hates me, Pilar. She blames me. I know you blamed Jack when Juan died. How did you forgive him?"

"There was nothing to forgive. Not really. Jack didn't kill my brother, just like you didn't kill Caitlyn's friend. Sometimes when grief comes, we lash out at the closest person. We believe we deserve to be alone because we blame ourselves. I know Carlos is to blame for my brother's death. He's the one who actually killed him. But if I listened to my brother in the first place and stayed away from Carlos, he never would have come after Juan. He would have forgotten about us, and we would have been safe."

"It's not your fault," English told her.

"I know. Carlos was crazy, and if it wasn't my brother, it would have been someone else who died. He killed for sport. And I hate that he killed Juan, but when he died, I blamed myself. I pushed Jack away because I was falling in love while my brother was being tortured and killed. I felt like I traded his life for my happiness. I grieved for him alone because I wasn't willing to accept that they weren't linked. I could be happy without my brother, even though it felt impossible at the time."

"I don't know if Caitlyn will forgive me."

"She will. Go see her. Don't let her go through it alone. Even if she wants to hit you and yell at you, she needs to know you're there for her."

English drew a breath and looked up at her window again. A light was on inside. She was home. And she was alone.

"Thanks, Pilar. I really appreciate your advice."

"You're welcome. And I hope you take it."

English got out of his SUV and headed for the door. "I'm on my way right now. Enjoy the rest of your evening."

"We will. See you soon, English."

English hung up and pocketed his phone. He took the stairs two at a time and knocked on Caitlyn's door.

Silence.

He waited a few minutes and knocked again. Maybe she was sleeping. She definitely could have been ignoring him. He pressed his ear to the door and strained to hear something. No TV, no radio, nothing.

English knocked a third time. His heart thudded hard. What if someone took Caitlyn? He had to find out if she was inside.

He had his lock-picking kit in his pocket. He hadn't used it in a while, but he knew he could still do it. He glanced up and down the hallway and crouched in front of the door. Twenty seconds later, he was in her apartment. The chain wasn't on.

Which meant Caitlyn wasn't home.

He walked through every room in her apartment, telling himself as he called out and she didn't answer that he was wrong.

But he wasn't. She was gone.

English closed her door and went back to his SUV. He turned on his computer as he called Dex.

"Yeah?" Dex said.

"Caitlyn's gone."

"What do you mean gone?"

"She threw me out earlier. I went to the morgue and stayed away for the day to give her some space. I just got back to her place, and she's not here."

"Is her car there?"

English noticed it when he pulled in. It hadn't moved. "Yes."

"So, someone took her." It wasn't a question.

"Fuck. I need to find her."

"Okay, take a breath. Track her phone, and we'll go from there. Maybe she went out for a walk. Didn't you say people walk a lot around there?"

English waited while the program ran. When it showed her location, his entire body went cold. "She's at the church."

"What... Oh. Where her friend disappeared?"

"Yeah. I need to get over there. Someone has her. They have to. How the hell did this happen?" English tossed his computer into the passenger seat and cranked up the SUV. He tore out of the lot, tires squealing on the pavement as he turned onto the road.

"What can I do?" Dex asked. His voice was tense, desperate. Exactly how English felt.

"Can you get here earlier than tomorrow?" English asked. He knew it wouldn't matter. His team couldn't be there to go with him. To find Caitlyn. To save her. He was alone.

"Dex, look at this," Taylor said. "Isn't this Liam's friend?"

"Who's my friend?"

"Fucking hell, it's Caitlyn," Dex said.

"What? Where? What are you talking about?"

"She's live-streaming. She's in a garage or something. Someone is talking. I don't think he knows he's on camera."

"She's recording her own kidnapping?" English asked.

"Pull over. See if you recognize this place. Tay, let me call Dunn on your phone. I don't want to lose English."

"Okay. I'm going to pull this up on the computer. She's tough. I want to meet her." Taylor was impressed. If Caitlyn survived, English had to make sure they met.

English parked in a small lot and searched Caitlyn's social media until he found the livestream. It was dark, but she was definitely in a garage. And she was goading whoever she was talking to.

"Jeanine did tell me about you. She said you were a good fuck, but not great. She called you Lengthy Lefty. She never wanted me to know she was fucking you, though. I definitely would have told her to stop."

A loud slap echoed through the video.

"Jesus," Dex said.

English forgot about him. He was too focused on Caitlyn. Where was she? He didn't recognize the garage.

"English, we're rolling out. We're going to find a way to get to you ASAP. I don't know how, yet, but—"

"I have a friend with a plane. I'll call him," Taylor said.

"You have a friend with a plane?" Dex asked.

"Yeah, if he can... Yep, he'll meet you guys at the airport in twenty minutes. English, they're coming!"

"Thank you, Taylor," English said. "Thanks, Dex."

"Don't mention it. Be careful. I know you can't wait for us, but if you get any leads on where she is, send them our way."

"I will. Thanks."

English hung up with Dex and stared at the screen. Caitlyn's phone appeared to be underneath something. She hid it so the person who held her wouldn't see it. She was smart.

"Tell me where you are, baby," English said out loud.

"Why did you kill Jeanine? That's the only thing I haven't figured out. What did she do?"

"Jeanine. Jeanine was a lying whore. She told me she liked me. She said I was different. Then she laughed in my face when I asked her to marry me. Said she was fucking other men, and that she never told you about me. She didn't deserve me."

English knew the voice. He heard it more than once. He blinked at the screen and tried to see if he was right. How? And where?

He had to go. He had to find her. It would be easier with his team, but—

Adam. He forgot about Adam. He wasn't involved in the case, but he was part of the FBI, dammit. He would help. He had to.

English didn't stop staring at the screen while he tapped to call his cousin. It rang twice before Adam answered with a laugh.

"Hey. We were just having dinner with Holly. You want to join?"

"Caitlyn's been kidnapped."

"What?" Adam's voice changed instantly. A chair scraped the floor as background noise came through the speaker. "Caitlyn's been kidnapped?"

"Oh, my God," Holly said.

"By who?" Lorelei asked.

"Daniel West. And she's live-streaming it right now."

CAITLYN HAD no idea if her idea to livestream what was happening with Daniel was good, or if it was actually happening. When he found her, she was about to call Liam, but when he said he was going to frame her for Jeanine's death, Caitlyn knew there was a chance Daniel would get away with everything. After he killed her.

She worked blindly behind her back so Daniel didn't see the screen. When he moved closer to her, she tossed her phone to the side and crossed her fingers that it worked. It wasn't like she could ask him to hold on while she checked.

Then all she had to do was get him talking. That part was easier than she thought it would be.

"Are you honestly telling me you didn't know Jeanine was screwing half the town? That you really thought you were her one and only?" Caitlyn laughed.

"I'm the last one to ever fuck her, so as far as I'm concerned, I was her one and only."

"That might be true, but she was supposed to meet Mickey and John the night she came here. How did you convince her to change her plans?"

"You're lying! She was not going to meet them."

"Actually, she was." Caitlyn was against the wall, the one solid wall in the garage. The one without a window or a door. Not that she could have escaped if she was in a better position. Daniel had the upper hand. And a really big golf club.

"No, Jeanine had plans with me. I saw her that morning at the diner. We always talked when she was working."

"You never called her?" Caitlyn asked.

He sighed like he was bored. "I had no need to call her. We would make plans when I saw her. I knew her schedule. I always ate at the diner while she was working. And if she wasn't at the diner, I walked over to the church to see her."

"So, you were stalking her?"

"God dammit! You're a fucking bitch, you know that? Jeanine loved me. She was just scared. She thought people would judge her because I'm rich and successful and everyone loves me."

"Not everyone. Jeanine knew you weren't who you said you were. If she thought you were everything, she would have told the world you were together. She didn't want you."

Daniel swung the golf club, splintering the wooden shelf next to Caitlyn.

She screamed and jumped away.

"Jeanine would have been mine forever. She would have married me."

"You said she laughed at you when you proposed. What do you think? She would have just changed her mind one day?"

"She knew I would take care of her. She was a smart girl. She would have said yes eventually. But she laughed. The fucking bitch laughed. If she hadn't laughed, she would have married me. But she got what she deserved."

"So did John Valentine and Mickey Donnelly, huh? You killed them, too?"

"They touched her! They had no right to touch her. She belonged to me."

Caitlyn snorted and laughed. She laughed hard, keeping one eye on Daniel the entire time. "Jeanine fucked half the men in town. She slept with anyone who wanted no-strings-attached sex. She didn't care. And they paid her for it. She. Was. A. Fucking. Whore."

"You're lying!" Daniel swung again, and again, and again.

Caitlyn screamed and ran to the other side of the garage. Away from her phone and the livestream. If it was working.

Daniel swung the golf club in front of her, connecting solidly with her abdomen.

Caitlyn went down instantly. The pain knocked her breath away. Her side, still healing from the stitches, exploded in pain. She coughed, curling on her side and praying she didn't die alone like Jeanine did.

"Stop talking about Jeanine like that," Daniel growled.

"Okay. Then let's talk about John and Mickey. Did you kill them?" she croaked.

"Why do you care?"

A tear ran down Caitlyn's cheek. He wasn't going to let her go. He wasn't going to stop until she was dead. He told her that from the beginning. She had two things to hold on to. One, the truth. If she knew the whole story, she would die knowing she'd figured it out. And two, she had a minuscule amount of hope that her livestream worked and Liam might find her.

"I want to know why Jeanine had to die." Caitlyn fought through the pain to sit up. She leaned against the wall and looked up at Daniel.

Daniel sighed heavily like he was dealing with a petulant child. Caitlyn didn't think he'd tell her anything, but apparently he liked meek and broken-down instead of strong. Why the hell he liked Jeanine, Caitlyn didn't know.

"Liam told me John and Mickey were involved with her.

That she slept with them. She was mine. They should have known not to sleep with their boss's woman. So, they had to die. They didn't deserve to live."

"Did you cause their accident?"

Daniel laughed. "No, that was God. A sign for me. He agreed. He gave them to me so I could finish the job."

"How did you do it?"

"Potassium in the IVs. It was simple. No one pays any attention to the help. It's how I was able to get everything. Of course, when it's a fire, you don't really need anything. Those are my favorites."

"You set fire to Jeanine's place when Liam and I were there?"

"Yeah, but that one was easy. I didn't have to drug you first."

"Did you drug Jeanine?" Caitlyn asked, her voice soft.

Daniel shook his head slowly. He stared past Caitlyn. His eyes were glazed and unfocused. "She begged me not to. She said they would be better. But they wouldn't change. People don't change. He wasn't going to. I saw it in his eyes when I set the fire. I stayed in the room until the fire swallowed them up. It was quick, but not painless. She stayed with him. Choosing to protect their reputation instead of her own son. She deserved it as much as he did."

Caitlyn gasped. "Your parents? You killed your parents?"

He smiled. It was the kind of smile a person had on their wedding day. The kind that was full of bliss and joy. The kind that said everything in their world was exactly how it was supposed to be.

Except this smile was evil. He was smiling because he was a psychopath. Because he'd been killing people who wronged him for years. And getting away with it.

And Caitlyn was next.

"I think that's enough talking for now. We need to go."

Daniel walked over to Caitlyn and grabbed her arm. He yanked her roughly to stand, pain slicing through her stomach with the harsh movement.

"Ow!"

Daniel ignored her yelp and dragged her toward the door.

"Where are you taking me?" she shouted.

"To die, Caitlyn. It's time for you to die."

"Help!" she shouted. "Someone help me! I'm at Daniel West's house in East Charlottesville, Vermont. If you can hear me, please send help!"

Daniel spun her and slammed her back against the wall. It knocked the breath out of her already strained lungs. Caitlyn started to sink to the ground, but he dragged her upright again.

"Who the hell do you think is going to hear you? There's no one around for miles. That's why that stupid woman who saw me walk into my parents' house the night of the fire left town. I made sure she thought she was crazy. She would have ruined everything for me. You're not going to do the same. You're going to be a good girl and die nice and quiet."

"Fuck you," Caitlyn hissed.

He snorted and shook his head. "You're not my type. I don't like fatties."

Caitlyn swallowed back the tears. Even as she faced death, she was hurt by his words. It was the last thing that should matter, but it did. Because she mattered.

She was done hiding and pretending people didn't bother her. She was done letting people like Daniel and Heather walk all over her. And she was done not fighting back against the people who were full of hate.

They were almost to the garage door. Caitlyn knew her

only chance to get away was to knock him into the door and run like hell and hope he didn't catch her before she found someone. It wasn't much for a plan, but if she caught him off guard, it might work.

Daniel lifted the wood he blocked the door with and opened it. He stepped outside and looked around, then came back inside. He grabbed Caitlyn's arm and pushed her toward the door first.

Caitlyn waited, dragging her feet like she couldn't walk without assistance. Daniel stayed close, holding her arm tightly.

Caitlyn made it out the door. Daniel stepped toward her, his hand on the knob to close it behind them. It was now or never.

Caitlyn checked him with her hip, sending Daniel flying toward the door. He swore and sounded like he fell. Caitlyn took off. She ran as hard as she could toward the road.

He started screaming. Chasing her. His voice closer. His steps louder. Everything echoing in her ears.

She screamed for help.

Daniel screamed back. Threatening her. No longer caring who heard.

Because there was no one there. No one to help. No one to save her. No one to care when she died.

25

ENGLISH SIGNALED TO ADAM WHEN THEY HEARD CAITLYN scream in the garage. They parked their vehicles at the church and moved across the property toward the garage, but when Caitlyn shouted for help, English could barely hold himself back from bursting inside.

They didn't know where either of them were. They couldn't risk hurting Caitlyn or Daniel using her as a shield. He knew all that, but it was still almost impossible to stop himself.

When Caitlyn took off running toward the road, English was at the back of the garage, trying to see through the dingy window to get the layout. Adam was circling the front to make sure Daniel didn't get out that way. And Lorelei was in position behind Daniel's vehicle, a surprise if Daniel managed to get past Adam and English.

Caitlyn ran straight for Lorelei. English wanted to call out to her, but if he did, it would ruin the element of surprise. They wanted Daniel alive. They wanted him to pay for what he did. Five murders. That he admitted to.

Adam had people recording the livestream. There was

no telling how it would play out in court, but that kind of confession usually worked against a defendant. They needed everything they could get.

English hurried toward the front of the garage as Caitlyn and Daniel raced down the driveway. Caitlyn passed the SUV half a second before Daniel did. He reached out for her, grabbing her thick curls and yanking her to the ground. She yelped in pain, a thud sending a chill up English's spine.

"Freeze!" Lorelei shouted. "Let go of the woman, Daniel West. You're under arrest."

Daniel let go of Caitlyn and took a step back. "What? Why would I be under arrest? I found her trespassing in my garage, then she ran. She was trying to steal from me."

"Nice try, asshole," Adam said from behind Daniel. "We know everything."

Daniel smirked and crossed his arms over his chest. "I don't know what you're talking about."

English stepped forward, finally letting Daniel see him.

"Oh, Liam, I'm so happy you're here. Your cousin and this woman are trying to arrest me. I don't even know why. But Caitlyn...I'm sorry, Liam, but Ms. Powers is exactly who I told you she was. I caught her in my garage. She was here to steal from me. I told you she was a thief."

English walked over to Daniel. He was not gentle when he turned Daniel and slammed him against the side of his own vehicle. "You're under arrest for the murders of Jeanine Waterford, John Valentine, and Mickey Donnelly. And thanks to Caitlyn, I think we'll also be able to add charges for the murders of your parents, too."

"What are you talking about?" Daniel tried to push back, fighting against the hold English had on him.

"He's talking about this, you sick fucker," Lorelei said, sticking the video of the livestream in his face.

"Jeanine would have been mine forever. She would have married me."

"You said she laughed at you when you proposed. What do you think? She would have just changed her mind one day?"

"She knew I would take care of her. She was a smart girl. She would have said yes eventually. But she laughed. The fucking bitch laughed. If she hadn't laughed, she would have married me. But she got what she deserved."

"So did John Valentine and Mickey Donnelly, huh? You killed them, too?"

"They touched her! They had no right to touch her. She belonged to me."

Lorelei paused the video. "Sounds an awful lot like a confession to me."

"You can't do that. That's illegal."

"So's killing people, asshole," Adam said.

Daniel fought again, using his weight to push English away from the vehicle. Adam leaned on his other side, using his weight to help hold Daniel still.

Lorelei stepped between them and snapped on a pair of cuffs just as sirens echoed through the silent night.

"You can't do this to me! I'm a fucking god in this town. They'll never convict me," Daniel growled.

Adam nodded. "You're right. They probably won't. But don't worry. You won't be tried here. Kidnapping is a federal crime. And dumping Jeanine's body across the border definitely pulls things up a level, so we'll make sure we get you a really good jury of your peers far outside East Charlottesville."

English stepped back while Adam read Daniel his rights. He looked past Lorelei to where Caitlyn stood. Tears rolled down her cheeks. Her arms were crossed awkwardly around her stomach. She looked like hell. But she was alive.

"Hey," English said softly, moving closer to her.

"You saw it. I didn't know if it worked or not."

English nodded. "I saw it. You caught him."

"I had to. For Jeanine. He had her necklace. It was in the garage. I found it, and I was going to call you, but he was there."

"God, I was so fucking scared when I heard you talking to him. How did you figure out that he was Lengthy Lefty?"

"Heather. She went home with him last night. She said he was long and curved left, but that he was nuts. He called her Jeanine."

"Oh, God. He could have killed her."

"I wouldn't have worked so hard to find him if that were the case," Caitlyn mused.

English snorted. "No, but you found him anyway. You gave Jeanine the peace she needed."

Caitlyn nodded. She sniffed and ducked her head. Her shoulders shook.

English stepped forward and wrapped his arms around her. When she hugged him back, he took his first deep breath since he found her apartment empty.

"I thought you were gone," he admitted. "I went to see you and I thought…"

"I didn't think you'd believe me unless I had proof."

English pulled back and cupped her jaw. "I'm sorry I made you feel that way. I'm sorry for all the bad things that have happened since I got here."

"I never would have gotten this far without you. Thank you."

"I definitely need to be thanking you. None of this would have gotten resolved if it weren't for you."

"Liam, we need to go," Adam said.

English looked up from Caitlyn and nodded. He wanted to take her back to her apartment and show her how much he loved her, but they didn't have time for that. They needed to give official statements, Caitlyn needed to go to the hospital, and they needed to make sure Daniel did not get away.

It was going to be a long night.

ENGLISH FINALLY LEFT the police station at seven the next morning. His team showed up an hour after they brought Daniel in, and they took over the questioning and the case. Dunn called their FBI contacts and followed the letter of the law on everything to make sure Daniel couldn't exploit any loopholes and get away with any of the crimes he committed.

Adam and Lorelei stuck around to close out their case and to manage the FBI side of things temporarily.

English sent Rocky and Jack to the hospital with Caitlyn to get her checked out. They agreed to question her once her injuries were treated, then to stay with her until English could get there.

He was not expecting it to take so long.

Dex caught up to English as he was heading to the parking lot. "You going to get Caitlyn?"

English nodded. "This wouldn't have happened without her."

"Taylor is dying to meet her. I know what you have is new and whatever, but if she's looking for a change from this place, Taylor said she'll create a job for her. Anyone as clever as Caitlyn is someone Taylor wants working for her."

English shook his head and laughed. "I'll let her know."

"Good. Make sure you let her know you love her, too."

English nodded. "Top of the list."

Dex grinned and clapped English on the back.

English walked the mostly quiet halls of the hospital. His credentials got him in early, long before visiting hours started. He brought breakfast for Jack, Rocky, and Caitlyn.

Laughter was the first sign he was getting close. Jack couldn't sit in a room without making everyone laugh, especially a woman, even when he had bruised ribs. English could only hope Caitlyn didn't fall for his unavailable teammate in the hours they were together.

"Morning," English said from the doorway. "I thought I might find some hungry people."

"Hell, yeah. I'm starving. Hospital food sucks," Jack said.

"It's not that bad," Rocky argued.

"I clearly have no problem with any food," Caitlyn said.

"You know you're hot. Own it," Jack told her.

Caitlyn smiled up at him. "Pilar is a lucky woman."

"I tell her that all the time," Jack quipped.

Caitlyn laughed, then looked up and met English's gaze. She was happy, relaxed. Better than he'd seen her look since he walked back into her life.

"Hi," she said softly.

"Hi."

English moved into the room toward her. Jack grabbed the bag of food and vacated the seat next to Caitlyn with a wince and a hand on his side. He dug through the bag and found sandwiches for him and Rocky. The two of them made excuses to stretch their legs and leave the room while English ignored them and sat next to Caitlyn.

"How are you?"

"Bruised ribs like Jack. I needed some new stitches. I should be able to leave today."

"Good. How were those two?"

"They're great. And so are Pilar, Nikki, and Sylvester."

English's brows drew together. "How do you know that?"

"They called them last night. I also met Taylor, Lily and baby Tessa, Ashleigh and Junior, Kayleigh, Megan, and Kyra. Oh, and Howler." She rubbed her ear.

English laughed. "Sounds like you're part of the crowd now."

She shrugged and picked at the sandwich in front of her. "They're nice."

English nodded. "They are. They're my family. The people whose opinions really matter to me. I love them."

"I can understand why," Caitlyn said softly. "I've never had people in my life like them."

"You can. If you want to."

"What do you mean?"

"They're not the only ones I love, Caitlyn. And I know you talked about leaving East Charlottesville, and I don't know if you know where you want to go, but I want you to move to Niagara Falls. I want you to come home with me. Meet my friends, my family. Get to know them, and me."

"Why would I do that? You haven't said you love me or anything." The side of her mouth twitched.

"I love you, Caitlyn Powers. I love your sassiness and your sweetness. I love the way you care about people. I love that you were willing to risk your safety to take down someone else, although I don't want you doing that again. I love everything about you. And I want you with me every day, for as long as you'll have me."

She tapped a finger against her lip. She narrowed her eyes. Then she laughed. "I love you so much. I don't deserve you."

"You're right. You deserve better than me. But I'm hoping I'll do."

"You'll more than do. Kiss me."

English leaned forward and pressed his lips to hers. She was everything he'd ever hoped to find. And she was his.

CAITLYN DIDN'T WASTE any time packing up her meager belongings and moving them into Liam's house in Niagara Falls. Taylor offered her a job, which she happily accepted. Reconnecting with Liam changed her life in ways she never imagined it could.

The man himself walked into the bedroom and caught her gaze in the mirror. "You almost ready to go?"

She nodded. Taylor was having a party at her house. Dex officially moved in, something sped up by Caitlyn moving in with Liam, but Dex and Taylor were thrilled. They wanted to celebrate with a party and invited the whole team, including wives and girlfriends, and some of Caitlyn's new coworkers.

She couldn't remember the last time she went to a party. She was excited to talk to people and show off her new look, compliments of *Birds of a Feather*. Taylor not only gave her a job, but she hired Caitlyn to be their in-house model once she learned about Caitlyn's background.

Caitlyn approached Liam at the door and tilted her head to the side when he didn't move. "Everything okay?"

"I have something to tell you," he said.

His voice was serious. The kind of tone that had all the hair on Caitlyn's body standing on end and her heart ready to make a break for it.

"I found your mother."

"What? How?"

"I'm really good with computers. I was angry when you told me she stole all your money, and I wanted to find her and tell her what a horrible person she is, but I wasn't sure how you would feel about me getting involved, so—"

"I love you," Caitlyn said, going up on her tiptoes to kiss Liam. "Thank you. But I'm done with her. I'm letting go of the pain she caused me. She was never a good mother, or a good person, and she taught me to be better. I don't care about her anymore."

Liam smiled and kissed her. "You're a better person than I am. I was tempted to drain all her accounts and donate all the money to charity."

Caitlyn snorted. "That would be funny. But I don't care about her. If she's rich, hopefully she does something good with it. If not, she got what she deserved."

Liam nodded. "I love you."

"I love you. Now, let's go. I don't want to be late."

Liam laughed and let her lead the way outside. He drove to Dex and Taylor's and parked at the street. His hand was warm and soothing on her lower back as they walked up the driveway and let themselves in. The grill outside was going and everyone was talking and laughing and enjoying the day.

Caitlyn said hello to Taylor and Jessica, Taylor's assistant. Jessica was becoming a good friend of Caitlyn's already.

"Where's Braden?" Caitlyn asked Jessica.

Jessica blushed and widened her eyes with a nod toward Taylor.

"He'll be here in an hour. He worked last night. I'm trying to talk her into asking him out, but she's trying to pretend she doesn't know what I'm talking about," Taylor said.

Caitlyn snorted. "I think everyone at work knows."

"Knows what?" another woman asked. She hugged Taylor.

"That Jessica is in love with my stupid brother, and he's too oblivious to have any idea," Taylor said. "By the way, Stacey, this is Caitlyn. She just moved here. She's my new model."

Stacey smiled at Caitlyn. She was pretty, but there was a sadness in her eyes that broke Caitlyn's heart. "Nice to meet you."

"You, too. Are you Taylor's sister?"

Stacey shook her head. "My husband and Braden are best friends. They grew up together and now work together. Taylor was nice enough to invite us today. I think she's on a mission."

"I don't know what you're talking about," Taylor said, not at all innocently.

Stacey sighed heavily. "I need a drink." Taylor handed over her glass. Stacey took a healthy sip of it and forced a smile for Caitlyn. "My husband almost gambled away everything a few months ago. Taylor is trying to get me to give him another chance."

"Because he's sorry."

"He could have gotten us killed."

"But he didn't. And he didn't know it was that bad. Braden said he's a totally different guy now."

Stacey snorted. "I'm sure he's on a tight leash at work. I'm just not sure I can get over it. I'm trying, but..."

"Okay, no more talk about the mistakes men have made. This is a party," Jessica said. "Come on, Stacey, let's get a drink."

Jessica led Stacey away from Taylor and Caitlyn. Taylor watched them go, then turned to Caitlyn. "Ever since Dex and I got together, I want to see everyone I know paired up and happy. It's like a compulsion. But I know not everyone is ready for something."

"Your brother?"

Taylor snorted. "God, no. Braden is just dense. He has no idea Jessica likes him. There have been times I think he likes her, but I can't get a read on him. I meant Stacey and Wray. I've known Wray forever, and I adore Stacey. They were happy for a long time, but I'm afraid she'll never let him back in. I hate that for them."

Caitlyn nodded. "That's sad."

Taylor watched Stacey and Jessica. "It is. Those two women are like sisters to me in a lot of ways. I just want to see them happy."

"Hopefully they will be one day. Something tells me you're not going to give up on helping them."

Taylor laughed. "You already know me too well."

EVERYONE ATE and drank and talked. Caitlyn was sprawled over English's lap, his hand running through her hair. She was pink-cheeked and happy.

Just their team was left at the party. Taylor's employees and other friends had things they needed to get back to, but the team didn't budge. They slowly circled together until they were all paired off in front of the fire pit. Dex found marshmallows and sticks for s'mores, and they all huddled close as night fell and the temperature dropped.

"What's your nickname again?" Caitlyn asked Rocky.

"Rocky."

"Wait, I thought that was your real name."

Rocky shook his head. "My name is Adrian."

"Ooh, Rocky's better. And that's why your son is Sylvester?" Caitlyn clarified.

Nikki nodded. "I didn't know his real name. I knew Rocky was a nickname, and I wanted to name him after his dad. I never thought I'd see him again, though."

"It was fate," Megan said.

"It was," Nikki agreed.

"Your nickname is Slade," Caitlyn continued around the circle.

"Yep."

"English?" Caitlyn nudged English.

"Yep. I fit the part."

"Dex? Because you're so smart?"

Dex chuckled and nodded. "That's what they tell me."

"You guys don't use your nicknames. Pres, Squirrel, and Hulk?" Caitlyn pointed to them.

They all shook their heads.

"You should get new nicknames. Ones you like. Let's see, you'd be Eagle," Caitlyn told Dunn.

"Eagle?" he asked.

Caitlyn nodded. "You keep your cool, just overseeing everything. You're in charge, but you're also very chill."

"I like that," Ashleigh agreed. "He's even that way with Junior. I don't have that kind of easygoing attitude about anything."

"Jack would definitely be Casanova," Lily said. "He's flirted with all of us."

"Oh, yes, that's perfect," Pilar agreed. "And I think Archer would be Zeus. Powerful and strong, a fierce protector."

Lily smiled up at her husband. "That's perfect for him.

What about Jaymes and Mason. You two don't have nicknames."

"I'm not really a part of the team," Jaymes argued.

Everyone around the fire protested.

"You've saved all our asses at one time or another," Dunn said. "You're one of us. She's right. You both need nicknames."

"The Eagle has spoken," Jack teased.

"And Casanova agreed," Dunn said back.

The others laughed.

"Do you have a nickname, Mason? From your Team?" Slade asked.

Mason shook his head. "I'm not that man anymore."

English reached for Caitlyn's hand and squeezed. He couldn't imagine what Mason had been through, and after almost losing Caitlyn, he understood even more how painful it had to have been.

"Jaymes should be Snake. Because he's sneaky and crafty, but only strikes when he has no other choice," Kyra said quietly.

"That's good. So true. Pretty badass, too," Kayleigh agreed.

Jaymes leaned over and kissed Kayleigh. They whispered something no one else could hear and kissed again.

"I think Mason should be Stay-Puft because he's big and bad but soft in the middle," Kayleigh said.

Mason shook his head at her. "Please don't help them."

"Maybe S'mores," Jack teased.

"Or Teddy Bear," Archer said.

"Twinkie," Rocky added. "Mushy in the middle."

All of them laughed, including Mason. He shook his head and looked down at Megan. "I don't care what you call me. She's the only one whose words matter."

"Megan, give us a name for Mason," Slade said to his sister.

"Padre. That's who he is. To both of us," Megan said, staring at Mason.

Mason kissed her softly and nodded.

"Maybe that should be abuelo since he's so old," Jack teased. Pilar slapped his shoulder.

Mason shot him a dirty look softened with a grin. "I'm not that much older than you."

"Yeah, but you are older," Jack replied.

"It's decided," Dunn said. "But no matter what we call each other, the most important thing is that we're family."

The others around the fire nodded. Family.

THANK **you** for reading English and Caitlyn's story! This story is purely fiction but was inspired by an actual church in Vermont that sits on the Canadian border. How cool is that? English was always one of my favorites, and it was hard to wait for someone who deserved him, but Caitlyn was worth the wait!

Sadly, this was the last book in *F-BOMB: SEALs Love Curves.* I hate to say goodbye to these characters, but it's not goodbye forever. Remember Stacey and Wray? And Jessica and Braden? How about Adam, Lorelei, and even Captain Patrick. They are all getting stories in the new *F-BOMB: Curvy Vigilantes* series!

Stacey thought Wray was her forever. He picked her, but he lied and he stole and he broke her. There would never be anyone else for her, but without trust, what did they have? Wray won't give up on them so easily, especially when he learns someone is threatening their family. *FURY* is available now!

NEED MORE NOW? Newsletter subscribers get *exclusive* bonuses like short stories, bonus scenes, and a first look at everything new. Sign up for my newsletter today so you never miss a thing!

WANT EVEN MORE? Mandy is a curvy girl who doesn't need, or want, a man in her life. Xander is out of her league but determined to get to know Mandy, no matter how many times she runs away from him. Read Chubby & Charming for free now!

ABOUT THE AUTHOR

USA TODAY Bestselling Author Mary E. Thompson spent most of her childhood wishing she had a few less curves. She hid between the pages of books because her favorite characters never cared what size her clothes were. Now, neither does Mary, and she writes stories about women like her. Real women who have curves, chase dreams, and find love, because we should all be happy, no matter what size we are.

When Mary's not reading or crafting stories, she's playing with her two kids or living out her own real life romance with her amazing, curve-loving hubby. She has a weakness for chocolate and will fight you for the last peanut butter cup. Unless you trade her for a glass of wine. Then everyone can be friends.

Visit https://MaryEThompson.com/subscribe/ to sign up for Mary's newsletter, **Romancing the Curves**. You'll get free ebooks and other fun stuff, like exclusive, members only content and giveaways, plus be the first to know about new releases and sales!

For even more great stuff, find me at:
MaryEThompson.com